Charlotte MacLeod
WRITING AS
ALISA CRAIG

THE WRONG RITE

AVON BOOKS ◆ NEW YORK

AVON BOOKS
A division of
The Hearst Corporation
1350 Avenue of the Americas
New York, New York 10019

Copyright © 1992 by Alisa Craig
Published by arrangement with the author
Library of Congress Catalog Card Number: 91-30374
ISBN: 0-380-71043-9

Published in hardcover by William Morrow and Company, Inc.; for information address Permissions Department, William Morrow and Company, Inc., 1350 Avenue of the Americas, New York, New York 10019.

First Avon Books Printing: January 1993

AVON TRADEMARK REG. U.S. PAT. OFF. AND IN OTHER COUNTRIES, MARCA REGISTRADA, HECHO EN U.S.A.

Printed in the U.S.A.

RA 10 9 8 7 6 5 4 3 2 1

CRITICAL ACCLAIM FOR

Charlotte MacLeod
WRITING AS
ALISA CRAIG

A Madoc and
Janet Rhys Mystery

THE WRONG RITE

"MacLeod is an expert in the crazy cozy"
Washington Post Book World

"Delicious detail . . .
The portrayal of old Welsh customs and
engaging family eccentrics is delightful"
Publishers Weekly

"It's always a pleasure to visit
with Janet Rhys and her Mountie husband, Madoc"
The Washington Times

"When it comes to the comic mystery,
it's hard to beat Charlotte MacLeod.
Wonderful, weird characters, plenty of wit . . .
clever and cunning."
The Globe and Mail (Toronto)

"Charlotte MacLeod is beyond doubt
one of the most delightful of mystery writers . . .
A radiant roster of delightful folk
with heaps of fragrant Welsh cakes . . .
and villians with their just desserts."
The Drood Review of Mystery

"All the vintage Christie elements are in place . . ."
Chicago Tribune

Affectionately dedicated to Peg and Bill
Logan . . . with special thanks to the ghost of
Uncle Tommy; to Peggy Emmerson for her
inspirational tea and Welsh cakes; and most
gratefully to Donald Daniel of Wales, for his
inestimable help and patience in checking
this book through its various drafts and
ramifications.

All the characters and their doings, even
some of the place names, are figments of the
author's imagination. Any resemblance to
actual persons or events may be attributed
either to coincidence or to sorcery.

SIR CARADOC RHYS, BARONET

His Immediate Family

Huw, his son and heir
apparent, a sheep
farmer

Elen, Huw's wife

Owain, their son, Huw's
assistant

Mavis, Owain's wife

Their five children

Sir Emlyn Rhys, Knight,
Sir Caradoc's nephew

Silvestrine, Lady Rhys,
his wife

Their children:

Dafydd, a tenor

Madoc, detective inspector,
RCMP
Janet (Jenny), his wife
Dorothy, their daughter

Gwendolyn, a clarinetist

His Relatives and Guests

Bob Rhys, a distant cousin, a friend of the lesser demons

Mary, Bob's sister, a gem-cutter and fire-leaper

Dai, their nephew, the sorcerers' apprentice

Lisa (Mrs. Arthur) Ellis, widow of a murdered man
Tib, her young daughter
Tom Feste, her visiting stepbrother

Iseult Rhys, an actress
Reuel Williams, her scriptwriter

His Household

Iowerth, butler and poet laureate

Betty, cook and housekeeper
Megan, Alice, her nieces who help out

Danny the Boots, shoeshine boy and general factotum

Padarn, a superannuated sheepman

Footmen, sheepmen, et al.

Prologue

It was a dark and stormy night.

A filthy night to be robbing a corpse. Particularly a corpse of one's own dispatching. One did wish this beastly rain would quit dripping down inside one's collar. One was not nervous, exactly. It was unlikely that the gendarmerie would be so tactless as to come poking around the alley behind Madame Fifine's high-class bawdy house, for surely she must pay them well. There was, however, the possibility of being accosted by some other person of less elevated principles. One did not want to be mugged and robbed oneself, not after all the bother one had gone to.

Hunting down these black silk gloves, for instance. So pleasant on the hands—one did like the feel of real silk. One supposed one ought to get rid of them somewhere afterward. Poke them down a grating, wasn't that the standard procedure? One ought to observe the conventions, particularly with so distinguished a stiff as Arthur. Arthur had always been punctilious about the conventions.

Where the bloody hell had he stashed his little budget of boodle? One had always been given to understand persons in his profession let the things roll around loose in their pockets. Not Arthur, unfortunately. Taped inside his socks, perhaps, or stuck into his navel. No, that wouldn't be Arthur's way. Navels were uncouth.

A money belt around the waist, more likely, or a chamois bag around his fat—aha!—neck. On a neat, braided thong reaching all the way down to his—tut-tut, Arthur! More to you than had met the eye. One must hope the thong was not connected to a midget burglar alarm.

Leave the engraved calling cards and the no doubt paid-up credit cards scattered artistically about the body, make it easy for the *flics*. Leave the cosh, too; one wouldn't be needing it again. Take the money and walk, don't run. Resist the temptation to hail a taxi; one mustn't gamble on getting a driver with a short memory. One had been so very careful, so astounding clever; one must forgo small comforts for great gains. One wouldn't squander any of Arthur's money on the morning papers; one would hear soon enough about the prominent gem dealer found robbed and slain.

Or slain and robbed, as the case might be. *Tant pis*, Arthur. *Addio*, Arturo. For once, one didn't mind at all being left to hold the bag.

Chapter 1

"**I**s it a cup of tea you will be having to drink?"

Betty the Cakes must have put the kettle on the stove as soon as she heard the gate squeak; Betty had ears like a hare. Madoc Rhys, who'd known Uncle Caradoc's cook all his life, gave her a bear hug and a smack on the cheek.

"It is the baby we will be needing to change, Betty *fach*, and the bags to take upstairs."

"Ach, Danny the Boots will carry the bags, and we will change the wee one here by the warmth of the fire, God bless it and the devil miss it. Let me give you a clean towel on the table for her to lie on, Mrs. Madoc. She has your sweet mouth, but her taddi's dark eyes. And it is Dorothy you named her?"

"After my mother." Janet Wadman Rhys didn't at all mind hearing her baby's name pronounced Torothy, here where Madoc was Matoc. "I'll bet my husband's had his nappies changed on this very spot."

"Indeed he has, and many the time," Betty answered, "I have changed him myself, when his fine English nanny would let me. Sit down, lad, and keep out of the way. This is women's work."

"Not at our house." Janet was dealing capably with

her firstborn. "I don't hold with these disposable diapers as a rule, but they're handy for traveling."

"She is young to have come so far."

"Eight months on the day before yesterday," said Madoc. "We could hardly expect Uncle Caradoc to postpone his ninetieth birthday till Dorothy grew up. Anyway, she was good as gold all the way."

Flying first class had been hideously expensive, but worth the difference. It had been a long journey from New Brunswick, Canada, to a place in Wales that barely rated a dot on the map. Once off the plane and through the nightmare of Customs, there'd been a train. Then Madoc's elder brother, Dafydd, had met them in an elderly but sumptuous borrowed Daimler with a bar in the back and a blonde of Wagnerian proportions in the front.

Going off with blondes seemed to be a hobby of Dafydd's, though he could manage with a brunette or a redhead and, according to international rumor, often did.

He'd be around for the birthday but would have to sleep down the road at the house of a distant cousin named Lisa Ellis. Ancestral piles didn't come all that big in Wales as a rule, Sir Caradoc hadn't enough rooms for everybody who'd asked to come, and Dafydd was merely a world-famous opera star.

Madoc was a policeman, a detective inspector in the Royal Canadian Mounted Police. This was a rank seldom attained by anybody at all, let alone a soft-spoken wisp of a chap still in his thirties; but Madoc had been training for it all his life. In Canada, he was something of a legend. Over here, he'd been merely an amiable younger son who'd sought no special attention and got no more than his relatively meager due.

But last time around, he'd boosted his stock by showing up with a blushing and beautiful bride. Now, with the addition of a lawfully begotten baby daughter, he was getting the full red-carpet treatment. Quite literally, in fact; he and Janet were to have the red room, right next to Uncle Caradoc himself. Danny the Boots had already carried down the ancestral cradle from the box-room for Dorothy to sleep in and kindled a fire to warm her infant toes, Welsh weather being what it was even on the next-to-last day of April.

But first there was to be tea. Already an infinitude of cups had been set out at the far end of the table. The loaf and the knife were on the breadboard, the butter in a lordly dish, softening up to be spreadable. The Welsh cakes, fresh-baked and smelling wonderfully of currants, were heaped upon the big pewter salver from which they'd been served since time immemorial; the milk was in the pitcher and the sugar in the bowl. Janet had barely managed to get Dorothy comfortable and Betty to fill the pot when some atavistic tribal instinct alerted Rhyses one and all that it was time for tea.

People who live in great houses, and even in houses not so great, are supposed to have their tea served to them in drawing rooms or libraries by butlers, footmen, parlormaids, or some tasteful combination thereof. At Sir Caradoc's, everybody piled into the kitchen and helped himself. Madoc's sister, Gwendolyn, led the pack.

"You're here! Why didn't that idiot Dafydd let you off at the front door so we'd see you coming? Aunt Elen and Uncle Huw can't come to dinner, but you're to pop up to the farmhouse tomorrow morning without fail. They're itching to see the baby. Is this my angel niece? Come and give Auntie a great big kiss."

"Watch out for your *embouchure*," Madoc cautioned. "She's got a tooth."

"Ah, she wouldn't bite her Auntie Gwen. Would you,

precious? Look, Jenny, she's smiling at me. Does she remember me, do you think?"

Gwen, a clarinetist with the Albert Hall Symphony, had been in Canada on tour three months previously and managed to sandwich in an overnight visit to Fredericton. Janet smiled and lied.

"Of course she does, why wouldn't she? When did you get here, Gwen, and how long are you staying?"

"I've a whole fortnight, isn't it lovely? How about you?"

"Madoc doesn't have to be back till the twelfth, so that gives us lots of time to visit. You're looking marvelous, as always."

"So are you."

Marriage and motherhood had done well by Janet. Orphaned at twelve, she'd been living on the family farm in New Brunswick with her married older brother and his family when Madoc had first met her, thin, pale, and badly scared. While trying to recover from a ruptured appendix, she'd come upon two murder victims and been justifiably concerned as to whether she herself might become a third. He'd thought her lovely even then; now she was beautiful. There was a serenity in her face, a steadiness in her hazel eyes, a dignity to her carriage, a note of quiet amusement in her gentle voice that fooled some people into thinking she was a pushover, but not for long. Janet could pack more clout into a quiet word or a quelling glance than even Madoc's father, a choral conductor who seldom spoke above a pianissimo and could cow a whole mixed chorus and orchestra with one lift of an eyebrow.

Sir Emlyn was in the kitchen now, kissing his daughter-in-law, smiling at the son whom he loved in spite of the fact that Madoc couldn't carry a tune in a basket, and demanding quite aggressively, for him, that Dorothy come to Grandda. The young lady was pleased to oblige; she enchanted her grandpa with a cascade of fairly melodious gurgles, then flung herself cheerfully into the eager arms of Madoc's mother.

Lady Rhys took full credit for Dorothy's existence. It was she, after all, who'd proposed on her son's behalf after she'd eaten three of the then Miss Wadman's home-made lemon cheese tarts. She didn't mind a bit that the baby hadn't been named for her. Silvestrine was not a name to be wished on any innocent child and her parents might have known she'd wind up being called Sillie, a nickname wholly out of keeping with her husband's position. Position was important in a Welsh village; Janet had been relieved to learn on her previous visit that, as Mrs. Rhys the Mountie, daughter-in-law to a knight whose uncle was a baronet, she rated right up there with Mrs. Doctor Jones.

Surnames in Wales are shared by many members of its relatively few families, so everybody gets a nickname. Dafydd was the Song, Tom Feetu, who owned the Daim-ler (and, for all Janet knew, the blonde) and had something to do with the cinema, was Tom the Flicks. Tom's stepsister, the widow with whom he and Dafydd were staying, was Lisa the Tortoise, not from any slowness of locomotion or thickness of carapace, but because she wrote and illustrated a highly successful series of children's books about a very with-it tortoise named Tessie. An old man called Padarn the Dogs trained the collies and corgis that either assisted Sir Caradoc's several shepherds or were assisted by them, depending on whether you regarded the matter from the shepherds' or the dogs' point of view.

All of them sang, as the Welsh always do; some tunefully, some just loudly. A fair number wrote poetry; the rest recited it, dissected it, and argued about it with a fervor that in Canada would have been reserved for hockey or the government. Right now the poets and singers were clumping in from the fields and the barns, having first kicked their boots clean of mud and manure on the stone steps outside because Betty ran a tight ship. The stately Silvestrine was cutting them slices off the big loaf; Gwen, all sparkles, was pouring milk in the cups for their tea. Janet sat like a queen with Dorothy on her lap, accepting their homage while Betty refilled the big brown pot yet another time. It was lovely, just lovely, to be here.

Sir Caradoc was late in arriving; he'd been extending welcome to the three blind mice: small, scurrying figures clad in fuzzy grays and browns. All had sharp pink noses and splayed-out pink hands; all wore the sort of eyeglasses that turn dark in the light and light in the dark. One was, or appeared to be, female; Janet deduced that the other were her husband and her son. Janet was wrong; the fat mouse with the silly little fanned-out chin whiskers was her brother, and the twitchy young one her nephew.

They were, of course, Rhyses, in some remote degree that would no doubt be discussed at length over the table. It was no longer the custom for Welshmen to gather on hillsides of a Sunday afternoon and recite their genealogies all the way back to Adam and Eve or in some cases, it was suspected, to the serpent. Nevertheless, families still liked to keep their relationships sorted out.

The she-mouse was Mary, not Mary the Anything, just Mary. The brother was Bob and the nephew was Dai. Bob the Blob and Dai the Eye. Janet didn't care much for the way that young pipsqueak was staring at her, though it might just be the lamplight reflecting on those oversized glasses.

Sir Caradoc was turning the lot of them over to Sil-

16

vestrine, who could always be counted on to do the done thing, so that he himself could get on with the more important matter of making gentle clucking noises at Dorothy and beaming in ecstasy when she accepted his outheld finger and showed him her tooth.

"Ah, you are a beauty! Will you let me hold you while Mam drinks her tea? It is a long time since I danced a pretty young girl on my knee. Will she cry if I take her, Jenny?"

"Oh no, she'll love it. Here, sit down and I'll hand her to you."

Sir Caradoc was tall as the Rhyses went, fairish and quiet-spoken like the men of the North. He carried his four-score years and ten minus two days without much stooping, and moved easily enough though Betty had never managed to pad his big bones with enough fat to grease a griddle. Few now alive could recall what color Caradoc Rhys's hair had been before it turned to bright silver; he still had a magnificent headful. As he bent to kiss the wee one in her red sacque, she managed to grab a fistful and give it a tug. For that moment, it would have been hard to say which was the younger. Janet, now snugged into the curve of Madoc's arm, felt his clasp tighten and her eyes begin to smart. How right they'd been to bring the baby; she didn't begrudge that stupendous air fare one penny.

Dorothy had slept on the train, and Janet had fed her in the car, but she was, after all, only eight months and a bit. Nobody was surprised when she showed signs of working up to a fuss.

"Come on, baby, I think it's time for your nap." Janet was beginning to feel she could use a short lie-down herself. "We haven't even been up to our room yet. Thanks for the tea, Betty. We'll see you in a while. Coming, Madoc?"

As she and Madoc climbed the stairs—the front ones, of course, in view of their guest-of-honor status—somebody else was just arriving.

Too bad Dafydd had gone off with the blonde, Janet thought as she peeked down over the banisters. The woman directly underneath had a head of hair like a heap of new copper pennies; if the rest of her was up to the hair, she must be a knockout.

The redhead had a man in tow, naturally. At least her companion was wearing a Burberry and one of those floppy tweed caps Welshmen seemed to favor, though a person might think he'd have taken it off once he was inside somebody else's house. Ah well, one shouldn't pass judgment. Maybe the man had both hands full of his lady's suitcases. Janet only hoped her and Madoc's own luggage was where it ought to be. They had been in their traveling clothes too darned long for comfort, or even for respectability.

Danny the Boots had done them proud. The red room was, if not yet toasty, at least adequately warmed against the chilly drizzle that so often betokened sweet springtime in Wales. The cradle, already made up with the whitest and tiniest of linen sheets and pillow slips and the fleeciest of lambswool baby blankets, was near but not too near the welcoming fireplace. Dorothy, divested of her outer layers, made not a whimper as she nestled down into this wonderful cocoon and shut the eyes that were so like her dad's.

Now to unpack. No, that wouldn't be necessary. Some of their garments were already shaken out and hung inside the oaken wardrobe that had never yet felt the woodworm's tooth, thanks to a protective spell laid on it a few centuries ago by a visiting Archdruid. Others were folded neatly into the drawers of a pleasant mahogany chiffonnier bought at an estate sale in 1930 by

Great-uncle Caradoc's late mother, who'd always known a good thing when she saw it. Janet could have cried for joy.

"God bless Danny the Boots."

"Not Danny," said Madoc. "He's strict Chapel—he'd think it a black sin to be handling another man's wife's underwear." Madoc himself was kicking off his shoes and slinging his trousers over the foot of the bed. "Either Uncle Caradoc's hired a new housemaid or else the fairies have been around. We must remember to leave a saucer of milk on the hearth tonight. Come here, darling."

Two hearts may beat as one when love is true, but jet lag conquers even the most devoted. It was Dorothy who woke them; she wanted her supper, and she wanted it now. That was no problem; Janet didn't even have on a blouse to unbutton.

"Enjoy it while you can, precious. One more tooth and this milk bar's going to shut down."

Dorothy burped and went on nursing.

"What are we going to do with her at dinnertime, Madoc? You'll want to be with the family. Maybe I'd better just have my supper here on a tray, if there's anybody to bring it."

"Not to worry, love. Betty will have set something up. I'm going to have a quick bath and get dressed, then I'll go see."

"Don't take all the hot water. I want one too."

"There'll be plenty."

The Romans had introduced the concept of indoor plumbing to Wales sometime after A.D. 50. There might be places here as in Canada where it still hadn't quite caught on, but in Sir Caradoc's house, at least in the less ancient parts, the amenities were not lacking. Madoc was shaving and Janet, wearing a tricot robe bought

19

for the trip because it would pack well and wishing she'd brought her old blue fleece instead, was getting her child into fresh sleepers when Lady Rhys knocked at their door. Cowering behind her was a rosy-cheeked lass of about sixteen.

"This is Megan. She's going to sit with Dorothy while you go down to dinner."

"Oh good, we were wondering how to manage. Are you used to babies, Megan?"

"Yes'm."

"She's Betty's great-niece and the eldest of six, she's been to nanny college, and she doesn't have anything contagious," Lady Rhys amplified. "Isn't that so, Megan?"

"Yes'm."

After all, they'd be right downstairs. Janet needn't fuss. "Then why don't you come back in about twenty minutes, Megan, after I've had a chance to get dressed? Was it you who unpacked for us so nicely, by the way?"

"Yes'm."

"That's two things we have to thank you for, then. What time does Uncle Caradoc want us downstairs, Mother?"

Not having a mother of her own, Janet had fallen easily into the familial form of address. "Lady Rhys" would have been too formal toward someone she had every reason to love, "Silvestrine" was too much of a mouthful, and she could never have brought herself to say "Sillie," even if Sir Emlyn did.

"Dinner's at eight, but come as soon as you're ready. There'll be drinks in the hall, and people will be wanting to chat."

People would already be chatting, Janet was sure. Awkward silences were never a problem at Sir Caradoc's. Janet had got by last time mostly on nods and smiles and had therefore been a smash hit from the first; she had no qualms about meeting a fresh batch of relatives, even that one with the hair. Madoc was out of the bathroom now; she gave him a smile and a nod for practice and went to take her bath.

Chapter 2

The redhead turned out to be Iseult Rhys, Madoc's father's second cousin once or twice removed. The chap who'd come with her was not a Rhys, and gave the impression that he wouldn't have wanted to be. So far he'd shown no degree of cordiality except toward the waiter who'd brought him a drink; at the moment he was over by the sideboard consuming cheese straws in gloomy silence. Iseult, on the other hand, was standing directly under the crystal chandelier. Its light was catching her hair; the hair was catching Dafydd's eye. Iseult was an actress, Janet had learned; Dafydd was clearly warming up to play Tristan. Women did tend to go in and out of Dafydd's life with startling rapidity.

They made a handsome pair, Dafydd tall as Uncle Caradoc, elegant in the tailcoat and white tie he wore for his concert performances; Iseult in a long gown of emerald green with her white bosom swelling out—quite a long way out—of the skimpy bodice. "She looks like an upside-down leek," Madoc murmured, and Janet felt warmed and comforted.

She herself was feeling pretty darned classy tonight, for a girl from Pitcherville, New Brunswick; she'd welcomed the prospect of dressing up for the dinners at which Uncle Caradoc liked to retain the formal customs of earlier days.

Being a nursing mother and being Janet, she hadn't frittered away any great fortune on clothes she wouldn't get much use out of back home. Instead, she'd gone shopping for some interesting materials and, with her sister-in-law's help, run up a couple of simple, rather medieval-looking gowns that fell to her feet in soft, un-interrupted folds from modestly scooped-out yokes. To-night's was a midnight-blue silk in a rough weave that caught the candlelight with a genteel hint of a shimmer. Her arms were bare, but Annabelle had stitched a left-over strip of the material into a long stole that could fall loosely or be wrapped snugly around her shoulders, depending. Her jewels were the heirloom diamond ring that Lady Rhys had taken off her own finger to seal her son's impromptu engagement, the pearls Madoc had given her the next day, and the diamond-stud earrings—not vulgarly big ones, of course—that Sir Emlyn him-self, all on his own, had gone out and bought her to celebrate the birth of his first grandchild.

Compared to the designer model and the freight of gold and emeralds Iseult was wearing, Janet's modest toilette wasn't much; but it was enough. Even the in-scrutable type who'd come with Iseult was resting his eyes on Janet with a certain air of relief. His name, it transpired, was Reuel Williams, and he was a writer. He must, Janet decided, be the kind of writer whose name you're supposed to recognize, and if you don't, you try not to let on. Nobody was letting on; nobody knew either what his relationship to Iseult was, though it stood to reason that there was a certain amount of wonderment going around.

Anyway, Reuel didn't appear to be much bothered

by the attention Dafydd was paying his lady, if in fact she was his lady. Maybe Iseult was one of Tom's actresses and Reuel a scriptwriter or something. He wasn't a bad-looking man, though rather pale and haughty-nosed like somebody who spent most of his time indoors feeling superior. To other writers, Janet wondered, or to the world in general?

Maybe Reuel Williams wasn't a writer but a critic. Now that he'd had his fill of ogling Janet, he was casting a connoisseur's eye over the other women in the room. Gwen in scarlet silk with ropes of pearls down to her knees and a red satin headache band confining her curly black hair got a long, thoughtful stare. Tall, handsome Lady Rhys in black lace and lots of diamonds was well worth looking at; Mary the Mouse in dowdy gray was easy to ignore. Lisa's pretty daughter, Tib, ruffled like a yellow double daffodil, drew a reluctant smile. But it was Lisa herself, standing a little apart from the rest, wearing a stiff, somewhat arty-looking long brown dress with a high cowled neckline, whom Reuel chose as the object of his attention.

Janet felt a twinge of annoyance at his doing so; she herself had been hoping for the chance to chat with Lisa before dinner. She'd liked what little she'd seen of the youngish widow while they were being introduced; she thought Dafydd was lucky to have so attractive a hostess and wondered why he wasn't paying Lisa more attention.

Lisa was a few inches taller than Janet, perhaps five foot five or six. She had lots of fine brown hair worn in an old-fashioned psyche knot, hazel eyes with delicate black rims around the irises, one of those divine British complexions compounded of cream and roses, and a voice that made a person think of still waters running deep. She gave Reuel a polite smile when he addressed her, and made some inconsequential remark.

Whatever Reuel said in reply had a most peculiar effect. Lisa went chalk white, then seemed to disappear. Even though she hadn't moved a muscle, Janet got the distinct impression that she'd drawn her head down inside that upstanding brown cowl and didn't intend to come out.

Was Lisa having some kind of turn? Janet was wondering whether she ought to do something when Tib fluttered up quick as a butterfly, slid an arm around her mother's waist, and began chattering at Reuel nineteen to the dozen. A second or two later, Dafydd had remembered his duty as a guest, excused himself to Iseult, and made the trio a foursome. So that was all taken care of. Janet decided she might as well go be nice to Mary the Mouse.

Mary was not difficult to strike up a chat with, nor was she all that mousy once she got going. She was, Janet learned, agog over Great-uncle Caradoc's upcoming birthday gala, not because of him but because it fell on Beltane, the old May Day, when bonfires must be lighted and folk who understood the importance of these ancient rites must jump over them to protect the land from sorcery and assure good crops for the harvest. Mary herself had been among the leapers on numerous occasions; she had even, she admitted with a decent pretense of modesty, received accolades for her agility in the cause of fertility.

Mary warmed to her subject, describing in detail various Beltane fires she had hurdled. She did not hold with the degenerate custom of just lighting two bonfires side by side and running between them; although this sounded to Janet like a much more sensible thing to do, if one happened to be seriously concerned about baneful warlocks in the neighborhood. Janet couldn't recall that her brother Bert ever was.

Bert did burn over his pastures now and then. Often enough, as a kid, Janet herself had been one of the bunch stationed along the edges with wet sacks and old brooms to keep the fire from spreading. She'd enjoyed the excitement and the good-smelling smoke and the fun of beating out errant sparks. She'd realized the grass always grew better after a burning, but she'd never been aware that she was participating in a fertility rite. Janet thought perhaps she'd better not mention this back at the farm. Now that young Bert was stuck on the second Williamson girl, Annabelle was waxing a trifle edgy about fertility rites.

Reuel Williams was at her elbow again. Wickedly and deliberately Janet drew him into the Beltane fires, then slid away herself for a few words with the patriarch.

"Will you talk to me now, Uncle Caradoc? I barely got to say hello at teatime before you left me for a younger woman."

"An infant enchantress! Is it sleeping our Dorothy is now?"

"I hope so. I'm going to run up before we go in to dinner. Betty's great-niece Megan is baby-sitting. She seems like a nice kid."

"Oh yes, Megan is a good child. She will be Dorothy's seventh cousin once removed, you can be easy about her. Come now, I have a new treasure to show you."

"Not another silver crosier?"

"No, not that. Such discoveries do not happen more than once. How well I remember the pride in my father's voice as he told of drawing that beautiful thing forth from the dark, secret hole in which it had lain hidden for so many long years."

Janet knew how many: all the way back to the twelfth century and the reign of Henry II, when Rhys ap Gruffyd, the Lord Rhys, had been the most prominent man in Wales. The Lord Rhys had been among those who had favored the Cistercian monasteries; these had greatly flourished and multiplied, then gradually declined. Four centuries later, by the time of the Dissolution under Henry VIII, the buildings and the monks had been in sad state. The neighbors hadn't seemed to mourn overmuch at seeing the few remaining Cistercians ousted, but had set about lugging off their building stones to erect memorials in the utilitarian shapes of cottage walls and pigsties.

Janet hadn't been told and didn't quite like to ask how her husband's branch of the Rhyses had come to build their manor house around the monks' former dining hall, the one part that had always been kept in repair while outbuildings crumbled and even the chapel showed signs of decay. Various Rhyses had added to the manor from time to time, using what lay at hand. There were still a few oddments of ruins left here and there about the grounds, never removed nor dismantled lest some heir or other might take a notion to tack on another ell or build another cow barn.

With all the tearing down and rebuilding, various interesting artifacts had come to light. Some had been more than interesting, for the Cistercians in their heyday had waxed rich and spent freely to the greater glory of their God and the awe of the populace. It had been some Caradoc back around George IV's time who'd discovered the cryptic parchment; but nobody had caught on to what it meant until the present Sir Caradoc's grandfather had got a brainstorm one day and lowered his twelve-year-old son, Sir Caradoc's father, on a rope through a curtain of spiderwebs down a half-ruined stairwell, with a miner's lamp on his cap and a crowbar lashed to his belt.

Sir Caradoc's lilt rose almost to a song, chanting of how the young lad had found the stone with the crooked line carved into it, pried it out with his crowbar, stuck in his arm as far as it would go, and finally, croaked in the voice of a bullfrog, "Send down the basket, Father!"

Treasure trove must perforce be reported to the Crown and investigated by a coroner appointed to maintain the royal private properties. There was no way word of the great find would not have got around to the servants, no way they wouldn't have repeated it at the pub, no way that sole basketful wouldn't have been multiplied many times over in the telling. The coroner assigned to the Rhyses had been an Englishman, holding to the then-current belief among his peers that Wales was the armpit of the empire, that all Welshmen were liars and petty pilferers, and that no good thing could come out of a Welsh monastery because Henry VIII's trusty emissaries had well and duly snaffled everything worth taking three centuries before.

Wales had not then started to gear up for the tourist trade. The road had been vile, the inn worse. The coroner's bed had been not only lumpy but also verminous. The food had been unfit to mention, much less eat. Being thus in a filthy temper and bearing in mind that, while the Crown was entitled to seize any treasure it had a mind to, it must also pay the finder full value for what it took, the coroner had condemned the golden chalice as copper and its jewels as bogus. He'd reviled the badly tarnished crosier as a pitiful attempt to deceive, and declared the fist-size uncut emerald set into its crook to be in fact no more than a lump of Roman glass.

Told to take his junk away and dump it where he'd found it, Sir Caradoc's grandfather had humbly agreed with the coroner that he was just a stupid Taffy who hadn't known any better. The stupid Taffy had then placated the clever Englishman with a few noggins of homemade mead and talked him into writing a letter to the effect that there was nothing of value left at the site of the former monastery and no Rhys was ever again to pester the Crown with any more nonsense about hidden treasure. The Englishman had then departed with a sense of duty done and a slight buzzing in his ears. The crestfallen Welshman had watched him go, then slunk away to enjoy a quiet snicker while he wiped the carefully applied dirt off the golden chalice and got out the silver polish for the crosier.

Sir Caradoc's grandfather hadn't even bothered to mention the two golden sickles. That fine gentleman of a Sais wouldn't have been interested. Besides, they dated from the long-ago time when Wales had been still a sovereign nation, perhaps even from before the Romans. Why should those smart-mouthed Londoners put any claim to them anyway? It had been Welsh artisans who'd beaten the little sickles out of the native gold, Welsh Druids who'd used them to gather with due ceremony the all-healing mistletoe off the oak trees on which it grew.

Gathering mistletoe had been a major industry among the Druids. Not only deemed to be good for whatever ailed you, the pretty parasite also came in handy around the house as a picklock, a lightning conductor, and a good-luck charm for the dairy. The mere gracious gesture of bestowing a bouquet of mistletoe on the first cow to drop her calf after the New Year would put a crimp in the plans of any witch bent on curdling the milk or laying an antibutter spell on the churn. There might still be farmhouses around where a bunch of mistletoe could be seen gathering dust on the chimney piece. The very monks who'd done the cooking here when the house was yet a monastery would likely have kept some on hand, just in case.

Just why they'd collected the golden sickles was open to conjecture. Sir Caradoc thought it likely, as had his father and grandfather before him, that some abbot had confiscated the pretty things and tucked them away in his treasure hole as part of an effort to stamp out the old religion. Why they hadn't been melted down and the gold used for purposes the abbot deemed holier was anybody's guess. Maybe he hadn't needed the gold at the time, or maybe he hadn't had the heart to destroy the sickles.

That the Cistercians could actually have employed these pagan instruments for the purpose of gathering mistletoe would have been hard to credit, were it not that strange things had happened in those last, lax years so long after the founders of their houses had vowed themselves to poverty, holiness, and good works. According to history, a monk had been caught doing a tidy business in counterfeit coins, which he'd forged in his own cell. Rumors had even been bandied about that some of the monks in another monastery had turned out not to be males.

Anyway, for whatever reason, it was certain that somebody—the abbot, one of his flock, or all of them together—had been more than a bit interested in Druidic golden sickles. There'd been two of them in with the chalice and the crosier. Sir Caradoc's father, never forgetting that supreme moment at the end of his rope, had spent many hours thereafter prowling among the ruins, which were more abundant then than later, looking for another mystic mark. On the very eve of his eldest son's birth, he had come upon a stone marked with that same little crook, and behind it another sickle. Now, in his old age, Sir Caradoc had quite literally stumbled upon yet a fourth. Just before his birthday, too. Now, wasn't that a wonderful present for an old man?

He had it with him this very moment, a charming thing no bigger than a man's hand. "You see, Jenny? The blade is the shape of the crescent moon, for reasons Robert Graves has no doubt discussed in that wonderful but occasionally tedious book of his about the White Goddess."

"You could ask Mary," Janet suggested slyly.

"So I could." Sir Caradoc made no move to do so. "Would you like to hold it?"

"Oh, may I?"

This was the first time Janet had had any of the relics in her hand. The chalice was long gone. Sir Caradoc's grandfather, upon reflection, had decided that the coroner, though wrong about everything else, had been right in calling it ugly. Nevertheless, he'd figured that so much gold, so many jewels, and so impeccable a provenance must have their appeal for some wealthy collector. Being a resourceful man, he'd found one. The proceeds from the sale he'd so cannily invested that his heirs and assigns had so far never even needed to think of selling the crosier or the sickles.

The treasures were still where the old man had put them, back in the monks' dining hall, in a niche high on the wall that had most probably been there since the time of building, made to house a sacred relic of some sort. Sir Caradoc's grandfather had installed a wrought-iron grille to protect his finds. When his son had added his own two sickles, he'd also lined the grille with a sheet of heavy plate glass. Sir Caradoc was keeping the key in his inside waistcoat pocket by day and under his pillow by night. If, by an evil sleight, some rogue should succeed in stealing the treasures, Madoc could go and get them back.

If only Uncle Caradoc might hang on long enough for Dorothy to hear the story from his own lips! Selfish of her to be thinking about an old man's life in such terms, Janet realized, but maybe mothers couldn't help it. She'd better just run upstairs and make sure Megan hadn't run into any problems. With a twinge of regret, she handed back the newest golden sickle.

"Yes, you couldn't have had a more beautiful birthday present. Thank you for letting me hold it. Is there still time enough before dinner for me to take a peek at the baby?"

"Dinner will wait for you."

"Oh no, please. I shan't be five minutes."

As she headed for the stairs, Madoc, who'd been annexed by Iseult, managed to break away and intercept her. "What's up, Jenny? Are you all right?"

"I'm fine. I just thought I'd better check on Dorothy before we sit down."

"I'll go."

"And what if she's hungry? Fat lot of help you'd be. This is women's work, Betty said so. I'll be right back. go talk to Iseult some more."

"What about?"

"Ask her if she's read any good books lately."

Janet gave him a peck on the cheek and moved on. Once away from the drawing room, she picked up her skirts and ran, not that there was really anything to hurry for, but it did seem a long time since she'd left Dorothy up there alone with a stranger who was hardly more than a child herself.

Chapter 3

Janet needn't have been in a rush. When she opened the red-room door, silently so as not to startle the baby, Dorothy wasn't making a peep. The fire was burning just right, the room was just pleasantly warm. Megan was sitting on a low stool beside the cradle, rocking it gently, crooning a lullaby. At least Janet supposed this must be a lullaby; the young nanny was singing in Welsh, so she couldn't be sure. Anyway, the gentle sounds must be doing their job; Dorothy was curled up in her elegant nest with one fist to her cheek and her eyes tight shut. Nothing to worry about here. Janet smiled down at Megan, and Megan smiled timidly back.

"Everything all right?" she murmured.

"Yes'm," Megan whispered.

"Good, then I'll go on to dinner. Did Betty give you something to eat before you came up?"

"Yes'm."

She must know more English than this; most Welsh people were either bilingual or exclusively Anglophonic. Maybe Megan just didn't care to chat with strangers. As was right and proper. Janet wouldn't want Dorothy talking to strangers, either. She adjusted Dorothy's blanket a whisker, not that it hadn't been fine the way it was but a mother had to get in a bit of mothering, assured Megan that she'd be back in a while, and left the girls together.

This being the new wing, its general flavor was early Victorian. Woodwork was mahogany, doors had shiny brass knobs, draperies were plush with scads of fringe. Floors were heavily carpeted, even out here in the hall. Why all these big cabbage roses? Roses were for England. The daffodil was the flower of Wales. Daffodils probably weren't much in favor with carpet makers.

Anyway, the thick pile was agreeable to walk in. The heels of Janet's blue evening slippers weren't making a sound, even though she was walking briskly so as not to keep dinner waiting. In spite of all the food they'd been plied with in first class, the snack they'd had on the train, and Betty's Welsh cakes at tea, she found herself quite ready to eat again. It must be something in the air. She was almost to the stairs when she saw the monk.

Of all the foolishness! The hooded figure in the long gray robe was lurking, silent and foglike, at the other end of the hallway, trying to look spooky. Danny the Boots, she assumed; according to Betty in her more acerbic moments, Danny's mental capacity was about threepence to the pound. He'd better not go poking his head into the red room to scare Megan and wake the baby. Should she tell him so? As Janet hesitated with her hand on the newel post, the monk faded gently from view.

"Well, I'll be darned. He must have been real."

Or rather not real. Janet supposed she ought to feel scared; instead she was rather pleased. It would be something to tell at the dinner table.

Then again, maybe it wouldn't. There was no sense

in getting anybody all worked up over a perfectly harmless ghost. Whoever was sleeping at that end of the hall might be the nervous type. She'd better just mention the incident quietly to Madoc or Uncle Caradoc and see what they thought. In her own opinion, the ghost had picked a silly time and place to manifest itself. If it was looking to make an effect, why couldn't it have skinned down to the dining hall and floated in behind the soup?

Downstairs, couples were being sorted out to go in to dinner, and it appeared that she was to be belle of the ball. Janet hurried to lay her hand on the arm that Uncle Caradoc had been reserving for her, noticing with some small relief that Madoc was taking his mother and not Iseult. Dafydd had been assigned to Lisa, as was right and proper considering that she'd been kind enough to offer him a place to sleep during his visit. It was Tom Feste who'd drawn the sumptuous redhead. Tom's track record with actresses had so far been rather spectacularly unsuccessful, according to Silvestrine. He was said to be paying alimony to two or three. One might have thought he'd have developed an allergy by now, but he seemed pleased enough with his companion.

Lisa's pretty daughter had been paired with the youngest mouse, Dai being the only male of suitable age in the party. Sir Emlyn had got stuck with Mary and the Beltane fires. That was all right, he'd rehearse some Handel oratorio or other in his head while she ran on. Neither would impinge on the other's pleasure and both would leave the table with a sense of time well spent. That left Gwen the only unattached woman, with Reuel Williams and Bob the Blob left over. Far too wily to choose, she gave an arm to each and swept into the dining hall like a female privateer running her prizes into port.

Since his wife's death eight years or so before, Sir Caradoc had got into the habit of asking his nephew's wife to play hostess whenever she happened to be in residence. Lady Rhys took her place at the far end and got everybody seated to her satisfaction. Not entirely to theirs, perhaps, but when one had to cope with a man too many, one did the best one could.

Lady Rhys had done well by her daughter-in-law, anyway. Comfortable between Sir Caradoc and Sir Emlyn, Janet was mildly entertained to see Dafydd parked beside Mary the Fires and Iseult tucked away on the opposite side of the long banqueting board. She leaned back in her ancient but mercifully cushioned oaken chair and waited for Sir Caradoc to say grace and the footmen to start bringing around the soup, which old Iowerth the butler was serving from a vast silver tureen at the sideboard.

It was interesting to see how many liveried servitors could manifest themselves on formal occasions. Janet had not so far discovered where they went or what they did between dinnertimes. Stayed in their rooms and wrote poetry, perhaps. Or went out on the hillsides and sang to the sheep.

Actually there were only two waiting tonight beside the butler. Fifteen at table required no great retinue, this was rather a paltry turnout in a house where the old Welsh tradition of hospitality was scrupulously maintained.

Caradoc Rhys had been one of four. Born in 1902, he'd been too young to fight in the Great War that had taken his elder brother and left him in line to be fourteenth baronet. His parents and a sister had all died in the terrible influenza epidemic of 1918. Not yet of age, he'd found himself Sir Caradoc, lord of the manor and thrall to the countless cares and responsibilities of a large estate, some thousands of sheep, a tenantry who regarded him as their appointed guardian angel and fount of every blessing; along with a younger brother who showed great promise as a musician and none whatsoever as a farmer.

Caradoc had done his duty and done it well. There had been money enough, thanks to the chalice and his forbears' good stewardship. His workers had been decently paid, his sheep well fed, his brother's music lessons paid for. He'd married young and well, a girl from the county with a little money of her own and no great slew of relatives to add to the weight of his burdens. The late Lady Rhys hadn't been everybody's cup of tea, but she'd been Caradoc's to love and to cherish, and she'd loved him and cherished him back.

Sir Caradoc's brother had fulfilled his early promise, become a concert violinist, and married his accompanist. Emlyn had been their only child. During the war, as the blitz hotted up, they'd sent him for safety to the manor, where he'd have Caradoc's son, Huw, also an only child and just a year or two older, as a companion. When one of Hitler's buzz bombs had found the stage on which Emlyn's parents had been performing, the new-made orphan had stayed on, regarding the manor as his home and Huw as more a brother than a cousin. In time, each had been best man at the other's wedding. Huw and his Elen had wanted a big family, but they'd managed to produce just two, a boy and a girl.

Huw's daughter, an anthropologist, was in Africa with her husband and some other scientists; they were sorry to miss the party but would be home for Christmas. Her brother, Owain, Huw's right hand and eventual heir, had never wanted to do anything other than the work he was born to. He'd done an agricultural course and married as soon as he decently could, a girl of Welsh descent whose forbears had emigrated to Argentina during the nineteenth century and joined the Welsh sheep-farming colony in Patagonia. Owain and his Mavis had lost no time building up the family stock, they and their four offspring were just now back from visiting Mavis's relatives with a Patagonian niece and nephew along for ballast. The two young Patagonians spoke good English and Welsh, Sir Caradoc said, but with a Spanish accent. Janet would enjoy them.

Janet was sure she would. She thought she wouldn't bring up her monk while Uncle Caradoc was so happy talking about his family. She waited till Silvestrine turned the table, and told Sir Emlyn instead.

It cannot be easy to upstage Handel, but Janet succeeded; her father-in-law was intrigued. "A monk in the west wing? Jenny, that's most unusual. I don't recall anybody's ever seeing one except here in the dining hall or out among the ruins."

"That's what I'd have expected. He did seem terribly out of place up there among all that plush and mahogany. Some overstuffed Victorian who'd died of too many nine-course dinners would have been more in keeping, wouldn't you say?" Janet couldn't stop herself from glancing over at Bob the Blob, who was shoveling in lamb and new peas at double speed for fear a footman might snatch away his plate while there was still food to be had.

Sir Emlyn smiled. "Far more appropriate. You must have been startled."

"Not really. I thought it was just somebody trying to be funny. I was all set to lay him out about not scaring Megan and waking the baby when he simply vanished. Then I realized I must have seen a ghost."

Toward the other end of the table, Dafydd was behaving badly. Instead of turning to chat with Mary as etiquette demanded, he had not even pretended to listen when she'd ventured an opening remark or two, but applied himself in sullen silence to his glass and his food. Given the cold shoulder, Mary had no recourse but to eat her dinner in chilly isolation or to eavesdrop on Sir Emlyn and Janet. She eavesdropped; she gasped. She interrupted.

"You saw a *ghost*?"

"That was my impression at the time," replied Janet, wishing to goodness Mary wouldn't talk so loud. "At first I thought it was somebody playing a trick, but then it vanished. All the bedroom doors were closed, and there was nowhere else it could have gone. But it was nothing to be scared of."

"Scared? Oh no. No indeed. This is marvelous, simply marvelous! Bob! Bob, listen. Mrs. Madoc's seen a ghost."

Incredibly, Bob the Blob stopped eating. With the last forkful of peas halfway to his mouth, he sat for a moment rapt in what looked like catalepsy but turned out to be unalloyed rapture. When he uttered, his voice was surprisingly authoritarian. "A ghost? Describe it me, pray, Mrs. Madoc."

By this time, the whole table and even the footmen were listening; Janet had no recourse but to start over from the beginning. The episode had been thin enough at the start; as she talked, it sounded thinner and sillier. Reuel Williams was sneering, Dai was trying to but hadn't quite got the knack. Tib was agog, Gwen enraptured, Tom amused, Lisa taking it calmly. Iseult seemed annoyed, Lady Rhys just a tad alarmed, Sir Caradoc pleased as punch. Madoc pushed back his chair.

"If you'll excuse me, I think I'll just run up and have a look."

"Let's all go!" cried Tib.

Her grandfather raised a staying hand. "That would not do at all, Tib. Ghosts are tetchy creatures, and so is our Betty. She would take it greatly amiss if we raced out before the meal is over. Let me tell you about the first ghost I ever saw. It was right about where you are sitting now, and I was only ten years old."

Sir Caradoc's story had little more substance than Janet's but he told it far better, keeping a tight hold on everybody's attention until Madoc was back among them. He hadn't run into anything in the supernatural line but had peeked in on the baby and was in a position to assure everyone, meaning principally Janet, that Dorothy was rapt in peaceful infant slumber. That was excellent news for her, now they could talk about something else.

But no, Bob was as tenacious of the subject as he'd been of his plate. "Sir Caradoc, what color was your ghost?"

"Color? Why, no color, as far as I can remember. Whitish, or pale gray, I suppose. Cistercians were known as the Grey Monks or the White Monks, to differentiate them from the Cluny and other Black Monks."

"But over the white habit, a Cistercian would have worn a black apron or scapular, the scapular being most probably a short cape or stole. Was there no black whatever about your ghost?"

"I really could not say, such a long time has passed. What about yours, Janet?"

"Oh, just ordinary ghost color, sort of like fog. I'm sorry to disappoint you, Bob."

"But you do not disappoint me, Mrs. Madoc. On the contrary, you elate me. My hypothesis is confirmed. What you and our honored kinsman saw could have been no monk. That was, on the contrary, a Druid!"

Janet started to laugh. Bob's pronouncement was

just too pedantically bombastic. What possible difference could a ghost's religion make?

Quite a lot, evidently. Mary was hooting like a stage whistle. "I knew it! I knew it! It's the sickle. He's come to take back his golden sickle!"

At last she'd caught Dafydd's attention. He turned in his chair and looked down upon her with about the same kind of interest he'd have shown a worm in his salad. "Then what was he haunting the west wing for? The sickles are all down here."

"Not the newest one. Sir Caradoc's been carrying it around. The Druid must have followed him up to his room."

"Then why didn't it have sense enough to follow him back?" Janet argued. "Uncle Caradoc was in the drawing room when I saw the ghost."

And so, come to think of it, was everybody else in the party. She'd been the last one down, they'd been lined up ready to come to the table. So if there had by any chance been a human agent behind that eerie manifestation, he or she couldn't be anybody here.

Mary wasn't ready to yield the floor. "Maybe it thought Sir Caradoc had left the sickle in his bedroom when he changed for dinner."

"I did not," Sir Caradoc assured her. "The sickle is in a safe place. You need not worry, we have a policeman in the house. Tomorrow Madoc will perhaps be kind enough to help me put it up there with the others."

"Of course," said Madoc. "Whenever you say. Ah, I see Betty's done us proud."

Nobody would expect to get out of Wales without having at least once eaten trifle. There are trifles and trifles: some of them are excellent, some of them are so-so, some of them are downright awful. Betty's was no trifling matter. Its base was not the usual sponge cake but a delectable gateau soaked in Sir Caradoc's best sherry. Its jelly was homemade currant, tart and firm and glowing like rubies. Its fruits were fresh and ripe, jazzed up with a drop of rum. Its custard was smooth and thick and just a touch nutmeggy. Its whipped cream was subtly flavored with Grand Marnier and piled up like summer clouds over Snowdon. Iowerth had an extra jug of heavy cream ready to pour on lest anybody find the trifle not quite rich enough already.

For Janet there was a special portion in a small glass bowl. "There is no spirits in this, ma'am," the footman murmured as he set it before her. Clever Betty, she didn't want Dorothy getting drunk any more than Janet did.

Suspecting that something like this might happen, Janet had gone easy on the lamb. She mustn't hurt Betty's feelings by not eating it all, God help her.

Orange juice on the gateau, a hint of lemon with the fruit. Lovely. Now if only Dai would quit staring across the table at her through those owl-eye glasses and Bob glancing up to make sure that she hadn't got more trifle than he, and if Mary would ever quit harping on the Druid's sickle! Driven to desperation, Janet gave each pesty mouse one of her looks and asked Sir Emlyn in a good, clear voice why Handel's oratorios had continued to be performed so much oftener than his operas.

That perked even Dafydd up. The conversation became general and often heated. They gravitated in a bunch to the grand piano in the drawing room and wound up with everybody singing excerpts from the *Messiah, The Creation,* and a number of lesser-known works which of course everybody but Janet and Madoc had down cold. Dafydd was in wonderful voice, as was only expected. Surprisingly, so was Bob the Blob. Even when she could no longer stop her yawns, Janet hated to leave the party.

42

Chapter 4

Madoc woke early. Really early, early enough to have beaten the sun by a good way. But not before the birds. They were having a high old time out there. Some of them, anyway. Tone-deaf as he was, he couldn't make out their calls very well, but this racket could hardly be an exaltation of larks, much less a deception of lapwings. Uncle Caradoc had taught him the ancient terms ages ago; being Madoc, he'd remembered.

A bevy of peacocks? No, Uncle Caradoc refused to keep peacocks because they sang too raucously off-key. A building of rooks? Not possible, there'd never been a rookery at the manor, nobody knew why. Madoc slid out of bed, cautiously so as not to wake Janet, and slipped over to the window in his bare feet. The floor was cold as banished hope, the fire was down to a few ashy coals. Outside, the mist was thick over the ground; he couldn't see any birds, but they were out there, squawking their beaks off.

Janet hadn't been able to sleep much on the plane, but Madoc was trained to nod off when and where he could. He'd had all the rest he needed, no sense in going back to bed; he'd only start fidgeting and wake the ladies. No need to make up the fire, the room would get warm enough once the sun was up. He dragged on trousers and an anorak over his pajamas, stuck dry socks in his pocket, slung thick-soled brogues around his neck by their laces. He let himself out the window, pulled it shut after him, and climbed down the ivy for auld lang syne.

The noise was coming from up beyond the farmhouse, the separate dwelling where Uncle Huw and Aunt Elen lived. Over among the ruins, Madoc guessed. Only the chapel had been kept in some kind of repair, it still had a door and most of its roof. He headed that way and was right to have done so. Now he could see them through the mist, great black birds, bigger than any blackbird, flapping in and out through the unglazed windows. Too big for rooks, not big enough for ravens. A flock—no, a *murder* of crows. Carrion crows, fighting each other to get in, flying back out with dripping red gobbets in their beaks.

He'd seen them like this at highway kills, swarming over each other to get at the carcass, tearing at the open wounds with their powerful black beaks, not budging from their feast until the next car was almost upon them. He ran to see what they were eating.

Only a sheep, thank God! Or what was left of one. Blood and wool were all over the floor, black wings filling the chapel with their frenzied beating. As he entered, stepping carefully to avoid what he could of the mess, the clever, cautious marauders took flight and went streaming and squawking out through the windows and the hole in the roof. Madoc could see it clearly, the mangled body on the eroded stone floor, the blood puddled deeper in the low spots. It was mainly at the neck they'd been pecking; the head was off by itself, standing up on its stump atop the altar, with a tatty brown cloth cap cocked over its left horn and a badly charred briar pipe stuck in its mouth.

Padarn's cap, Padarn's pipe. Madoc would have known them in Tierra del Fuego, he'd never seen Uncle Caradoc's oldest sheepman without them. Padarn couldn't be many years younger than the baronet whose liege man he'd been since the day he was born, in a thatched stone cottage beyond the ruins where his father and grandfather and not a few before them had lived and died in the service of the Rhyses.

Padarn could never have committed this outrage, not with one of Sir Caradoc's sheep. His ram, rather, the huge curled horns and the splotch of ruddle on its exposed left hip—distinguishable from a bloodstain, though only just—told Madoc that. Padarn would not have destroyed his patron's animal unless by his patron's orders. Padarn would not have desecrated even an abandoned chapel, he was strict Chapel himself. Padarn would never, not ever, have lent his own cap and pipe to so impious a display. Nor would he have parted from them willingly in any case. What in God's name had happened to him?

There was hardly any place to search. Madoc found the old shepherd in a matter of seconds, down behind the carved stone altar. He was lying on his side, his knees drawn up to his chest, his arms wrapped around his head as if to protect it from the crows. Crows liked to peck out eyeballs, Padarn would know that. Madoc drew a shuddering breath and knelt beside him.

"Padarn! Padarn, it's Madoc. Madoc Rhys, can you hear me?"

He got no answer, he took hold of the hand that was on top. It was clammy from the damp and ice-cold, but not that kind of cold, not cold and rigid. "It's all right,

Padarn, the crows are gone. They won't get at you. What's happened here?"

Gently Madoc drew the old man's arms away from his face. Padarn's knees relaxed a bit; he rolled over on his back, his eyes wide open, staring up into the cobweb-snarled, bat-hung, stone-buttressed ceiling. His lips moved a bit, but nothing came out.

Madoc knew shock when he saw it. No use in trying to make the poor chap talk sense yet. He felt quickly for injuries, saw no blood, found no apparent damage except one great lump on the head. Padarn must have been hit with his cap still on, thank God; the skull seemed to be intact. It was probably safe enough to move him— he couldn't stay here in the damp, not with all this blood splashed about. Take him into the farmhouse, get him warm, give him stimulants, send for the doctor. Padarn had never been a big man; age had whittled him down to a wisp. Madoc picked up the old sheepman easily enough, he was steering a path to the door through the carnage when his uncle arrived.

"Madoc! What in God's name is going on here? What are you doing with Padarn?"

"Hello, Uncle Huw. I was bringing him to you, actually. He's badly in shock and probably concussed."

"How did it happen?"

"As you see, somebody's been up to nasty tricks. I'd guess that Padarn heard the ram in trouble, came to see what was wrong, and got knocked on the head. He's got a lump the size of a doorknob, it's a mercy his skull isn't fractured. We'd best get him warm and send for the doctor. And the police."

"No! Give him to me and go back to the manor."

"I can't do that, Uncle Huw."

"Then you will do as I say. I am not having my father's ninetieth birthday ruined by some damned fool playing at witchcraft—Padarn will be best in his own bed. We will light him a fire and give him hot tea to drink. Then we will come back and clean up this unspeakable mess before the mist lifts and others come to see what the crows are fussing about. Then I will go back to Padarn. If he does not come to himself in an hour or so, I will drive him to hospital and tell some awful lie about an accident. You will say not one word of this to any living soul, nor shall I. After the party is over and done with, I will see that all steps are taken to track down and punish the culprit."

By the time the party was over, the culprit could be over the hills and far away. Madoc knew better than to argue. Uncle Caradoc had, ten years ago, yielded over to his son all responsibility for the vast sheep farm as well as his hereditary position as local magistrate. One of these days, Huw would be fifteenth baronet and lord of the manor. As a policeman, Madoc deplored Huw Rhys's decision. As a Rhys, he could not but think his uncle was right in putting the family first. When Huw offered to take the old sheepman's limp body from him, he shook his head and followed his uncle, docile as a sheep himself, to Padarn's cottage.

The place was tiny, its inside walls were blackened from many an open fire, but it was no hovel. Electricity had been laid on and Padarn's creature comforts not neglected. The bed had a decent mattress and was neatly made up with clean sheets and good woolen blankets, all smooth and snug.

"Looks as though he never went to bed last night," Huw grunted. "All those hours in the cold and damp. Make up the fire, Madoc, and boil the kettle."

A shiny little electric kettle was sitting on the shelf by the sink, left filled with water in the practical way of country folk. Madoc plugged it in and went to tend the fire while Huw, gently as a mother, eased Padarn out of his clammy garments and into a flannel nightshirt, chafed his feet to get the blood flowing, and covered them with socks of Padarn's own knitting to keep in the warmth. The kettle boiled, Madoc made tea, sugared it well, filled a stoneware jug with the rest of the hot water and slipped it into the bed.

Padarn must have been tough as an old boot. By the time Madoc's fire was up to a good blaze and Huw had got a few spoonfuls of sweet, strong tea into him, the patient had begun to stir.

"Ah, that's the way of it. Can you talk, *bach*?" Huw begged. "Can you tell us what happened, then?"

"Witches." A frightened whisper. "Witches, coming at me through the air. Great flapping things with eyes of fire and terrible cries. It is doomed I am surely."

"No, Padarn. It was crows you saw, only crows. It is the old ram from the lower pasture that is dead, and the crows coming to peck at him. Only the crows, *bach*, you know I would never lie to you. Is it hungry you are? Could you eat something?"

"It is more tea I could be drinking."

The voice was stronger, not much, but enough to wipe the anguish off Huw Rhys's face. "Here you are, then. Hot and strong, to put the heart back into you. Can you hold the cup yourself?"

Padarn could, and did. He handed it back empty with a small sigh of content, and closed his eyes. The other two men stayed just long enough to make sure his breathing was regular, the kettle unplugged, and the fire drawing well; then they hurried back to the chapel carrying what they could find in the way of cleaning tools.

The crows were back. Madoc felt a savage impulse to pelt them with stones from the ruins, he fought it down. One could barely blame wild creatures for snatching their chance at a square meal. No doubt the best solution from the crows' point of view would have been to carry the ram's remains to some secluded place and leave them to be picked clean. Huw wasn't having that.

"Among the ruins is an old well that went dry and was boarded up long before you were born. We'll dump the body there and cover it over with stones. As for Padarn's pipe and cap"—he shrugged—"I'll wash them off, and perhaps he won't remember."

"We ought to carry it in a tarpaulin or something so we shan't get bloody ourselves and give the show away," said Madoc. "And something to soak up this mess on the floor."

"Sawdust. I'll go."

Huw strode off toward the big barn, vigorous and hale despite his sixty-odd years. He was still a tall man, broad-shouldered and fair-skinned; this was the way Madoc remembered Sir Caradoc from earlier visits. Huw was looking more and more like his father as time passed, taking on his guise as well as his responsibilities.

Madoc had responsibilities, too. A policeman couldn't just destroy the evidence of a crime without first trying to learn what he could from what there was. Could this have been the work of one person alone? A big ram would have been hard to handle, even an old one, Madoc knew that from painful firsthand experience. One experienced sheep handler with a well-trained dog might have managed it, he supposed, or a psychopath in a frenzy of blood lust; but he wouldn't care to bet on either just yet. More likely a pack of necromantic nuts celebrating some rite of spring.

Thinking of dogs, where was Padarn's? He'd always had one of his own, always a female called Fan after his long-dead wife. Last time Madoc and Janet were here, the most recent Fan had been fairly gray around the muzzle. Perhaps she'd died and Padarn hadn't yet replaced her. He'd ask Uncle Huw later on; just now he'd better scout around for clues, if any.

He did find a few bloody footprints, but they didn't tell him much. From the crude shapes and fuzzy texture, he deduced that the culprit or culprits must have been wearing the sort of cheap cloth scuffs that could have been bought almost anywhere and discarded once the gory deed was done. Wear disposable gloves as well, strip yourself otherwise naked, wash off the grue after the slaughter was over, under the pump or in Aunt Elen's lily pond, get dressed and go home, and who'd be the wiser?

It was hard to envision a bona fide warlock in rubber gloves and fuzzy slippers and nothing in between. The cap and pipe suggested less a primeval ceremony than a vicious act of spite or vandalism trying to pass itself off as a practical joke, but one never knew. Madoc was still looking when Huw came back on the dead run with a bucket of sawdust and a shovel and a big canvas sheet.

"Mist's beginning to rise," he panted. "Folk will be stirring, we'd best work fast."

They did. In a matter of minutes the ram and the sweepings were down the well and the cover back on. Huw went to see how Padarn was doing. Madoc sluiced a few bucketfuls of water over the chapel floor and altar, made sure he hadn't collected any telltale stains, took the bucket back to the barn, went back to the manor, and swarmed up the ivy. The window he'd been so careful to close behind him wouldn't open. Janet had to get up and let him in, laughing fit to kill.

"Hi, Tarzan. Me Jane. What in the world have you been up to?"

"Just taking a little morning climb. I hope I didn't wake you."

"Not really. What time is it?"

"Getting on toward six, I expect. Why don't you go back to bed for a bit? I'm going to shave."

Madoc took his time in the bathroom, he felt the need of a cleansing soak. Like as not, the gloves and slippers would turn up in the pond if anyone ever got around to dragging it. The knife or cleaver used for that rather competent beheading might well be there also. He didn't suppose any of the things would help much, but a start had to be made somewhere.

He might as well quit champing at the bit. Uncle Huw wasn't going to budge, and Madoc couldn't really blame him. Not with so many being gathered together for so momentous an occasion. Not with the Rhyses all working their heads off to get ready.

He wished he could forget about heads off, at least for now. He wished he could tell Janet, he might feel better. And make her feel worse. The day after tomorrow would be time enough. It would have to be. He heaved himself out of the tub at last and picked up his razor. He was doing the fussy bit under his nose when Janet tapped at the door.

"Were you planning to spend the day in there? I'm getting up."

Getting themselves and the baby put together took a while, but they were down in the kitchen not long after seven. Betty had tea in front of them before they'd even sat themselves down.

"Is it up so early you are, then? We thought you'd be sleeping till noon."

"And waste a day like this?" said Janet. "Just one piece of toast for me please, Betty. I ate far too much last night. Oh, and thanks for making me that special trifle. I practically licked the dish. Are we the first ones down?"

"Oh no, Master will be along. It is his eggs I am cooking now. He just stepped out to be taking a look at the weather. Will you have eggs, Madoc?"

While they were settling the question of Madoc's breakfast, Sir Caradoc came in through the back entry. Dorothy, already conversant with the Welsh tradition of hospitality, offered him a bite of the rusk Betty had given her to try out her tooth on. After a while, he got around to noticing her parents.

"And what are your plans for this beautiful day?"

"I'd like to go up to the farm for a while," said Janet. "We'd like Aunt Elen and Uncle Huw to see the baby, and we thought we might help out a bit with the party."

"Such a fuss because an old man has grown a year older." Sir Caradoc looked pretty smug about the fuss. "There is to be a Maypole, Mary tells me."

"How nice, I've never seen one. What happens? Do the children dance around it?"

"Probably not, but it is pretty to see. Dorothy shall be our Queen of the May, with a crown of daisies around her sweet head."

"She's a bit young to be crowned," Madoc protested. "Why don't we just pin a couple of leeks to her nappy?"

"Daddy's making fun of you, Dorothy," said Janet. "What about the Beltane fire, Uncle Caradoc? Will there be one?"

"I suppose so." The old man didn't sound particularly elated by that part of the program. "It is always a worry to me. There will have been drink taken by then, you see. Some of the young fellows may get silly. And some of the girls also."

"Well, I expect we girls here will be in bed by then. What do you say, Madoc? Do you suppose we'd be too early if we went to the farm right after you've finished your breakfast?"

"Oh no, they'll have been up before us. Unless you'd like me to put the sickle into the niche for you, Uncle Caradoc."

"There is no hurry about that. We can do it at dinnertime. Maybe the ghost will come and watch."

"Then Bob can tell for sure whether he's a monk or a Druid," said Janet, "though I personally can't see what difference it makes."

"Oh, it would make a difference. The Druids were not such gentle creatures as those folklore chaps make them out."

Betty was setting a huge plateful of bacon, eggs, fried bread, and home-cured sausage in front of Sir Caradoc. "There you are then, Master, and may the food lie easy in your stomach."

"Thank you, Betty. Your food always agrees with me, you know that."

If a man Uncle Caradoc's age could down a meal the size of that one every morning, he was probably good for another decade or two, Janet thought. While Madoc finished his paltry single egg and sausage, she tied on Dorothy's white bonnet and buttoned up the pink sweater with bunnies on it that Silvestrine had knitted while Sir Emlyn was conducting rehearsals in Edinburgh. The day would surely be warm once the sun got high, but the thermometer still had a way to go, and God forbid that the Queen of the May should come down with a sniffle.

The mist was dissipated by now; the tits and the finches were making merry in the hedgerows; the sun was offering a handsome apology for yesterday's sullen streak. Madoc took Dorothy on one arm and Janet on the other, just to feel them safe with him.

Uncle Huw couldn't have told Aunt Elen about Padarn. She was all smiles when she met them at the farmhouse door. "Come in! Oh, what a love! Come, Dorothy, give Auntie a kiss. Have you eaten breakfast?"

"We had something with Uncle Caradoc," Janet temporized. They'd had quite enough, but there was no way they were going to get out of having more. She sat down at the long table and looked expectant, as courtesy demanded, while Elen whipped fresh buns out of the oven and poured boiling water into the teapot. "Where's all the family, Aunt Elen?"

"Owain's off to the sheep. The kids are still asleep, the lazy creatures. Huw's around somewhere, he'll be in for his tea. Mavis is out at the high barn, dusting off about a hundred ugly old plates Huw's grandmother bought at a sale years ago. I suppose they're antiques by now. We store them away in one of the grain bins; they come in handy every so often for a major bash."

"Can we help?"

"Not on your life! You sit right here and talk to me. Have you finished your house? Were the icebergs bad in the river this year? Is Dorothy teething yet? Did you bring any snaps?"

Janet had expected just such questions. She was showing Elen a view of the lovely St. John River with not a floe in sight and Sir Emlyn in waders and an old felt hat stuck all over with dry flies, reeling in a salmon, when Huw came in. He put on a decent show of surprise and pleasure. "Ah, Madoc, welcome home. Jenny, it's good to see you again. And this is your little one! Would she have a hug for her uncle Huw, do you think?"

She would. Huw kept her on his knee while he drank two cups of tea and ate one of Elen's buns. His wife was all for showing him Janet's snapshots, but he shook his head.

"Let's save them for when I've time to enjoy them. Madoc, I was thinking you and I might clean up the chapel. Give the floor a good scrubbing and brush down some of the cobwebs. Folk will be wandering in, you know. Elen, would you have a cloth we could drape over the altar? Nothing special, just something to give a spot of color."

And hide the bloodstains from the severed head that must have soaked into the stone. There were no flies on Huw Rhys. Madoc nodded.

"I'll be glad to help, Uncle Huw. Where do you keep your mops and things, Aunt Elen?"

"In the closet over there. Help yourselves. I'll find you a scrap of something, Huw. Jenny, you might like to pick flowers if you've nothing else on just now. They'd be pretty on the altar."

Elen was a tallish woman, more Saxon than Celt, she wore her silver-gray hair in a thick coronet. Even in an old-fashioned print housedress and lisle stockings, with a scrubbing pail in one hand and a mop in the other, she had a presence about her. "Here you are, then. Now scat, all of you. I've pies to make."

"I can help with them after I've done the flowers," Janet offered.

"No, Mavis will be back from doing the plates. Pick lots, Jenny, it would be nice to see that gloomy old place looking cheerful for once. Here, take my snippers and this rug for Dorothy to crawl around on."

Huw and Madoc went off to the great barn. Janet put Dorothy down on the rug and let her crawl around in the sun while she herself cut sprays of bloom from places where they wouldn't show too much, and laid them carefully in the basket. A perfect chore for an all-but-perfect day. Dorothy was practically nose-to-nose with a butterfly that had lit on the rug, too bad Madoc wasn't here to see.

Well, there'd be other butterflies, and perhaps other

babies. Janet could feel herself calming down, mellowing out, starting to yawn. She'd better get these flowers into water before temptation overcame her and she flaked out on the rug with Dorothy and the butterfly. She picked up her child, the rug, and the basket all together; they made a big armload, but she hadn't far to go.

Elen had a row of jam pots already lined up beside the sink, she was fussing around with some pieces of faded velvet. "I thought one of these might do for the altar, we wouldn't want anything new-looking. What do you think, Jenny, the red or the blue?"

"How about that funny greenish piece? It would look springy and blend with the flowers." Janet was working with her pickings, not trying to be fancy, just bunging them into the jam pots and giving them water to keep them happy overnight. "Would you have any candlesticks that aren't worth stealing? I personally wouldn't put anything out there that I cared about."

"Neither would I. This pair might do, wouldn't you think? I picked them up ages ago at a jumble sale. I don't think I've ever used them."

"They'll be fine." The candlesticks were just cheap green glass chunks that wouldn't show up much against the cloth anyway. "I suppose the candles ought to be white or cream-colored."

"Oh yes, otherwise Mary and Bob will be suspecting us of practicing witchcraft without a license. Here, take these white ones, they're a little bit used and battered-looking."

"Perfect. Maybe I'd better empty the water out of these jars and fill them up later. They'll be awfully heavy to carry if I don't."

"Oh, leave it in, and trundle them up in the wheelbarrow. Wheel it right up to the sink, this floor will have to be washed later anyway. Jenny, will you look at that now? Dorothy's trying to pull herself up by the table leg. I'll mind her here if you don't mind going alone to the chapel. They should have the worst cleared away by this time."

"If they don't, I'll wait outside. Thank you, Aunt Elen. It's the building just past that broken wall, isn't it? The one that still has most of its roof?"

"That's right. See you in a bit, then. You'll be ready for your *teabach*. Would Dorothy like some porridge, do you think?"

"A little, maybe. She had a chopped egg for breakfast. She and Betty's cat, I should say. I suspect the cat got the lion's share."

"You can be sure he did, the old glutton. Here, let me help you over the sill."

Chapter 5

"**I**s it safe to come in?"

That was Janet, with the flowers. Not to worry, Madoc had done a more thorough job on the floor this time, it was as clean as it was likely to get. He sloshed the scrubbing water out a window so that she wouldn't notice how red it was, and went to meet her.

"Just in time, love. Watch the floor, it may be slippery. Where's the kid?"

"Aunt Elen's giving her another breakfast. That makes three so far. She got cozy with a butterfly while I was picking, I'm afraid she's turned into an awful flirt."

"Gets it from you." He pulled her against him and sought her mouth.

"So this is what Welshmen do in chapel," she panted when she could get her breath back. "Where's Uncle Huw? What did he do, stick you with the dirty work and slide off?"

"That's just what he did do." Padarn was fairly rational now, Huw had popped back for a minute to report. He could remember dropping off while listening in on the wireless, waking up and stepping out to take a look at the weather, hearing some small commotion over by the chapel and coming to see what it was. The last Fan had been put down in March and Padarn wouldn't have another dog. He said he was too old. Huw said he spent much of his time these days in the manor kitchen, fetching wood for Betty and chinning about old times with Uncle Caradoc, God bless them all.

"Didn't you bring the flowers?" he asked.

"They're outside, in the wheelbarrow. I'll get them."

"I'll do it, Jenny." It would be a refreshing change from scrubbing clotted gore out of the cracks in flagstones. Madoc went to fetch in the jam pots while Janet stood pondering where to put them.

Those latter-day Cistercians appeared to have lavished more care on their dining hall than they had on their chapel, or else it had been thoroughly sacked by Henry VIII's men. It was ancient but otherwise nothing special: just a narrow room perhaps thirty feet long with roughly dressed stone walls that had two small windows knocked into them on either side. They might have been glazed at some time or other; if so, the glass was long gone. Heavy black oak beams held up what was left of the roof.

The monks and the villagers who came to attend their services would have sat in pews or on backless benches made from other great oaks, Janet supposed. Any furnishings must have rotted away or, more likely, been carried away ages ago. The altar was a slab of the native slate, carved all over in the intricate squiggles beloved of the ancient Celts, laid across a couple of dressed granite blocks that must have taken a good deal of muscle or perhaps a spot of wizardry to set up. Janet unfolded Elen's remnant of bronzy green velvet, most likely part of an old drapery, and spread it over the slab.

"There, that's not too bad. Hand me that biggest potful of flowers, will you?"

Flowers in the middle, candles at the sides; she fitted

them into their undistinguished holders and teased the sprays of bloom into a spread-out fan. "How does this look?"

"A vast improvement. What happens with these others?"

"Aunt Elen said to put them in the window niches, but I'm afraid they'd get blown down and smashed. I'll just set them here in front of the altar."

Janet was glad she'd picked so many. The masses of white and pink and yellow and green were making a difference, their fragrance masking the vaguely disagreeable odor she'd noticed when she'd first come in. She fussed with the bouquets, loosening them up to make more of a splash.

Masses of cobwebs still clung to the rafters. She herself would have swiped them down with a broom tied to a long stick; but she wasn't going to mention them now. They'd bring a shower of dust along with them and the place would have to be cleaned all over again. Anyway, why disturb the ancestral spiders? At least something was getting some good out of the chapel.

"There," she said at last, "that's the best I can do. I'll come back in the morning with Aunt Elen's watering pot and give them another drink."

"Yes, love."

Madoc put his arm around her again. The two of them stood there, facing the altar with its air of springtime. A rite of exorcism, Janet thought, though she couldn't imagine why. What in heaven's name had come over her?

It must be something in the air around here. She'd be trying to ride a broomstick next. Speaking of which, here came Mary the Fires. She and Madoc made their manners like good little Rhyses.

Mary only stood there, glaring. "These flowers are not

going to do any good. You should have used mistletoe."

Madoc gave this suddenly belligerent mouse one of his mildest glances. "In a Christian church? The Anglicans wouldn't notice, I don't suppose, but the chapelgoers might be inclined to take umbrage, wouldn't you think?"

"Who cares about them? Why do you think the Druid walked last night? Why do you think Sir Caradoc happened upon the last of the golden sickles just at Beltane? Why do you think—" Mary sucked air in a great, loud gulp. "This place is not safe, I tell you! The emanations are terrible. I must go and talk to my brother." She galloped off, not bothering to say good-bye.

The person to talk to was Uncle Caradoc, Janet thought, but she didn't say so. Uncle Huw wouldn't want his father pestered by a goofy distant relation with a bee in her bonnet.

"Oh gosh, Madoc. I hope that poor woman's not going to make a nuisance of herself. We'd better alert your mother to keep an eye on her. What sort of relation is Mary to you?"

"A damned annoying one, since you ask." Madoc didn't often use even the mildest of cusswords, he must be finding Mary one straw too many. "She and Bob are the children of Lisa's grandfather's stepsister. Lisa's grandfather was a second cousin to my grandfather. You figure it out."

"What for?" said Janet. "It sounds to me as though you and they aren't related at all."

"Oh, we're bound to be, one way or another. Anyway, I believe the stepsister and my grandmother, or Lisa's grandmother, or at any rate somebody's grandmother, were bosom friends, which makes up the difference, you see."

"No, I don't see, but I'll work on it. Madoc, do you

think Mary was just being oracular, or—" Janet didn't quite know what she'd meant to say.

Madoc didn't know, either. "I think it's quite possible that Mary wandered out here last night hoping to see the Druid walking or to catch the fairy queen having it off with the fairy knave, and got scared off by—I don't know. An owl or a bat, perhaps. I can't think why else she'd be yammering for mistletoe. Once she'd heard about your ghost, she was bound to start having psychic twinges."

"I'm sorry I ever mentioned the darned thing."

"Jenny love, don't feel that way. Over here, an apparition is regarded as a status symbol. We'd all have felt a bit cheated if some spook or other hadn't rolled out for the occasion."

"Then why didn't the silly thing do its haunting downstairs where everyone could see? It was pure happenstance that I came along just when I did."

"Who knows? Maybe it's not a particularly sociable ghost, or maybe this was just a rehearsal for the main event."

"Somebody practicing up to give Uncle Caradoc a thrill on his birthday, you mean? I can't see how."

"Easily enough, I should think. It must have taken a bit of rigging, but then all the operator had to do was stand behind those heavy draperies at the end of the hall ready to twiddle the wires or strings, as the case may have been. You wouldn't have noticed them in that dim light, against the dark woodwork and busy carpeting. Exactly where were you when you spotted the thing?"

"Almost to the stairs."

"Just the right spot. The operator saw you coming up the hall and had plenty of time to wiggle the whatsits. You were on your way down and it was odds-on you'd mention the ghost at dinner, as who wouldn't?"

"Well, of course. Why didn't I think of that? It must have been nothing more than a piece of gray chiffon or tulle draped over a thin wire to give it shape. I suppose I stood there gawking for a second or so. As soon as the joker was sure I'd noticed, he just dropped the thing to the floor and whisked it under the drapery. I should have gone over and investigated, but Uncle Caradoc had said they'd hold dinner till I got back from checking the baby. I'd asked him not to, but I was still afraid he might, and didn't want to keep the rest waiting. You didn't happen to notice who followed me upstairs?"

"Nobody did."

"What makes you so sure?"

"Darling, do you have any idea what an effect you made in that blue gown? There wasn't an eyeball in the place that wasn't straining after you, my own included. Believe me, I'd have noticed."

"Which means it was either some outsider or one of the help?"

Janet spoke rather brusquely, being a cynosure was not the Canadian way. Now she'd be embarrassed to wear that blue gown again, and she did love it so. "I can't see that meek little Megan working the fiddle, unless she had fishlines strung the whole length of the hall. Anyway, she doesn't strike me as the type. What about Danny the Boots? Is he inclined to go in for practical jokes?"

Danny the Boots had been playing second footman. Madoc didn't tell Janet so. "I shouldn't be surprised. Come on, let's go see whether Dorothy's worn out her welcome with Aunt Elen yet."

She hadn't, of course; she was sitting on the floor making goo-goo eyes at her Uncle Dafydd, of all people. Dafydd was eyeing her back as he might have eyed a mermaid in his bathtub; charming to look at, but what was one supposed to do about her? He greeted his brother with noticeable relief and some degree of puzzlement.

"Madoc, did you actually produce this kid all by yourself?"

"Oh no, Jenny helped a bit. What got you up so early?"

"Tib was after me to go horseback riding with her."

"And did you go?"

"God, no! What do you think I'm made of? I told her I had to see Uncle Huw on urgent business. Namely conning Aunt Elen into cooking my eggs. Lisa wouldn't feed me, she's got a gaggle of minions over there chopping leeks for tomorrow's pies. Thank you, Auntie love, this is beautiful. Want a bite, Jenny?"

"No thanks, I'm on a strict diet of tea and Welsh cakes. I've tried making them at home, but for some reason mine never come out the way Aunt Elen's do."

That was just for manners, Janet's cakes were as good as anybody's. Even Sir Emlyn said so, and he should know if anybody did. Who the heck did Dafydd think he was, coaxing her to eat from his plate like the princess and the frog? Or the prince and the frogess? The great Dafydd Rhys gave her a pain where she'd never had an ache. One of these days she was going to tell him so.

Which was mean, rotten, and uncharitable, and she ought to show more compassion. Maybe he was just trying to be brotherly. That glamorous life Dafydd led must in fact be rather a lonesome one at times, when you came right down to it. Being a star meant always having to shine, being so much in demand meant being on the road too often for comfort. Having a different woman panting after him every time he turned around meant that he never really got to know any of them.

Except, perhaps, in the biblical sense. "Come on, Dorothy," she said. "Quit teasing Uncle Dafydd and let him eat his breakfast in peace. Where can I change her, Aunt Elen?"

"I'll show you."

Bathrooms had come to the farm during the brief but opulent reign of Edward VII; nice, commodious ones with plenty of room to do what needed to be done. Dorothy enjoyed herself hugely. When they finally got back to the kitchen, Tom the Flicks was there too. Tom Feste, actually; she'd finally learned his real name though not yet his precise connection with the Rhyses. Not that it mattered, they all appeared to call each other cousins regardless of degree.

Madoc was still the best-looking, Janet decided, comparing the three of them together. Dafydd was the handsomest, an entirely different thing. That made Tom the ugly duckling, which wasn't fair. He wasn't so bad, if you liked them tall and skinny and oozing personality from every pore. Magnetic, that was the word. Like those fancy gadgets that well-meaning people gave you at Christmas to stick on your refrigerator door. And about as useful, from what little she'd seen of him so far. His job on the films was supposed to involve production, but nobody seemed all that clear as to what he produced.

Dorothy didn't think much of Tom, that was plain enough. When he tried to chuck her under the chin, she turned her head away and primmed up her mouth, so exactly like her mother when Janet was miffed about something that Madoc burst out laughing.

"Let her alone, Tom, she's too young for you. What happened to Patricia, by the way?"

"Good question. What happened to Patricia, Dafydd?"

That must have been the blonde in the Daimler, trust Madoc to remember her name. Apparently Dafydd didn't; he looked blank for a moment, then shrugged. "Oh yes, Patricia. She wanted to go to Swansea, so I drove her to the station and put her on the train. I assumed you knew."

"Clever you."

Meaning, Janet supposed, that Tom admired the way Dafydd had thwarted Patricia's hope of being driven to Swansea in the Daimler. Or that Tom was pleased at having got the woman off his hands so effortlessly. Or that Tom was not pleased, and wanted Dafydd to know it. This wasn't Janet's kind of conversation. She stood up and reached for the diaper bag.

"This has been lovely, but I expect Betty will be wondering where we've got to. We'll see you later on, won't we? Madoc, do you want to stay and visit awhile longer?"

"No, I promised Uncle Caradoc I'd help him hang up his new sickle. Come on, Dorothy, say thanks to Aunt Elen and Uncle Huw. Let us know if there's anything we can do to help this afternoon."

There would be, for sure. They left the farm with their consciences clear and dawdled back toward the big house, taking time to sniff the apple blossoms along the way.

After a while, Madoc asked, "How does Dafydd strike you this trip, Jenny? He seems a bit down in the mouth, don't you think?"

"It could be that he's worn-out from the rackety life he leads; but if you really want to know, I'm wondering whether he might be plain jealous."

"Jealous? Of whom?"

"You, of course."

"That's a switch. What makes you say that? Is it because of you?"

"I suppose I'm part of it, in a way. I expect it's more seeing everybody making a fuss over Dorothy, and us being so well settled in our own house and, oh, you know. Dafydd's used to being cock of the walk; now you've got something to crow about that he doesn't. Dafydd's what? Thirty-eight?"

"Thirty-nine. Six years older than I. Good Lord, he'll be forty his next birthday. I see what you mean."

"Then you'd better take him aside and give him a little brotherly talking-to about growing up, don't you think?"

"No, you do it. You know him better than I."

"Madoc, that's ridiculous! I've seen Dafydd maybe half a dozen times in the four years we've been married: once here, once that time when he stayed overnight with us in Fredericton right after we'd bought the house, and occasionally for dinner in St. John or someplace when he happened to be passing through."

"But he talks to you."

"He flirts with me. Not because he's interested, just from force of habit. I don't think I've ever had two minutes' worth of serious discussion with Dafydd about anything at all."

"Neither have I, that I can remember. Dafydd was just that much older, you see. When I was a kid in Canada, he was off at school in England. When I was at school in Winnipeg, he was already studying voice in London; and so it went. You know, love, it's a funny thing. Back at your brother's farm, I can wander out to the barn with Bert and pretty soon we'll be sitting on a couple of upended milk pails. We'll get to talking about taxes or plumbing or whatever, and wind up solving the riddle of the universe. With Dafydd, it's just polite chit-chat. We've nothing in common except our parents and the relatives. I'm fond of him, I suppose; but when it comes down to cases, Jenny, I don't really know my own brother at all."

Chapter 6

"**W**ell, it's his loss, not yours." Janet couldn't bear to see Madoc looking glum on such a lovely morning, not over a lightweight like Dafydd. "I expect sooner or later some nice, tough-minded woman a lot like your mother's going to take him in hand and straighten him out. What about your cousin Tom, or whatever he is? Are he and Dafydd friendly? Really friendly, I mean, like you and Bert. I should think they'd have more in common, both being in the entertainment field, in a manner of speaking."

"Perhaps they do, though you'd better not let Mother hear you calling grand opera 'the entertainment field.'" Madoc was smiling now. "Tom's no relation to us, but he and Dafydd knew each other as kids. Whether they pour out their souls to each other, I couldn't say. What they really appear to have in common these days is a taste for flashy cars and persuadable women, though at least Dafydd has sense enough not to marry every third one who comes along. God knows what Tom's paid out in alimony by now."

"It doesn't seem to have made much of a dent in his pocketbook, if that Daimler's any sign."

"Oh, they make big money on the flicks. Besides, if

Tom gets hard up, he can always come and sponge on Lisa."

"Does he?"

"He comes. I don't know whether he sponges. I wouldn't put it past him."

Making judgmental remarks unsupported by evidence was not a habit of Madoc's. Janet wondered a bit, then changed the subject.

"Speaking of Lisa, she wants us to visit. Are we supposed to drop in whenever we feel like it, or wait to be properly invited?"

"Let's get Dorothy bedded down for her nap, then drop. If Lisa's still chopping leeks, we can say we're just out for a walk and mustn't stay because Betty expects us back to lick the spoons."

"I hope she doesn't."

Uncle Caradoc's kitchen door was standing open now; the day had turned warm as they'd known it would. Somebody was holding forth inside; Janet recognized the plummy voice as Bob's. She raised her eyebrows at Madoc, he shrugged back as best he could with Dorothy trying to climb over his shoulder, and they went in.

"Properly speaking, the *coelcerth* should be ignited by a spark achieved by rubbing two pieces of oak together," Bob was insisting.

"This is after the nine men with no money in their pockets and no buckles on their belts have collected the sticks from the nine different kinds of trees?" That was Gwen, being flip.

Bob might not have realized she was pulling his leg. Anyway, he refused to be disconcerted. " 'With no metal on their persons' would perhaps be the apter phrase. The sticks would by now have been more or less symmetrically arranged within the perimeter of a circle cut in the turf. One stick would catch the spark and be used as a torch to kindle the *coelcerth*."

"The *coelcerth* being the Beltane fire, right?"

"Or the balefire, as it is sometimes called. There may be two fires instead of one."

"Oh, not two fires!" That was Mary, all set to pout. "You're not going to do two fires, Bob?"

"My only hope is that there will be sticks enough for the one fire, since we are unable to assemble nine men to do the gathering."

So this was the real reason why Dafydd and Tom were hiding out at Uncle Huw's, and why Bob was casting that baleful glance at Madoc.

"But you're still going to rub the two pieces of oak together, aren't you?" Gwen really was a minx. "How long will it take you to get a spark?"

"Till hell freezes over," muttered Dai. "He'll use a match, he always does. Plenty of matches, and maybe a dash of petrol."

"Not petrol, Dai," Madoc protested, "unless your uncle's planning to commit a particularly unpleasant form of suicide. I'll make him a fuzz stick, Canadian style."

"How jolly, the fuzz will make a fuzz stick. You are fuzz, aren't you, Madoc?"

Dai, who'd barely opened his mouth all last evening, must suddenly have decided to be the life of the party. Janet wished he'd go back to being sullen. Madoc was taking the callow youth in stride.

"Oh yes, I'm fuzz, if you don't like the sound of policeman. We get called worse, often enough. A fuzz stick isn't a truncheon, if that's what you're thinking; just a piece of kindling wood that's been frayed around the edges to make it ignite more quickly."

Gwen skipped over to the box where Betty kept bits of kindling she might need to restart the coal fire in the

Aga should it go out, which it seldom did, winter or summer. "Here's a likely faggot. Let's see you fuzz it."

"Very well, Gwen, on to the fray."

Madoc took out his jackknife and began making short, slantwise cuts into the wood, keeping them close together and not detaching them so that they curled back and would indeed present a tempting snack for any spark ambitious to become a blaze. He worked neatly and quickly; by the time he was through, the stick was a mass of whitish curls.

"Ooh, that's lovely!" cried his sister. "Much too pretty to burn; it's like a miniature tree. Does he make them for you, Jenny?"

"Sometimes. He whittled a whole grove of baby ones this past Christmas to hang on our tree as a present for Dorothy. Fuzz sticks are mostly for when you're out camping and can't find any dry tinder. This isn't one of Madoc's better efforts; you may have it for the Beltane fire if you want, Dai."

Neither Dai nor Bob appeared to be overwhelmed with gratitude, but Mary was ecstatic. "Thank you, *cefnder*. This will be my first time to jump over a fuzz stick."

"I have tried to explain, Mary"—Bob spoke with the weary impatience of one who has had to say the same thing far too many times—"that it is inappropriate for you to anticipate. The correct procedure is for cakes to be baked, some of oatmeal and some of brown meal, then broken into fourths and placed in a bag. Each person in the gathering should draw a piece without looking, and only those who get the brown pieces should leap three times through the fire. However, as it appears we are not to have our oatmeal cakes nor our brown cakes and the fire will not have been laid with proper ceremony, this may as well become just another case of who wants to leap and who does not."

"Count me among the nots." Iseult had finally graced the gathering, in cream-colored gabardine pants and a matching tunic that had its neckline cut in a capital V. She also wore a good many golden chains, presumably to keep her pectoral area warm. "Where's Reuel?"

"He asked for sandwiches and went off to the downs." Betty was putting great platters of sliced meats and salad on the table. "It is yourselves you must be helping, I have more to do. And no time to be baking white and brown cakes for heathen rites," she added rather snappishly. "What is it that Dorothy will be wanting to eat, Mrs. Madoc?"

"Nothing, thank you, Betty. She had porridge at Aunt Elen's. I'll just take her upstairs, she usually has her nap about now."

Sir Caradoc and Sir Emlyn volunteered in chorus, bass and baritone, to sit with her if Janet and Madoc wanted to go off somewhere. Janet was charmed.

"Why don't you do it together? She'd love having two handsome men all to herself. Wouldn't you, Dorothy?"

Sir Caradoc would drop off, too, Janet suspected. So would Sir Emlyn, like as not. And what if they did? Surely one or the other would wake up if the baby cried. Lady Rhys was indicating that she'd be downstairs in the drawing room fixing the flowers, or else in the dining hall scraping up candle wax. She'd come to the rescue should her services be required, as they very likely would.

While they were settling the baby-sitting question, Madoc had been making Janet a lovely sandwich to take upstairs with her. She thanked him and excused herself.

"Come up in half an hour or so, whenever you're ready. I doubt whether Dorothy will take long to drop off, after the busy morning she's had."

She'd had to raise her own voice to make herself heard over Bob's, he was still on about the Beltane fires.

"It is sympathetic magic, you know. Symbolically, the fire is meant to burn up the witches."

"That doesn't sound madly sympathetic to me," drawled Iseult. "Would somebody pass the mustard?"

Presumably someone did. Janet couldn't wait to find out, Dorothy was beginning to fuss.

It was thoughtful of Betty to have put them in the red room, pleasant to be alone with her baby for a while, to sit in a low slipper chair by the window with the soft breeze coming in, to watch the sun turning the hills to golden green, to eat her good sandwich while Dorothy kneaded and sucked and made gentle grunting noises like a happy piglet. A neat illustration of supply and demand.

She'd got the baby tucked into the cradle and herself decent by the time the proud grandfather and the delighted great-great-uncle tiptoed in like two policemen strayed from *The Pirates of Penzance*, and she was free to go. She gave them each a kiss, reminded them to yell for Lady Rhys if their charge should wake up, and left them to cope as they might.

Her husband was, as she'd expected, still in the kitchen. Megan had appeared from somewhere and was washing pots for Betty, Madoc was trying to help and getting the shy girl all flustered. Janet chased him off to make another fuzz stick and offered to take over the pot-washing. However, that only flustered Megan further, they might as well go fluster Lisa instead.

Madoc was quite willing, this was not a day to be

sitting around the kitchen stove. He presented his fuzz stick to Betty, who tucked it up carefully in a corner of the dresser next to the Staffordshire cow, and they went.

"How far is it to Lisa's?" Janet asked. "I didn't even get to meet her before, did I? I didn't remember her at all."

"It's not much more than half a mile. You won't mind walking that far, will you? And no, we didn't see Lisa last time. She was off somewhere. Looking at tortoises, probably. I told you about Tessie, didn't I?"

"Yes, you did. We'll have to get some of her books for Dorothy when she's old enough to read."

"I'm not so sure about that, love. Tessie's a fairly uninhibited type, as tortoises go, we don't want to give the kid notions. Jenny, do you think it's going to be tough on her, having a cop for a father?"

"I expect likely she'll manage. Look at that sheep, smack in the middle of the road. It's got blue paint on its neck. That's not Uncle Caradoc's mark, is it?"

"No, his is a red splotch on the left hip." Madoc remembered that all too well. "I don't know whose this one would be. Somebody will cope with it, sooner or later."

On her previous visit, Janet had marveled over the way sheep were allowed to graze wherever they took the notion. She'd seen them in dooryards, churchyards, along roadsides, on the lawn of the town hall. She'd been startled one morning in Bangor, where they were staying at a rather classy hotel, to see a sheep with its nose pressed against the bathroom window, watching her brush her teeth. She didn't see much point in trying to shoo this one over into the meadow, it would only wander back again if it took the notion. Drivers in rural areas were used to keeping a lookout for sheep; if they weren't, they soon learned.

"Good thing they're such docile creatures," she remarked.

"Not always." Madoc wished the subject hadn't come up. "A ram can be as mean as a billy goat. Worse, because they look so sheepish you don't think anything's going to happen. One of Uncle Caradoc's rams got me in the seat of the pants when I was a kid. I flew about six feet and landed in a mudhole. Mother was not pleased. She'd have thought I knew better than to go around teasing a poor, innocent sheep."

"You must have been a sore trial." Janet slipped her arm through his and rubbed her cheek on his sleeve.

"Oh, I was. You're not planning to leap the balefire, are you?"

"Perish the thought. I've got nothing against witches. I wouldn't mind watching Mary, though. It'll be tomorrow, won't it? How late will they start?"

"Not late. Shortly after the sun goes down, I expect. Perhaps the idea is to bring back the light. I'm not much up on folklore myself, I hear enough of it from crooks. Anyway, there's no reason why we shouldn't go and watch, if you want to. We could take Dorothy, for that matter. At least in later years she can say she's been."

"You're thinking this might be the last time, aren't you?"

"I suppose so, Jenny. How could I help it?"

"Uncle Caradoc looks fairly spry to me, dear. Of course we never know what's going to happen." Janet could hardly help thinking of her own parents and that logging truck her father hadn't happened to notice quite soon enough. "Uncle Huw wouldn't want to keep up the Beltane fires?"

"I shouldn't think so, he's not too big on pagan rites. I suspect the main reason he and Aunt Elen stayed away from dinner last night is that Uncle Huw finds Bob's gassing about folklore something of a pain, and particularly can't stand Mary when she gets on about her leaping."

"Which shows his good taste, in my opinion. I expect I could work up a fairly healthy scunner to that pair myself, if I had to be around them long. How long are they planning to stay, do you know?"

"Just through tomorrow night, I hope. Mother said something at dinner about their having an urgent appointment to haunt a house. I think she was being facetious, but I'm not quite sure. Well, well, look who's coming. What's the matter, Dafydd, did Aunt Elen throw you out for singing bawdy ballads? Where's Tom?"

"Peering interestedly down the front of Iseult's blouse, the last I saw of him," the elder brother replied. "Where did you park the kid?"

"She's taking a nap. Tad and Uncle Caradoc are baby-sitting."

"*Chacun à son goût.* Where are you off to?"

"We thought we might pop in and say hello to Lisa, if she's not too busy baking brown and white cakes."

"Why brown and white?"

"That's Bob's latest crotchet. He was nagging Betty to bake a batch for some extra bit of hocus-pocus he wanted to tack on tomorrow night at the bonfire. She wasn't interested."

"I'm sure Lisa wouldn't be, either. Bob does tend to make one feel there's something to be said for human sacrifice, don't you think? Jenny, if you were delegated to hurl somebody into the fire tomorrow night, which would you pick: Bob or Mary?"

"Well, I shouldn't pick Bob because he has a nice

singing voice even if he is a bore. And there'd be no point in my picking Mary because, from the way she's been talking, she'd already be in it. Besides, it's not polite to shove people into bonfires."

"Really? I hadn't thought to consider that aspect of the question. But then I'm a rude fellow, as you must have noticed. Not a bit like my brother."

"That's all right, Dafydd. I'm not much like my brother, either. How long are you here for?"

"Is that Canadian for 'How long do you intend to stay'?"

"Yes, we don't like to waste words. We save our breath to call the polar bears."

"And what do you do with the polar bears once you've got them?"

"Nothing, they never come. We just like to exercise those old Celtic yearnings for the unattainable that I'll bet somebody around here's just finished writing a poem about."

"Ah, you've been reading romantic novels about Welsh poets."

Actually Janet's tastes in reading tended to be on the scholarly side, but she wasn't about to belabor the issue. "Well, I can't read the poems themselves because they're all in Welsh, and Madoc won't translate for me because it makes him feel silly. Is anybody writing a poem for Uncle Caradoc's birthday, I wonder?"

Dafydd laughed. "Is anybody *not* would be the more pertinent question, and you're going to be sorry you asked. Prepare yourself for at least two solid hours of bardry tomorrow afternoon, Jenny darling. What do Canadians yearn for, by the way?"

"Blubber and tallow candles. You ought to know that, you've been to Canada often enough. What does Reuel Williams write?"

"Scripts for the sort of movie Iseult plays in. Which is a dreadful thing to say about anybody, but there it is. I can't think why she dragged him along, unless he's planning to use us all as characters in his next horror story. Hello, Tib. Looking for me?"

Chapter 7

"**M**other sent me to find you. She's steaming because you left that great monster of Uncle Tom's parked behind her bug. She can't get out to go to the shops and they're desperate for flour in the kitchen."

"Oh God! I gave the keys back to Tom, and he's gone wondering off somewhere with Iseult."

"Then you'd better find him, unless you want to find snakes in your bed tonight."

The pretty teenager was enjoying herself, this must be Tib's revenge for Dafydd's refusal to ride with her this morning. Poor Dafydd, Janet thought, he was getting it both barrels this trip. An idol was not without worshipers save among his own relatives. Too bad for him.

"Madoc," she said out of pity, "can't you jump-start the Daimler and move it out of the way?"

"Not I, love. I'm not messing around with anything that pricey. Come on, Tib, let's saddle up the horses and gallop into town western-style. I'll be the hitching post while you buy the flour."

"Super! Come on, then."

Tib raced off without a backward glance. Dafydd's

scowl would have looked just right on Baron Scarpia, hardly a role for a tenor.

"I suppose I'll have to go fetch those blasted keys or I'll never hear the end of it. Want to come with me, Jenny?"

"Thanks, but I'm beginning to feel I've done enough walking for today. Good hunting, Dafydd. They probably haven't gone far, Iseult's wearing high-heeled sandals. I'll see you in a while, then."

Her brother-in-law didn't bother to say good-bye, just turned around and started back the way he'd come. Left alone, Janet took time for a good look at Lisa's house. This was exactly the sort of place one might expect a writer who had a tortoise as her heroine to live in: low and wandering; part stone, part half-timbered; with little diamond-shaped windowed bays jutting out in odd places. She was wondering which of the many doors to knock at when Lisa herself dashed out of the one at the farthest end.

"Dafydd! Dafydd! Oh, that *beastly* man! What's he running off for? Didn't Tib tell him to move the car? Jenny, how nice of you to come. Isn't Madoc with you?"

Janet explained, Lisa chuckled.

"Trust Madoc! And never, never trust Dafydd. He has a positive gift for turning the simplest errand into a full-scale flap. The operatic temperament, I suppose. Come and meet the tortoises."

"Please don't feel you have to play hostess, Lisa. We just came to see if we could help with the cooking."

"You can't. I've three ladies from the Women's Institute in there chopping leeks for the pies. We can't start making the paste till Madoc gallops back with the flour, bless his ears and whiskers."

They were around behind the house now, in what Janet supposed must be the kitchen garden. "Insouciant" would be as good a description of its layout as any, she decided. The focal point was a somewhat helter-skelter ring of stones, in the midst of which were a few growing plants, a weathered structure that resembled a miniature doghouse or else a large birdhouse, and five lumps of brown shell.

"Here we are," said Lisa. "That's Tessie under the geranium. The big chap's her boyfriend, Jonathan, the three little ones are Bip, Bop, and Boo. They don't do much; but they're rather sweet, don't you think?"

"We have snapping turtles in the pond back home on my brother's farm, but these are much prettier." Janet didn't feel at all disloyal in saying so, no snapping turtle would ever be hanged for its beauty. "Is a turtle a kind of tortoise, or is it the other way around?"

"No, you got it right the first time. Yours would be freshwater turtles, I assume; these are land tortoises. I don't know whether you have any in Canada."

"Come to think of it, neither do I. I'll have to check them out when I get home. Oh look, Bip's putting his head out. Or is that Boo?"

"Actually I think it's Bop. I mix them up myself if I don't have my specs on. Here, ducky, have a nibble of lettuce. All right then, don't. Little wretch! Why is it animals and children will never perform when one wants them to?"

"General cussedness, I expect. I understand you write books about a tortoise."

"Write, illustrate, and peddle from door to door if my American publisher has his way. He's yammering for me to go over and do something he calls a tour, but I'm not going. My tortoises need me. Don't you, loves? Well, anyway, I like to think they do. Besides, I'm scared green of flying. I sit there with my hands riveted to the armrests, holding up the plane the whole way. I suppose you're brave as anything."

"Not really, but it's not the flying that bothers me. I'm too busy stewing over whether we'll ever get our luggage back."

Lisa chuckled. "There is that. I see we have a lot in common. What's the matter with Dafydd? He's been grouchy as an old bear ever since he got here."

Janet thought she'd better skate warily over this one. "Has he? You must know him far better than I. Better than Madoc, for that matter. They never saw much of each other when they were growing up, and of course they still don't, with us in New Brunswick and Dafydd on the go all the time. You don't suppose he's coming down with something? So much traveling and having to be a celebrity both onstage and off must be awfully wearing on a person. It's not as though Dafydd were a young kid. Madoc told me he'll be forty his next birthday."

"Forty's still young, or so I keep trying to convince myself. Not so terribly young for a singer, I suppose. But it's still early for him to start worrying about his voice. That should be good for another ten or fifteen years in opera, then he can do concerts or television spectaculars if he wants to. Even if his voice ever did give out, he could skid by on his looks and reputation. Dafydd will always be a smasher, like Uncle Caradoc. Or he could conduct, like his father. Dafydd's often said he'd like to conduct. Still, forty's a milestone, as well I know. I had mine in March, and I was in the dumps for two solid weeks. We'll have to think of a way to buck him up."

"Tib seems to be in favor of putting snakes in his bed. I think she's a bit miffed because he ducked out of riding with her."

"Oh, furious. Or was earlier on. I expect she's over it by now. Tib has a mad crush on Dafydd, needless to say. Unless she's transferred it to Madoc by now. I simply cannot get over the change in that man! Madoc used to be so—I don't quite know how to put it. One just tended not to remember he was around. Now all of a sudden he's handsome and fun and, unfortunately for us poor old Welsh widows, possessed of a gorgeous wife and an adorable baby. Also a lovely house, according to Aunt Sillie. The house, I mean. That is to say—oh dear, what do I mean?"

"The house isn't all that special." Janet reached into the pocket where she'd stashed her photographs. "We bought it mainly on account of the cupola. I do have some snapshots with me that I brought to show Aunt Elen. You don't have to look at them."

"Oh but I want to, I'm a dreadful snoop. We could sit down over there on the bench if you don't object to a few bird droppings."

"Not a bit. A person doesn't dress up much if she's toting a young one around. I learned that back when I used to baby-sit my brother's kids."

"Tell me about them. How do they like their new cousin?"

The two were deep into the stack of photographs, Lisa asking questions faster than Janet could answer them, when Madoc and Tib galloped back with the flour. Lisa offered lemonade, but Janet decided they'd better let her get on with her leek pies and go back to relieve their baby-sitters. There'd be plenty of time to talk families after the birthday party was over.

"It's just as well you went for that flour when you did," Janet remarked as they started back to the big house. "Dafydd never did get back with Tom's car keys.

Lisa was asking me what's got into him. I just said she knew him better than I do."

"Sensible of you."

"Well, you know how it is with families. I didn't want to start anything. Oh, and Lisa thinks you're handsome all of a sudden. I can't imagine why she never noticed before. It was perfectly obvious to me even before you shaved off that silly red mustache. What happened to her husband, do you know?"

"As a matter of fact, I don't. Nobody ever wants to talk about Arthur to me, not even Mother. He died about eight years ago. In France, I believe, or possibly Spain. He was a dealer in precious gems and traveled a lot. I rather suspect Arthur's death may have occurred under less than dubious circumstances, and everyone keeps hushing it up for Lisa's and Tib's sakes."

"A heart attack in the wrong bedroom, for instance?"

"Your guess is as good as mine. I only met Arthur a few times—he generally managed to have urgent business elsewhere when the family were gathering. He was a big chap, quite a bit older than Lisa, as I recall, pleasant enough in a buttoned-up way, and seemed fond of her and Tib. Other than that, I can't remember much about him except that he wouldn't let me take his fingerprints."

Madoc smiled. "That was one of my less attractive hobbies as a kid, you know; I was always nutty about police work. I kept a file of everybody's prints who'd let me take them, and took careful notes on those who didn't, on the theory that they must have criminal records they didn't want me to know about. That may possibly have been the case with Arthur, come to think of it; I can't say I've ever seen Lisa crushed down by weight of woe to be rid of him. Of course he left her pots of money. She's spent a lot fixing up the house; it was in fairly bad shape when she inherited it. Her grandparents always used to have her here for summers; her own parents lived in London. They still do, as far as I know, but Lisa has always preferred Wales."

"I don't blame her. I hope I get to see inside the house before we leave."

"You will; she likes you. If she didn't, you'd know. Lisa has a strange way of getting the message across; she simply pulls in her head like one of her tortoises. I've seen her do it a time or two, it's not something you forget in a hurry."

"I know," said Janet. "I saw her myself, last night before dinner. That Williams fellow who came with your cousin Iseult went over and said something to her that must have upset her, though I don't suppose he meant to. She turned absolutely chalk white, then just seemed to go away, even though she hadn't stirred an inch. It was eerie to watch."

"Williams did that?" Madoc wrinkled his nose. "I'd had the impression he was a complete stranger to everybody but Iseult and Tom. Unless Iseult got him up to something, I wouldn't put it past her. What happened next?"

"Nothing much. I did think maybe I'd better go prop her up in case she was going to faint, but Tib beat me to it. She's a nice kid, isn't she? Then Dafydd went and took Lisa's arm and she snapped right out of it and went on chatting as though nothing had happened."

"To Williams?"

"No, he'd gone. To get another drink, like as not. He must have been embarrassed, he couldn't possibly not have noticed. I couldn't help wondering what he'd said to make her react so badly. Not that it's any of my business. And you've seen it before?"

"Yes. Once with Bob and once with Mary."

"That I can well believe. That pair would be enough to give Count Dracula the willies. Does anybody really like them?"

"They like themselves. And each other, I suppose. I can't say I care much for either of them myself, but their father was Uncle Caradoc's cousin, and one gets used to them. Anyway, they never stay long. You don't mind too much, do you?"

"It's hardly my place to mind, if Uncle Caradoc wants to entertain his own relatives in his own house. I can't say I'd be overjoyed to have them in ours, but I don't suppose they'd ever come. Or would they?"

"Not unless we sent them tickets. Bob's too cheap to pay his own way, and too much the petty tyrant to let Mary come without him. Should we form a bodyguard for Lisa tonight, do you think?"

"She's not coming. Dafydd and Tom are taking her and Tib out to dinner, as they darned well ought to since she's good enough to be putting them up."

It wouldn't break Janet's heart if Iseult and her boyfriend went too, but she didn't say so. Madoc had something on his mind, why disturb him with small talk? There'd be enough of that when they got back to the manor.

As she'd confidently expected, they found Madoc's parents, Uncle Caradoc, and an assortment of relatives and farmhands sitting around the kitchen drinking tea. Dorothy was perched up in an antique high chair that had been dragged out from somewhere, her grandmother was feeding her tiny sippets of bread and milk from a coin-silver coffee spoon in the neatest way possible. She smiled amiably at her mother and father, but showed no particular inclination to be picked up and hugged.

"She's not going to want to go home. Don't bother, Betty, I'll do it." Janet poured for Madoc and herself and went to sit beside Sir Emlyn, who'd nudged himself over on the settle to make a place for her. "How did the baby-sitting go?"

"Very well indeed. I think Dorothy is going to be a lyric soprano."

"Lovely. When should we start her lessons?"

"Oh, not for a while yet. Give the lungs time to develop."

"What makes you think they haven't? You should have been around when she used to wake up for a two o'clock feeding."

Janet helped herself to a Welsh cake, figuring she'd done enough walking today to balance the calories. But then she'd done a fair amount of eating as well. How did the Rhyses all manage to stay so svelte?

Except for Bob. He was eating bread and honey, smearing it over his various chins. Even Dorothy knew better than that. Somebody ought to grab that old pig by the ear and scrub his face with a scratchy washcloth. She'd do it herself, if she weren't company.

"Dafydd hasn't dropped in, by any chance? He went to find Tom and get the keys for the Daimler. It's blocking Lisa's drive, Madoc had to play cowboy."

Janet made a funny little story of the ride for the flour. Everybody laughed except Bob and Mary. They were reminded of scurrilous tales dating from Dai's early boyhood and keen to rehash them. Nobody else wanted to listen, so they wound up sputtering back and forth to each other while the rest either talked around them or got up in silence and left the kitchen. Dai was first among the leavers. Lady Rhys watched him go, frowning a bit.

"I hope that boy's having a good time," she murmured to Janet. Conductors' wives got used to playing mother to singers and musicians; she'd developed a keen awareness of moods and megrims. "He doesn't look happy to me." She raised her voice, a full, rich mezzo-soprano that had once sung "'Ah, Sweet Mystery of Life" for the Queen Mum. "Mary, what does your nephew do? Is he still at school?"

Interrupted in her litany of Dai's peccadillos, Mary blinked. "Oh, school? No, Dai has no inclination toward the academic life. He is my apprentice in gem-cutting."

"Then that's who you are." Reuel Williams had come in from his walk, sat down almost unnoticed at the far end of the table, and drunk his tea without a word to anybody. His sudden utterance drew everybody's attention, Williams didn't appear to mind.

"I've been trying to place you ever since last night, Miss Rhys. It's been a long time, of course. You've—er—done something different to your hair."

Whatever she'd done was a sad mistake, Janet thought. Mary could not fairly be called dirty or unkempt, but she could surely have used a shampoo and set. Better still, a wig and a face-lift. At the moment, however, she was preening herself like the Queen of the May.

"Mr. Williams! Yes, indeed it has been a time. You were a young man then, just starting as a writer of television scripts, were you not?"

"That's right, it was my first documentary. Unusual careers for women. You were the gem-cutter."

"And she still is." It was not to be supposed that Bob wouldn't horn in with his two cents' worth. "My sister is internationally renowned as a lapidary, both for her knowledge and for her skill."

Lady Rhys had a fairly sizable collection of diamonds herself, which she wore with éclat on every possible occasion out of respect for Sir Emlyn's position; she was naturally interested.

"Mary, I knew you were a lapidary; I had no idea you'd become so famous. Do you mean you actually travel all over the world splitting diamonds?"

Mary waved, an airy gesture of dismissal. "No indeed, the world comes to me. And I have no interest in diamonds. My special field of expertise is among the colored stones."

"Give her a ruby or a sapphire and there's nobody to beat her," cried Bob, dripping more honey in his enthusiasm.

"Really, brother dear, you might have mentioned emeralds and opals. Opals—those of gem quality, that is—are particular favorites of mine. You cannot imagine the exhilaration of cutting into a great, blazing chunk of Australian opal. Pliny placed the opal right after the emerald in importance, as do I myself. 'For in them you shall see the living fire of the ruby, the glorious purple of the amethyst, the green sea of the emerald, all glittering together in an incredible mixture of light.' Isn't that lovely?"

"But you do have a particular feeling for the living fire of the ruby," Bob insisted.

"How could I not? It stirs my very vitals. The emotion that grips me when I gaze into the green sea of the emerald is of a more transcendent quality. I can't wait to see the crosier taken down tonight for its annual polishing. You will let me examine the emerald, Uncle Caradoc? I've brought my loupe."

"Yes, Mary, since it gives you pleasure. And we shall all be happy to hear once again your pronouncement on the quality of the stone. But no, I still do not wish the emerald to be cut. Now may I offer you one of Betty's cakes?"

90

Chapter 8

Everybody was in the dining hall, though only for drinks and the opening of the grille. Huw and Elen, with Owain, Mavis, and their brood, would be going back to the farmhouse for dinner; Lisa and Tib whither Tom and Dafydd listed.

Megan was upstairs keeping an eye on Dorothy. Betty was in the kitchen, being visited by one and another of the family as the spirit moved them. Alice, another of Betty's nieces who obliged on special occasions, had blossomed out in the glory of a black silk dress, lace collar, ruffled white organdy apron starched stiff as a boot, and a fetching white maid's cap with a frill around it. She was busy supervising a lavish buffet of appetizers, keeping an eye on Danny the Boots, who was bartending at one end in his Sunday blacks, and occasionally venturing into the press with a trayful of tidbits to tempt the shy, the feeble, and the overpolite.

Everybody was dressed to the nines, as Sir Caradoc like to see them. Janet had on another of Annabelle's creations, cut from the same pattern as the first, though nobody but an expert would have noticed. This was a brocade the color of heavy cream, with an Empire waistline defined by a band of brocaded silk ribbon in sap green and gold. Its sleeves were long, tight, and intended to be plain; but Annabelle, inspired by a picture in a book of fairy tales that had been around the old farm since nobody could remember when, had added fat little armseye puffs and outlined them with more of the ribbon. Except for the small diamonds in her ears and the ring on her hand, the touch of green was Janet's only decoration; but it was enough. Even Bob the Blob bestirred himself to pass her a compliment of sorts.

"It is this gown you will be going to wear tomorrow? You will be needing a hennin."

"I wouldn't know where to find a hennin. Anyway, this wasn't exactly meant to be a masquerade costume."

That sounded awfully squelchy; Janet softened her words. "I hadn't realized people were going to wear fancy dress tomorrow. Will you be going as a Druid?"

"Oh no, that would not be at all the thing to do. I shall be wearing my usual."

Whatever that might be. Janet didn't care, her mother-in-law had it all arranged that the ladies of Sir Emlyn's entourage should appear in their Liberty lawn frocks with floppy straw garden-party hats that Gwen had picked up somewhere on tour and bedecked with silk flowers: daffodil yellow for herself, violet and mauve for her mother, shades of blue for Janet. Dorothy would have a wreath of tiny pink rosebuds around her white bonnet, and a pale pink dress with more rosebuds embroidered on the front. Just how long she'd stay pink remained to be seen; Janet had a blue dress ready and waiting, just in case. The weather was going to be beautiful, Lady Rhys had that all arranged too. If it wasn't, they'd just pretend it was and Madoc could help with the umbrellas.

Danny the Boots had deserted the bar, Huw was pinch-hitting, being careful not to load the drinks. He wasn't about to let anybody get tight and cast a cloud over the ceremony that meant so much to his father. And perhaps more to himself than Huw was willing to let on, Janet thought.

Now Danny was coming in with a tall wooden stepladder, making a big thing of placing it exactly under the tall, narrow iron door let into the stone wall. The assembled company were making way for Sir Caradoc to pass among them, carrying the little golden sickle and a big iron key. Dafydd walked a few respectful steps behind him, and Madoc behind Dafydd. At the ladder, they paused while the key was ceremoniously passed along to Madoc. He climbed up, squirted a drop of oil into the lock, and inserted the key.

The grille opened easily enough. Madoc spent a moment deciding where to hang the newest acquisition, another brief time affixing a small brass hanger to the velvet-covered backing, then went halfway back down the ladder to take the fourth golden sickle from Sir Caradoc's upraised hand.

What sets gold apart as the king of metals is that it never tarnishes. Reuel Williams cast a covetous eye upward and made a tactless remark.

"I wonder how much those would be worth melted down."

"Not much."

That was, of all people, Dai Rhys. His Uncle Bob turned on him. "And who are you, young jackanapes, to be uttering rash pronouncements in the presence of your elders and betters?"

For a wonder, Dai stuck to his guns. "Well, look at them. They're almost the color of Aunt Iseult's hair."

Iseult didn't care for the "Aunt." "And is that bad?"

"It simply means the gold's full of copper. British gold tends to be, and the ancient Celts didn't know how to refine it. Anyway, pure gold wouldn't have done the Druids any good, it's too soft to cut anything. The most valuable thing about those sickles is their age. And the workmanship. It's—right. You'd have to be bonkers to melt them down."

"Thank you, Dai," said Sir Caradoc. "You are quite right, the gold is the least of their value. And now, Madoc, the crosier."

Madoc reached in again, lifted out the great silver crosier, and handed it down to his brother. Dafydd, with a fine operatic flourish and a low bow, grasped the tarnished shaft in both hands and presented it to Sir Caradoc.

Janet was standing near enough to notice in detail what an impressive piece of work the crosier was. She estimated that it must be about four-and-a-half feet long, probably as tall as the abbot for whom it had been crafted although short in proportion to the old man who now held it aloft for all to see. The shaft was carved in the intricate Celtic style. The top was curved over and filled in with slender spokes to hold a huge, roughly hexagonal chunk of rather dull-looking green stone.

"That's the famous emerald?" Iseult was fingering her own spectacular necklace, looking disappointed. "It isn't very pretty."

"Not to you, perhaps."

Mary's superior smirk was enough to turn a person's stomach, though Janet supposed one shouldn't fault a person for knowing her own job. She had her bulbous little magnifier out, clearly she was champing at the bit to get in a spot of expertise on the stone.

Sir Caradoc was handling the crosier much the same way he'd cuddled Dorothy, carrying it over to a side table that had been set ready with soft padding, cleaning rags, and a bottle of silver polish.

"I know some antiquarians would say not to, but it is my fancy that the old monks would have kept the crosier bright for their revered abbot. Besides," he confessed, "I like to see it shine. Were the grille not so awkward to get at, I'd be polishing all the time, and the old monks would come back to haunt me for wearing away their chasing."

Everybody glanced sideways at Janet, she made haste to cover the awkwardness. "Where do you suppose the emerald came from, Uncle Caradoc?"

Greatly relieved, the old man picked up his discourse. "That is indeed the question. The Rhys manuscript states that it came from the temple of Solomon; I think that is a beautiful legend. The abbot's emerald could indeed have come from somewhere around the Mediterranean Sea, however. Mary has told me that the ancient source of emerald was Upper Egypt. Am I not right, Mary?"

"Oh yes, you are no doubt alluding to the so-called Cleopatra's Mines, which had in fact been worked for at least sixteen hundred years before the last and most promiscuous of the Cleopatras was born. It is my belief that the abbot's emerald must have been brought to Wales by one of the earliest missionaries, in the latter half of the fifth century."

"During the period known as the Age of the Saints," Bob the Blob amplified.

He was all set to go on, but Mary had the floor and meant to keep it. "As to why an emerald, I suspect it may have been simply that emerald, as precious gems go, is relatively soft and easy to work."

"A likelier explanation," Bob was grabbing the floor, after all, "is that emeralds were deemed to have medicinal virtues, as well as the power to drive away evil spirits, and a third virtue which would naturally be of paramount importance in a monastery; namely, the power to promote chasity."

"Do you suppose it really worked?"

That was Tom, speaking not quite sotto voce enough to Dafydd, who had retired to the buffet and got himself another drink. Janet didn't hear her brother-in-law's reply, which was perhaps just as well.

Mary was making a protracted business of dusting off the stone with a sable brush that Sir Caradoc evidently kept for that one express purpose. As she worked, she talked, discoursing on specific gravity and dispersive powers, and other things that nobody else wanted to hear about.

The scene here in the dining hall reminded Janet a little bit of a viewing at Ben Potts's funeral parlor back in Pitcherville. People would step reverently up to the table, stand for a moment gazing down at the now-gleaming crosier, then drift off to join some chattering group around the buffet. She herself stayed because she didn't think it would be polite not to, and because she sensed that Sir Caradoc liked having her there. He'd picked up one of the polishing cloths but wasn't trying to hurry Mary along as she checked over every millimeter of the gem with her loupe and a small but powerful penlight. He seemed happy enough just being so close to his beloved object, even if it did mean bearing the full brunt of Mary's monologue.

"Naturally the emerald would show to far greater advantage if I were granted the cutting and polishing of it," Mary was saying, "though I should hardly leave it in one piece like this if it were to be sold. Nobody's ordering any new crown jewels these days, that I know of" she tittered at her own mild witticism "and such a gem would be far too cumbersome for anyone to wear as jewelry."

That was a dig at Iseult, but the cinema actress only shook her redgold head and murmured, "Try me." Sensing that she was failing to hold her audience, Mary tried another ploy.

"Dai, come here. I want you to examine the emerald."

"Why should I?" The nephew wasn't liking Mary's peremptory tone, as who would. "You've already spoken the final word."

Nevertheless, he set down the drink that had perhaps given him the Dutch courage to bark back but not enough to disobey, and came forward to take the loupe Mary was holding out. Janet was interested; she'd never seen anybody literally black with rage before, though perhaps Dai's color was a trick of the fading daylight outside and the candlelight within. Anyway, he bent over the stone. Mary turned her little flashlight this way and that, lecturing all the while on what he ought to be seeing. The youngster—he couldn't be more than nineteen or so—replied only when she insisted, and then in sullen grunts.

It was a relief to those watching when Mary snatched back her loupe, tucked it into a gray flannel mitten, and shut it inside the black leather handbag whence it had come. Everybody was pretty sick of the emerald by now, except Iseult.

"What about those emeralds you won't get to cut out of the stone, Mary? How much would they have been worth all together?"

"The mind boggles. Millions. But one hardly likes to think of sacred relics in terms of cash."

"How high-minded of you, Mary." Iseult made it plain that she found Mary's attitude quaint, amusing, and implausible. "So one could simply prise out this great lump of rock, take it to a gem-cutter, wind up with a handful of gorgeous green emeralds, and nobody would know where they came from."

"It would not be that easy, Iseult. Gemstones have their individualities, an experienced lapidary can detect differences between one and another. I myself would certainly recognize any gem cut from this one, of whatever size and in whatever form."

"Oh yes," said Bob, who had continued to linger near his sister, "Mary would indeed be hard to fool. Is that not so, Dai lad?"

Dai only glared and turned his back. Bob pretended not to notice.

"And now, Sister Mary, what is your official pronouncement?"

"I pronounce Sir Caradoc's emerald as magnificent tonight as it has been throughout the ages, and I wish him continued joy of his stewardship."

"Thank you, Mary, for your good wishes and for your valued opinion. Jenny, my dear, I would ask you to help an old man with his polishing were it not for fear of spoiling your beautiful frock."

"Oh, don't worry about my dress. I'd love to help."

Madoc, policeman that he was, hadn't strayed far from the crosier since he'd got it down from the niche. As the well-trained son of a sometimes imperious mother, he'd put a neatly folded handkerchief in the breast pocket of the dinner jacket he'd inherited from his elder brother. Janet tweaked it away and tucked one corner into the neck of her gown.

"All fixed, Uncle Caradoc. You smear and I'll wipe."

They worked together happily, the old man applying the polish in reverent dabs, the young woman plying a soft cloth, bringing up the gentle sheen that only truly antique silver can achieve. It was ticklish, painstaking work wiping every trace of polish from the incised carving. Not that anybody would be apt to notice the odd smidge with the crosier up there above eye level behind its iron grille, but Janet was bound to do the job right for Sir Caradoc's sake.

Watching somebody else polish silver, even such silver as this, was at best only the mildest of diversions. By the time Sir Caradoc pronounced the crosier burnished to his satisfaction and asked Madoc to restore the magnificent relic to its place of safety, most of the party had drifted away to their respective dinner engagements. Elen had kindly asked Dai to join Owain's flock at the farm, Janet noticed with relief.

Alice had cleared away the buffet and picked up the empty glasses. Those staying for dinner were starting to cast hopeful glances at the now laid and waiting table. Danny the Boots carried away the ladder, Iowerth appeared through the swinging door.

"Dinner is ready to be served, my lady."

There was no formal procession tonight, Lady Rhys got the party seated in jigtime. Janet wound up next to Reuel Williams. Not having the faintest notion what to say, she began by putting her foot in her mouth.

"We thought maybe you and Iseult would be going out tonight with Tom's lot."

The writer only shrugged and went on drinking his soup, so she did likewise. Then she reflected that hers hadn't been a particularly tactful opening, and tried again.

"Are you gathering material for another play, or is this visit just for fun?"

"I never do anything just for fun." Reuel sounded quite indignant at the notion. "Of course I'm gathering material. Writers are always working, though I don't suppose you believe me."

"Oh, I believe you. What sort of work are you planning? You look as though you might write spy stories."

"Spy stories?" She'd startled him. "Whatever put that idea into your head?"

"I suppose it's just that one tends to think of spies as being suave and inscrutable."

That was a lie pure and simple. When Janet Wadman Rhys thought of spies, she thought of old Maw Fewter back in Pitcherville, with one ear to the ground and the other glued to the telephone for any scrap of gossip, however trivial, that she could spread around. Janet didn't suppose Reuel Williams would have cared much for being compared to Maw Fewter, but he was taking her polite fabrication well enough. She could see him turning suave and inscrutable before her very eyes. Then Mary leaned across the table and raised her voice to the pitch of an overexcited peacock's.

"Oh yes, Sir Caradoc, strange things happen in the world of gems. I'm sure Mr. Williams agrees with me. Don't you, Mr. Williams?"

Janet heard a noncommittal grunt followed by a grinding of teeth. "God!" muttered Williams. "Why hasn't somebody strangled that woman?"

Chapter 9

Sir Caradoc's birthday dawned fair and warm as a day in mid-June. It wouldn't have dared not to.

"Oh, Madoc, the weather's going to be perfect!"

Janet spoke before she noticed that the other half of the bed was empty. Smiling, she went to scoop Dorothy out of the cradle.

"Come on, Dody, time to get up. Your da's out climbing the ivy again."

She'd got her daughter bathed, fed, and dressed all but the gala frock and bonnet and was laying out fresh underwear for herself when Madoc entered prosaically through the door. She gave him a kiss on the left ear.

"Good morning, Merry Sunshine. Been doing a reconnaissance?"

"Just making sure the larks are all on the wing and the snails aren't muscling in on each other's thorns. What's up?"

"Us, almost. Keep an eye on Dorothy, will you? I've got to get organized."

Janet left Madoc playing with the baby and went into the bathroom. There was a shower of sorts, just a rubber tube that fitted over the bathtub spout and had a sprinkler head on the other end. It worked well enough for practical purposes. She soaped and rinsed, gave herself a quick shampoo, and toweled her head. A comb through and a push here and there were all the hairdressing she needed. Nature would handle the rest.

"I don't think I'll put my good clothes on yet," she said.

"Glad to hear it." Madoc plunked Dorothy back in the cradle, gave her a toy rabbit to chew on, and turned the cradle so that she couldn't see what was happening in the bed.

"That wasn't what I meant." Nevertheless, Janet allowed herself to be persuaded. After a while, she rubbed her lips against his thick, dark hair. "That was a pleasant way to start the day, I hope it stays this good. In a manner of speaking, that is. You were planning to shave, weren't you?"

"Yes, love, and I'd better get cracking before the rest are up and hogging all the hot water. You and Dorothy go on down to breakfast if you want."

"No rush. She's had her first course and my hair's still damp. I'll come and hold the hose if you want."

What with one thing and another, they didn't get to the kitchen until close on eight o'clock, by which time Sir Caradoc was on the scene and the birthday in full swing. Madoc's parents had already been for a short stroll; Lady Rhys had stuck a daisy in her hair and another in her husband's buttonhole.

"We walked up to the big barn," she reported, plucking Dorothy out of Madoc's arms for a morning hug. "Huw and Elen and the lot of them are buzzing around up there like a swarm of bees. Nobody's dressed for the party yet—they're planning to change before the guests start arriving."

"Which means the vicar and his wife will catch them

running around barefoot and pantless." Sir Emlyn helped himself complacently to strawberries. "I personally am as dressed as I'm going to get."

"So am I," said Sir Caradoc. "How do you like my birthday scarf, Jenny?"

"You both look just lovely."

The handsome but not too handsome silk scarves were exactly right, Lady Rhys must have picked them out. And tied them, too. She'd had so much experience improvising haberdashery for orchestra and chorus members who'd mislaid their luggage or run short of clean linen that she'd become a dab hand as a dresser.

"Is it a boiled egg you would like to eat this morning, Mrs. Madoc?" Betty was determined that nobody should go hungry.

"That would be nice. I'll cut some more bread for toast, shall I? Madoc, you want berries, don't you?"

Madoc wanted berries. Dorothy had a boiled egg like her mother's, she shared it with Betty's cat.

"Bartholomew," Betty fussed, "will you not be making a pest of yourself?"

Madoc wasn't hearing a word against the old malkin. "Let him alone, Betty, he's only trying to help. What the moggy catches on the way down, the floor doesn't."

This made excellent sense to everybody, especially Bartholomew. Things were going swimmingly when Bob and Mary appeared, in that order. The brother and sister were already dressed for the festivities, they could hardly have been more so.

Bob's usual, about which Janet had wondered a bit, turned out to be a black skullcap, a starched ruff, and a long-sleeved black robe of fine wool that hung down over his shoetops. Over the robe he wore a loose, short black surcoat with its full sleeves turned back. He was going to fry in that getup by noontime, Janet thought.

He'd have looked much like a pig's head on a platter sitting atop a tar barrel, if it hadn't been for the beard. Today, instead of the coquettish fan, he had his chin whiskers combed down into a point, for some reason he'd no doubt be telling them all about before they could turn him off.

The sister was in traditional Welsh garb: a black steeple hat worn over a white mobcap, full red flannel skirt, fitted black waistcoat, white blouse with a hand-crocheted lace collar, black shoes and stockings, and a rather handsome shawl woven in red and black checks. The ruffled cap hid her lank hair and softened her face, the tall hat relieved her dumpiness, the colorful skirt and shawl did far more for her sallow complexion than her customary muddy grays and browns. Janet felt Mary deserved a compliment, and was happy to give it.

That meant she had to say something nice to Bob also. She could hardly allude to the pig on the platter and couldn't quite bring herself to an outright lie, so she compromised on "What an interesting costume."

Bob smoothed his restructured facial adornment and rewarded her with a complacent nod. "This garb is indeed of great interest and also of much historical significance. Even you, from your savage land of howling wolves and eternal snow, will have realized that I am thus honoring the memory of the illustrious John Dee."

Actually Janet hadn't realized, but knew better than to say so. Bob was getting nicely wound up.

"You, in your benighted ignorance of Welsh history and lifelong exposure to English propaganda, will perhaps not be aware that this unparalled mathematician, cosmographer, astrologer, and some say necromancer; whom Queen Elizabeth the First called her philosopher, who himself had calculated by his art the most auspicious day for her coronation, who schooled her in the esoteric interpretation of his works, notably the *Proto-paedeumata aphoristica* and the *Monas hieroglyphica;* who assisted her in claiming for her realm those far lands that were being discovered by her subjects, was himself, though born in London, by blood a Welshman."

Janet did her best to look thunderstruck, hoping Bob had run out of subordinate clauses. She might have known he was only warming up for the smashing grand finale.

"And, look you, Mrs. Madoc, what is to me of the most immediate import is this." He leaned so far forward that the end of his beard narrowly missed a dunking in his teacup. "John Dee was my ancestor!"

"And mine!" Mary was not about to let her brother hog all the glory. "Through our mother," she added complacently, scoring a point for the distaff side and letting the Rhyses know they needn't think they could muscle in on the Dees.

"I had no idea."

That was the plain truth. Janet wasn't very well up on astrologers and necromancers, although she had known an alchemist of sorts back in Pitcherville. That one had been able to transform tubfuls of potato peelings and rotten turnips, plus a little burnt sugar and whatever other odds and ends might be lying around, into an implausible but far from feeble imitation of rye whiskey; until Madoc and the town marshal had found out what he was up to and made him stop. She didn't think Bob would be interested in hearing about the Pitcherville alchemist, she might as well finish her tea and go tend to her flowers.

"Come on, Dorothy, let's get you fixed and take you for a little walk."

"Where are you off to, then?" Mary was already half out of her chair.

"To the loo" would be rude. Janet merely smiled, wiped Dorothy's face with her napkin dipped in water, and took off the eggy bib. A change of diaper—nappy, rather; when in Britain one must change as the Brits changed—was probably indicated.

"Want me to take her, Jenny?"

Madoc was ready to oblige. So was Lady Rhys, but Janet was getting to feel she'd just as soon keep her baby to herself once in a while.

"Thanks, I'll manage. Say thank you to Betty, Dorothy. No, don't kiss her till you've had your face washed. All right, kiss the kitty if you want, I don't suppose he'll mind."

"It is unsanitary to kiss cats." Bob was miffed with Mrs. Madoc, most likely not so much because she was letting her daughter do what any reasonable child would naturally do as because she wouldn't stick around and listen to him yammer on about John Dee.

"No it isn't," Janet replied unfeelingly. "I've kissed cats myself, and never died of it yet."

She let Dorothy rub noses with Bartholomew a couple more times, then picked her up and headed for the bathroom. When she came back, Mary was still demanding to know where she intended to walk; it would be childish not to tell. "I'm just going to borrow Aunt Elen's watering pot and freshen up the flowers in the chapel."

"What kind of flowers? Why didn't you ask me? I would have done them. I shall go with you."

"Don't you want to finish your breakfast?"

Mary had taken a generous plateful of everything going, but had barely touched her food. Not that it would go to waste—Bob was already casting a lustful eye at his sister's sausages even though he hadn't yet finished his own. Nevertheless, Janet wished the woman would stay in the kitchen.

Night before last, Mary had been silly and tedious about her leaping. Last night, examining the great emerald, she'd been still a bore but something of a personage. Today she was almost manic, dancing about like a skittish racehorse at the post, straining to be off and running. Was it because tonight she was going to leap the Beltane fire?

Well, why not? If a woman had reached middle age and only got her crotch warmed once a year—Janet flushed and administered a silent rebuke to her wayward mind. That was the sort of vulgar, sexist remark her brother's hired man might get away with down at the Owls' Hall, but hardly the thing for a respectable married woman to be thinking in the presence of her in-laws, not to mention her own baby daughter.

Speaking of whom, if Janet thought she was going to monopolize Dorothy all morning, it was clear she'd have to think again. Sir Emlyn was letting it be known with a smile and a nod that he had a lap ready and waiting. Lady Rhys was more outspoken.

"Oh, look at that smile! Come, precious, don't you want to stay with Granny and Grandda and pat the pussy while Mam does her flowers? Jenny, you can't carry Dorothy and the watering pot both, wouldn't you like us to mind her for you? You'll be coming back soon to change for the party."

Janet had the sense to recognize an order, however politely disguised. She handed over the prize to the victors and perforce accepted Mary as a most unwelcome substitute.

Mary was as exasperating to walk with as she was to listen to, darting ahead or lagging back, grabbing

Janet's arm then pushing it away, urging her on or nagging her to slow down. Janet tuned her pestiferous companion out as best she could, and concentrated on the day and the scene.

There was plenty of activity around the farm. The kitchen door stood wide open; people were rushing in and out, carrying things up from the milking shed, into the house, out to the barn, back and forth, forth and back. Nobody had time to stop and chat. Elen's watering pot was standing on the long wooden bench outside the door, Janet filled it from the spigot and went on to the chapel.

Her flowers had held up pretty well, but it was surprising how much water they'd managed to drink. Janet went around tweaking out the wilted ones, nipping off a faded blossom here and there, moving a stem to make a better show, refilling the depleted jars. She didn't have to worry about spills, water couldn't hurt stone and that old curtain over the altar was too far gone to matter. It did make a pleasant effect, though, with Aunt Elen's candles, the big bouquet in the middle and the massed jam pots below.

Mary had, for a wonder, fallen silent while Janet worked. Now she erupted again. "Where is the mullein? I am seeing no mullein. There must be mullein."

"And where do you propose to find any this early in the year?" Janet snapped back. "Anyway, mullein isn't much to look at."

"But mullein is necessary."

Janet couldn't see why, nor did she care. "Then why don't you go see if you can find some?"

She might have known Mary wouldn't pay attention, "And bindweed."

"Bindweed? Do you mean wild morning glory?" Janet had seen some in the hedgerows: big white blossoms, much more impressive than the smaller pink-tinged ones she was used to in New Brunswick. "I know it's lovely but the flowers shut right up if you pick them."

"Three days before the new moon."

"Is it? I've lost track, what with all the traveling." Janet didn't see what relevance the moon had to bind-weed unless morning glories worked the night shift in Wales. Or unless Mary was just talking to hear herself talk.

"Oh, you did use toadflax. That's a relief." The bright handful of yellow and orange flowers, like tiny snapdragons crowded together on spiky stems, did make a pleasant splash of color against the dark gray stone. Perhaps that was what Mary meant, if in fact she meant anything at all.

"Our name for it back home is butter and eggs," said Janet. "When I was little, my father showed me how to make the blossoms open and close their mouths. I used to pretend they were talking to me. We had a great patch down behind the barn." Where the old backhouse used to be—she didn't have to include that detail. "An old neighbor of ours called them ramstead. She claimed it had been a Welshman named Ramstead who first brought the plants over to North America. Did you know that?"

Mary didn't answer; she was walking round and round the altar widdershins, mumbling something to herself. Janet pinched one little blossom gently at the sides so that she could see the toad's mouth open, then picked up the now-empty watering pot.

"There, that's done. I'd better get back to the big house and put on my glad rags. Are you coming, or do you want to go looking for mullein?"

Not that Mary'd be apt to find any, but at least the hunt would keep her busy for a while, which was a consummation devoutly to be wished. Janet had a beautiful thought.

"You know, Mary, that's really a marvelous outfit you have on. I was just thinking how picturesque you'd look rambling around the hilltop, where people could see you as they came up. Guests ought to begin arriving pretty soon, hadn't they?"

"Yes! Yes they will."

Without another word, Mary hared off up the slope. Janet breathed a sigh of relief, put the watering pot back where she'd found it, exchanged a few quick words with passing Rhyses, and went on down to Uncle Caradoc's. He and Sir Emlyn were having a companionable wander around the garden, Lady Rhys and Dorothy were nowhere in sight.

"What have you done with my daughter?" Janet asked them.

"Sillie took her up to get dressed for the party," her father-in-law answered. "Madoc's gone over to Lisa's on some kind of secret mission. How did you manage to shake Mary?"

"I sent her up on the hill to look picturesque. Actually she's trying to find some mullein and bindweed—she didn't think much of the way I did the flowers for the chapel. Except the toadflax, she approved of that. Did you know it was brought over to the colonies by a Welshman?"

"No, but I surmise why a Welshman might have wanted to have familiar plants growing around him," said Sir Caradoc. "Mary had better leave your flowers alone."

Janet couldn't have agreed more, but she did wonder why the old man spoke so sharply. Sharply for him, anyway. Perhaps he was as fed up with Mary as the rest of them were, it was high time for a change of subject.

"Where's Gwen this morning? I haven't seen her yet. Or Dai either, come to think of it."

"Gwen came down right after you left," Sir Emlyn told her. "She had some tea and went to fix her mother's hair. We're supposed to send you straight up the minute you get back, to have your hat fitted. Dai, I believe, got up very early and went to join Owain's lot."

"That's good, they'll keep him busy. I'd better hop along, then, before Gwen comes after me."

"You had indeed. Our Gwendolyn is not to be gainsaid." Uncle Caradoc was smiling down at her. "Jenny, it is a joy to have you here. I hope you will enjoy my birthday as much as I am doing."

"I fully intend to."

Just so Mary didn't go messing around in the chapel. Mullein and bindweed, forsooth! Either the woman was a little bit cracked or else she'd been watching some television program about flower arranging for the space age. Well, to heck with Mary. What if the hat didn't go with her dress?

Janet ran upstairs, changed into her Liberty lawn, grateful that she wouldn't have to wear winter woolies under it on a day like this, and rushed to see her hat. It was perfect. Gwen was an enchantment, Lady Rhys an empress in disguise, Dorothy a living doll. Now for the birthday party.

Chapter 10

Janet had been wondering how they were going to cope with Dorothy all day, she might have known Madoc would come up with the answer. He was back from Lisa's pushing a magnificent pram that must have been Tib's, complete with flounced pillows and an embroidered pink silk carriage robe, plus a more utilitarian one to spread on the grass for the baby to crawl around on. Janet was ecstatic.

"How good of Lisa! See, Dorothy, now you can take a nap whenever you want and nobody will have to miss the party watching you snooze. We'll just stick her diaper bag in at the foot, and a bottle of water in case she gets thirsty. There's bound to be something she can eat at the luncheon, Elen's got food enough for an army. Do you want to push, or shall I?"

"This is man's work, love."

"Pooh, you just want to show off in front of the family. Come on, Dody, in you go. Da's going to take you for a ride."

"Da."

"Madoc, she said it! That's a good little Welsh girl, now let's hear you say Mam."

But Dorothy was her father's daughter this morning.

Janet didn't care. She was happy enough to walk behind the pram with Gwen and her mother, pleasantly conscious of the picture they made in their flowered frocks and blooming hats, with white shoes and white gloves in the Windsor style. The gloves were just for fun, of course, they wouldn't stay on long. At least Janet's wouldn't.

Sir Caradoc should probably be up front leading their little parade, but he looked happy enough escorting three so elegant ladies. Sir Emlyn was right beside him, unobtrusively ready to lend a hand should one be needed. Most likely it wouldn't, the old baronet could probably outwalk them all.

Bob the Blob had attached himself to their tail end. And a strange appendage he must make, Janet thought, toiling along in his hot padded robe with his whiskers *en pointe* and an antique tome tucked under his arm to show how brainy he was. That couldn't actually be one of John Dee's works he was carrying, she didn't suppose. Maybe it was *Mrs. Beeton's Cookbook*, which would be equally appropriate. Anyway, she hoped Bob wasn't planning to read it to anybody; Mary was nuisance enough for the pair of them.

She was up there, sure enough, right on the crest of the hill. She did look quaint and picturesque in her steeple hat and scarlet petticoat, and she did appear to be clutching an assortment of vegetable matter. Janet made out a snaking stem or two, Mary must have found the bindweed. Well, good luck to her.

Now they were getting in among the throng. Not that it was all that much of a throng yet but more kept coming, some on foot, some in cars that Danny the Boots was making them park down at the foot of the drive. Somehow or other Janet found herself in an impromptu receiving line with Sir Caradoc, Lady Rhys, and Mavis doing the honors for the farm because Elen was too busy helping Lisa cut up the pies.

There was no earthly use trying to remember names. Janet just kept smiling and shaking hands, and saying no, she and Madoc hadn't been much bothered by polar bears during the winter. Madoc and Gwen were handy by, smiling and chatting with some of those who'd come through the receiving line. Janet couldn't help noticing awed glances being cast from Madoc to herself to Dorothy queening it in her borrowed pram.

Bob had wandered off, thank goodness. He'd buttonholed some poor soul of a minister, and was expounding something out of his book. Dafydd and Tom were here at last, Mavis said Lisa and Tib had come earlier in the estate car with the leek pies. Tib was now among Owain's pack, off a bit from the grown-ups, dressed in something mildly outlandish and managing to look adorable regardless. Dai was also with the young bloods, looking rather bloodless himself but less miserable than he'd no doubt have been made to feel with his aunt and uncle.

As usual, Dafydd had turned on the charm and begun cutting a swath. He seemed happy enough to be surrounded by admirers, though Janet though his smile looked a bit forced. What was eating that man, anyway?

Tom the Flicks had clearly appointed himself the life of the party. He breezed up to the receiving line resplendent in baggy white flannels, a mustard-colored jacket with a pinched-in waist and huge green tattersall checks, and a pink-striped shirt with a celluloid collar. A malacca cane hung over his arm, a straw boater was moored to his topmost buttonhole by a long elastic. Lady Rhys was only mildly amused.

"You look like a leftover chorus boy from *Charlot's Revue*, Tom. Do try not to trip over that cane." After he'd flitted on to find a more appreciative audience, she murmured to Janet, "Oh well, there's always one in every crowd. Huw will keep him in line. Cousin Glynis, how lovely to see you!"

Iseult and Reuel were almost the last to arrive even though they'd had the shortest distance to cover. Perhaps the film writer had been skittish about being plunged too early into a maelstrom of Rhyses, or perhaps the actress had run into delays getting her eyelashes on. Iseult did seem to be awfully lush about the eyeballs today. Hauling that freight of cilia up and down every time she batted her eyes at Dafydd must be hard on the eyelid muscles, Janet thought.

A person did have to admire Iseult's outfit, though; she was one long ripple of lime-green chiffon from neck to ankles, with a turban to match and a big emerald brooch stuck in the front of it. A relatively modest assortment of emerald bracelets and dangly earrings completed her simple toilette.

"Do you suppose she plans to tell fortunes?" Mavis whispered in Janet's ear between handshakes.

"Not mine," Janet murmured back, and went on being polite to the relatives.

Madoc was managing just fine; Dorothy was handling her own receiving line with grace and aplomb. The young boys in the party were especially charmed by the tiny May Queen in her nest of furbelows. Janet wasn't surprised, having seen her own nephews' reactions, but Madoc was all set to play the stern father if any of them tried to date his daughter up.

Now the guests were all assembled, Elen was getting ready to serve. The meal was to be a sit-down affair. Janet had wondered how the Rhyses were going to handle such a crowd until she'd seen the U-shaped table that had been built sometime in the past for just such occasions. It ran the entire length of the great barn on three sides, except for a few gaps where people could get in and out without having to crawl underneath. Chairs had been borrowed from all four of the local churches and white sheets for tablecloths from anybody who still had some to lend. Overlaps in the cloths had been camouflaged by wreaths of ivy with daisies tucked in here and there: the short-stemmed, rosy-tipped kind one never saw growing wild in Canada.

Betty's multiple nieces had done the flowers, robbing gardens and hedgerows to make a good show, and succeeding beautifully. The focal point was at the center of the room, where stood three tall golden harps, surrounded by great tubs of fern and flowering hawthorn. Three harpists all in cloth of gold or a reasonable facsimile, with wreaths of ivy crowning their heads, were plucking music that rippled like a cooling stream on a summer's day. The harpists must be Sir Emlyn's birthday present to his father, Janet thought; she hoped to goodness somebody was taking pictures.

Even Lady Rhys wouldn't have tried to seat a table this size, but it arranged itself quite easily. Families mostly stayed together. Guests either knew or were gently reminded who was entitled by ties of blood to sit where. Everybody sat with his back to the wall, facing out toward the harpists; servers simply remained on the outside and reached across the narrow tables. A great oak armchair wreathed in garlands of green had been set thronelike at the exact center of the middle table for Sir Caradoc. His own son and grandson took the places of honor at either side of him.

As the patriarch's only nephew, Sir Emlyn counted among the elect. A high chair with a single rosebud in a tiny vase on its tray had been placed at the far end of the head table, next to the gap, so that Dorothy could easily be coped with. Janet sat next to her, of course, with Madoc, Gwen, Dafydd, and Lady Rhys all in a row beside their illustrious paterfamilias. Betty had also been graced with a seat at the head table, Janet was glad to see.

Close but not all that close connections got the seats nearest the bends of the U, the rest took the leftovers and were glad to get them. Bob and Mary had managed to bag themselves chairs up near the corner but on the other side, Janet was relieved to note. Iseult and Reuel were at Dorothy's end. The writer must have been promoted to honorary fiancé for the occasion, Janet decided; she wondered how much he appreciated the honor. Anyway, Reuel had some third cousin's pretty daughter at his other side and looked to be settling in comfortably enough; though he did keep a hopeful eye on his champagne glass all through the grace, which was said in Welsh by three different ministers speaking in relays. Janet was relieved for him when Huw rose to give the birthday toast to his father and it was safe to take a drink.

As always, one toast led to another but the rhetoric was not allowed to interfere with the eating. Bowls and platters of food were simply put on the table at frequent intervals and everybody helped everybody else. Lisa's leek pie was superb. So were Elen's chicken pie, Betty's steak-and-kidney, and all the other pies and pastries, the sliced meats, the cold salmon, the fresh peas, the crisp salads, the edibles beyond enumeration. They vanished like the snows of yesteryear amid music and laughter and general rejoicing.

When at last even Bob had had enough, the tables were cleared, the cloths crumbed, and the desserts brought on. There were mounds of strawberries, jugs of cream, gateaux on stands, tarts on platters, mighty glass bowls of trifle, Welsh cakes in greater profusion than the daisies on the grass. There were epergnes spilling over with grapes and peaches, apples and figs, nuts and chocolates, and strong peppermints to ease the overstrained stomach. Janet took a peppermint.

Dorothy had behaved well enough during the long drawn-out meal, with one pit stop between courses; now she was beginning to flag. Madoc picked her up and cocked an eyebrow. Janet nodded. They went into the farmhouse, got their daughter comfortable, rested in the quiet parlor until she fell asleep, then took her back outside and bedded her down in the pram.

During their brief absence, family and guests had been drifting out of the barn to a broad lawn framed in blossoming hawthorn, mulberry, and apple trees. Here, chairs, rugs, and pillows had been carried out to make a sort of informal amphitheater, with a little knoll at one end as a natural dais where the Maypole had been raised, bedecked with garlands of ivy and streamers of gold. The oaken throne chair was sitting there now but Sir Caradoc was still mingling with his well-wishers. Lady Rhys had staked out a rug and some chairs at a strategic point close but not too close to the dais, in the shade of a not-too-shady tree. Trust her. Madoc trundled the pram over that way, the springs taking the bounces easily, Dorothy not so much as blinking. They got her parked, then sprawled on the rug as a change from too much sitting.

"Comfortable, Jenny love?"

"Wonderfully. What happens now?"

"Poetry, in Welsh. Think you can stick it?"

"Translate for me. Till I fall asleep, anyway. All that food in the middle of the day's making me drowsy."

"You and plenty of others. Want another cushion, or will you settle for my manly bosom?"

"I'd better take the cushion. This crowd seems to be about half ministers and Sunday School teachers, and you know how your mother feels about your father's position. Oh look, they're bringing out the harps."

The majestic carved and gilded instruments turned the picnic into a fairy tale. Gwen, her daffodil hat and frock gold as the harps in the afternoon sun, could easily have passed for a fairy princess if she hadn't happened to be sprawled none too decorously on the blue rug with her clarinet case open beside her, taking her instrument apart and squinting into one of the pieces. She'd be playing in a while.

Dafydd would sing, of course. He was next rug over with Lisa and Tom, Tib having taken Dai under her wing and steered him across to where Owain's lot had staked out a claim. Lisa was straightening Dafydd's new ascot for him. Antique gold with a pattern of scarlet griffins might have been a bit much on some men, it was just right for Dafydd Rhys. That celluloid collar of Tom's must have been cramping his windpipe, he'd swapped it for a shocking-pink ascot with green horseshoes. Janet wondered whether the vanished Patricia had picked it out for him. Too bad she'd had to miss the party; she'd seemed a friendly soul. Perhaps she was only a casual acquaintance, though; nobody had so much as mentioned her since that first evening.

No sprawling on rugs for Iseult; she was artfully arranged in one of the lawn chairs, watching her light green draperies undulate in the gentle breeze, idly turning her emerald bracelets to catch the light. Reuel was stretched out on the grass with an arm across his eyes. Half-asleep and half-seas over, Janet thought uncharitably.

Bob had a chair planted smack in front of the dais. He'd donned a panama hat over his skullcap and was

119

glowering out from under its brim at the harpists tuning their instruments, daring them to strike a false note. The empty chair beside him was presumably reserved for Mary, but she was in no hurry to take it. Janet could see her darting here and there among the guests, perspiring in her checked woolen shawl but showing no inclination to take it off. Oh dear, she was heading this way. Janet sat up and prepared to be civil if necessary, but Mary plumped herself down beside the semicomatose Reuel.

"Well, Mr. Williams, we meet again. Enjoying the revels? You were always a great one for revels, were you not? Or should I say fun and games?"

His answer was a less than civil grunt, it didn't put her off a whit.

"You found my little dissertation on Sir Caradoc's emerald last night interesting, did you not, Mr. Williams?"

"Oh yes. Very interesting." He yawned without bothering to cover his mouth, just so she'd know he really meant what he said.

"You made good use of my knowledge once before, didn't you? Remarkably good use. Isn't that right, Mr. Williams? Or was it in fact not at all right?"

Williams was sitting up now, looking at Mary as though he couldn't quite make out what she was. "The show went well enough, I suppose. It's been a long time."

"Indeed it has, and much has taken place since then. Arthur Ellis's death, for instance. We must have a talk, Mr. Williams. Later on, when you're fresh and rested. A good, long talk."

"Arthur Ellis? He was the gem buyer, right? The one who wouldn't let himself be photographed except with his back to the camera? What is there to talk about?"

"Come now, Mr. Williams. Don't be coy. You know what."

She bounced away, with an eldritch cackle that would have done any one of Macbeth's witches proud. Iseult was amused.

"Just can't keep them off, can you, Reuel? What was that all about?"

"God knows. The old hag must be drunk."

Mary was something, at any rate. Now she was scuttling back across the lawn, to where Dai appeared to be hitting it off pretty well with Mavis's Patagonian niece, a pretty girl of sixteen or so. His aunt was the last person he wanted to see just then, his attitude made that plain. Mary said something to him, he tried to turn away. She grabbed the lapel of his blazer and started berating him about something, wagging a finger in front of his nose.

The other young people were starting to draw away. Who could blame them? Janet could have cried for the poor misfit who wanted so badly to be one of the crowd. Even from here she could see how red Dai's face was getting, see him finally pull away and stalk off, looking for a hole to crawl into. Tib, bless her heart, was running after him, soothing him down, drawing him back to the pack. He'd be all right now, nobody was paying any attention to him. People were quieting down, finding their places, looking expectantly toward the dais where the harpists were poised to begin.

All but Mary. She was still flitting from one to another, making, as far as Janet could see, a thorough pest of herself. Finally Bob the Blob had literally to force her to sit down and behave herself. He was as angry and humiliated as Dai had been. What in the world had got into the woman?

Either Mary was deliberately out to make an enemy

of everybody present or else she'd popped her cork. Surely a little champagne wouldn't have done that; nobody had got more than a respectable amount at the table. Not even Reuel, hard as he'd tried. The writer might well have brought a pocket flask with him, but Janet couldn't believe he'd have shared it with a woman whom he so obviously considered a pain in the neck. Mary must be overexcited in anticipation of the Beltane fire. What else could it be?

And who cared? Old Iowerth, Sir Caradoc's lifelong friend and butler, was center front now, advancing to the dais with stately tread and lofty mien, a sheaf of papers in his hand. As the harpers struck up an overture, anticipatory murmurs ran through the crowd. Here in Wales, a poet was a personage, Iowerth was said to be one of the best. This could be his crowning achievement.

He began to read. Janet couldn't understand one word in twenty, but she could relish the cadence: now grave, now lightsome, always reflecting the love and admiration this man felt for the patriarch who was being honored today. It was more than a poem, it was a paean. Gradually it became a lullaby. Decorously propped against her husband's shoulder, her face screened by her garden-party hat, Janet slept.

Chapter 11

It was Dorothy who woke her, crawling around on the rug. The Queen of the May had been given a drink of water and a fresh nappy by her doting grandma, she was full of beans and eager to reign. Bob was on the dais delivering some kind of oration. It couldn't be poetry—at least it didn't sound like poetry.

"What's he talking about?" Janet whispered to Gwen.

"He's just gassing on about ancient rites, as when isn't he. If it's a cup of tea you're wanting to wake you up, they've set up a table under the ash tree."

Janet glanced at her watch. "Good heavens, it's almost five o'clock. I didn't realize I'd slept so long. I haven't missed the music, I hope."

"Oh no, that's next. Come along, I need to wet my whistle and freshen up."

"Won't it be rude to go milling around while he's still talking?"

"Not a bit. Bob's so full of himself he won't even notice. Iowerth's poem was superb, which was rather a shame since none of those that followed could come up to his. Some weren't so bad, though."

"I can see Madoc will have to teach me Welsh before we come again."

At least Janet would be able to appreciate the rest of the program. Her own family had been musical, after their fashion. When she'd been Dorothy's age and a bit older, her father had sung to her about three little owls sitting in the forest. Her mother had been lead soprano with the church choir, Janet herself would probably have joined if she'd stayed in Pitcherville. As it was, she sang to Dorothy or herself and went to concerts at the university with her neighbor.

Now that Janet had time and opportunity to listen, and the incentive of having married into such a family as Sir Emlyn's, music had become one of her great joys. She had a good ear and was learning fast; her one regret was that she couldn't share her pleasure with her tone-deaf husband. Madoc himself didn't mind a bit.

Sir Emlyn was getting that look on his face which meant he was rehearsing in his head. Lady Rhys was down on the rug, tickling Dorothy with a blade of grass, to their mutual delight.

"Go along with Gwen if you want to, Jenny. You might bring me back a cup of tea, and perhaps one of Betty's cakes if there are any left. Emmy won't want any."

Naturally not. Sir Emlyn never could eat before a performance, even an informal one like this. He gave his two daughters a vague smile and waved them off; he could say more with his hands than with his mouth. They straightened their hats and went.

Naturally Gwen and Janet ran into any number of other people who weren't listening to Bob either; naturally everybody wanted to stop and chat. When they finally got to the farmhouse and headed for the downstairs bathroom, they found half a dozen lined up before them. One was Mary, still in full cry. She had Mavis backed into a corner and was giving her the finer points on how to leap a Beltane fire. Mavis was looking a bit frantic, as well she might; a good deed was clearly in order.

"Oh there you are, Mavis," said Janet. "We've been looking for you. Could you come along with us now, please?"

"Yes, of course. What's up?"

"Nothing, really," said Gwen once they'd got clear of the others. "Janet and I just thought you'd like an out from the Beltane fire. Come along to the manor, unless you're really desperate."

"I couldn't be desperate enough to go back in there. What's wrong with that woman, anyway? I've always thought of her as the original Minnie Mouse."

Janet laughed. "So did I at first, woolly gray with a bright pink nose. But mice can be awful pests once you let them get inside the house. Has Mary always been like this, Gwen?"

"Actually, no. When I was a kid, I don't recall Mary's ever saying much except 'Yes, brother.' I believe they're twins, though they certainly don't look it."

"But is it true, all that about her being a famous gem-cutter?" Mavis asked.

"I don't know how famous; but yes, that's what she does. Mary used to do work for Lisa's husband. He was an importer of jewels—his father and hers had been in partnership or something. Anyway the Ellises bought the rough stones and the Rhyses cut them. I don't know whom she works for now. I think Arthur Ellis pretty much ran his out of his pocket, so there wasn't anybody to take over after he died."

"What about Bob? Doesn't he have something to do with the business?"

"Perish the thought, Bob's a gentleman. He's never done a stroke in his life, as far as I know, except talk and keep a firm clutch on the purse strings. The parents left something to both him and Mary, but Bob's always had the handling of it. I don't know whether he's mismanaged their estate or whether it never amounted to much in the first place, but I have the impression that they've been living pretty much on Mary's earnings lately. Perhaps that's why she's grown more self-assertive, in which case I'm all for her. Well, not quite all. Not enough to listen to any more of her silly gabble about the Beltane fires, at any rate. Thank goodness, they'll be leaving tomorrow. I'm driving them to the station myself, to make sure they get there."

Janet laughed. "We'll go with you and wave them off. Not to be nosy, but what really happened to Lisa's husband? Madoc doesn't know, which I must say isn't like him. He just says Mr. Ellis died somewhere abroad and nobody ever wants to talk about him."

"I know. They won't talk to me, either. Lisa keeps his photograph in her drawing room, but I have a feeling that's mostly for Tib's sake. On the other hand, I may be doing her an injustice. One never knows with Lisa. If anything gets too close to the bone, she just draws in her head like one of her tortoises. For all one can tell, she may still be grieving her heart out."

"Eight years is a long time to grieve," said Mavis, "though the shock of his being murdered—"

Gwen nodded. "It was pretty bad. I was in London at the time. I happened to turn on the news, and there it was. A British dealer in precious stones, named Arthur Ellis, found robbed and murdered in Marseilles. He was assumed to have been carrying jewels with him; the inference was that he'd got mixed up with a smuggling ring."

"So that's why everybody's so hush-hush about the way he died?" said Janet.

"Could be, though I still find it hard to believe. Arthur always struck me as such a Playing Fields of Eton type. I used to wonder how he and Lisa ever came to marry, though they seemed to get on well enough. Of course he wasn't around much, that may have helped. That beastly Tom Feste used to drop bitchy hints about Arthur's having mistresses scattered all over Europe, but I don't think anyone took him seriously. I suppose Tom can't help being spiteful about other people's marriages when his own are always blowing up in his face."

"How many has he had so far?" asked Mavis. "I never can keep track."

"Legally, only three, with a few near-misses. I thought there might be a fourth coming along when Tom appeared here day before yesterday with a voluptuous blonde on the string, but I gather that one went bust."

"I was wondering about that," said Janet. "Dafydd had her with him in Tom's car, you know, when he come to pick us up at the station."

"Precisely my point. If Tom's intentions had been serious, do you think he'd have let her within clutching distance of Dafydd?"

"Now, Gwen, don't be mean. All Dafydd did was drive her to the station so she could catch a train to Swansea."

"Then he must be coming down with something. Golly, I hope it's not a sore throat. Here Mavis, you take this loo, I'll nip upstairs. Coming, Jenny?"

"Yes, I want to pick up a cardigan for myself and something warmer for Dorothy. It's starting to cool off a bit. Would you like a shawl, Mavis?"

"Don't bother, Jenny. I can run in and grab a woolly at the farmhouse if the goose pimples start to rise. I'll be in and out anyway, helping to set out the supper after the music. It's just going to be a buffet of leftovers. Mam Elen thought another sit-down affair would be too much for Sir Caradoc and who needs it anyway? See you."

The red room felt less welcoming without Madoc and Dorothy. Janet did what she'd come for and left quickly. There was no ghost in the hall, she wasn't disappointed.

Mavis hadn't dawdled either. She was wandering around looking at a collection of etchings that showed slate miners at work: splitting slates, loading tramcars in tunnels, swinging on ropes from the precipitous sides of open quarries. There was one of two men carrying a rude stretcher between them; the body on it was covered up head and all. Plenty of miners must have been killed by falls or crushed by falling chunks of slate. A hard life, and nothing afterward for the widow and the kids. The coal mines had been worse, Madoc had told Janet. The Rhyses had done well to stick to farming.

Mavis was shaking her head over the print of the dead man being carried away from the quarry. "That's how my own great-grandfather went. My mam's grandfather, that was. Her uncle Ivor carried him home, with a neighbor helping. On their dinner break, so they wouldn't get docked for taking time off from the job. Uncle Ivor was fifteen at the time. That's why he emigrated to Patagonia when they were getting up a colony. Thank God my lot have something better to look forward to. Tell me, Jenny, what's wrong with Dafydd? He's not in some kind of jam, is he?"

"Frankly, Madoc and I have been wondering the same thing," Janet had to tell her. "You have to realize that, silly as it sounds, we don't know Dafydd all that well. Madoc was telling me only yesterday how little they'd seen of each other growing up. Dafydd's six years older, you know, and went to school over here while

Madoc stayed in Canada. Madoc's the only one of the three who was born there, you know. And of course their interests have always been completely different."

"Well, that's how it is in families sometimes. Gwen, aren't you ever coming? They'll be starting up again."

"Coming!"

Gwen cavorted downstairs with her face freshly done and her hat on backward; they returned to the revels. Sir Caradoc was back on his throne with a teacup and scone serving for orb and scepter. Sir Emlyn was standing beside his uncle, exuding that gentle patience which meant he was fuming to get on with the music.

The three harpists had taken a long break during the poetry reading; they were back in their places, tuning their instruments yet again. There were still people around the tea table; it was quite safe to stop for cups and cakes, not forgetting the promised extra for Lady Rhys. Gwen took only tea. She drank up in a hurry, collected the clarinet her mother and Dorothy had been minding for her, went to the dais, and took the chair that was set ready for her in front of the middle harp. To Janet's surprise, Sir Emlyn now opened a case that had been on the chair till Gwen handed it to him, and took out a violin she'd never seen him with before. Gwen gave him an A, he lifted his bow, and began tuning up.

"I didn't know Tad played too," Janet whispered to her mother-in-law.

"Oh yes, Emmy was a child prodigy of sorts. He was fiddling professionally before he ever began to conduct. He still enjoys having a go now and then, the old sweetie."

Lady Rhys blew her husband a kiss and raised her teacup in silent toast. He gave his bow a tiny flick. At once those who were still milling around took their places, even Mary the Fires. Dafydd went forward to stand beside his father. Sir Emlyn turned sideways so that everybody on the dais as well as those out front could watch his bow, and struck the opening note.

Janet recognized the tune; it was the well-beloved *"Llwyn On,"* "The Ash Grove." She even knew the English words for one of its many versions. "All hail to thee, Cambria, the land of my fathers ..." The violin carried the melody, the harps and the clarinet wove a magic veil around it. Then Sir Emlyn nodded to Dafydd, Dafydd gestured to the audience, and the whole meadow burst into song.

Nobody has ever been able to say for sure when the Welsh first learned to sing in harmony rather than in unison. Giraldus Cambrensis thought they might have caught the habit from the Vikings but had by his time sung this way for so long that it had become an innate characteristic of the race. According to him, even tiny Welsh babies instinctively babbled in parts as soon as they'd got past mere screaming. So far, Dorothy hadn't shown any sign of doing so, but then she wasn't much of a screamer either.

Whatever its origin, the sound was glorious to hear with Dafydd's magnificent tenor soaring above all the rest, then blending gently into the harmonious whole. Janet sang the English lyrics she knew, they seemed to work as well as any. She didn't know how many stanzas there were, she only wished there'd been more. But Dafydd swung them into a melody sweet and plaintive, then on to something brisk and funny, himself singing a few solo bars and the rest shouting back, over and over till they ran out of breath.

Then Sir Emlyn played alone, then Gwen, then the two together. Then the harps joined in, then all the instruments stopped at once and Dafydd sang without accompaniment and Janet forgot all the times she'd wanted to swat him. Then everybody sang a capella, then the harps came in one by one, then the clarinet, then the violin, and so it went, on and on, until Sir Emlyn signaled an intermission and everybody went to get another cup of tea.

Now it was back to the music, but now it was different. Bob the Blob sang a solo, and sang it very well, Janet had to admit. He got his round of applause and left the dais well satisfied with himself as always, but this time with good reason. Now Dafydd was beckoning Owain and Mavis and their four up front with the two Patagonians and Sir Emlyn was jigging out a ballad for them to sing, first in Spanish and English by Mavis and the kids, then in Welsh by Owain and Dafydd, with everybody, even Madoc, belting out each chorus in the language of his choice.

There were more performances by various Rhyses, then Dafydd came down to escort his mother up to the dais. Light opera had been Silvestrine's specialty back when she was performing; she still had a rich mezzo-soprano well suited to some of the familiar melodies of Victor Herbert, who, though not Welsh, had at least been a Celt. She sang alone, she sang with Dafydd, she sang with her husband's accompaniment, she sang with her daughter's. Then she said she was too hoarse to sing any more, and Dafydd brought her back to the rug amid tumultuous applause.

"Come along then, Jenny. You're on next."

Janet recoiled as though her brother-in-law's outstretched hand had been a cobra. "Me? I can't sing."

"Of course you can," said Lady Rhys. "You were caroling like a lark a while back. Go ahead, Jenny."

There was nothing to do, even Madoc was urging her on. Janet went. Dafydd turned her to face the onlookers.

"I expect you've all met my beautiful Canadian sister-in-law by now. Jenny, what do you sing over there?"

"Whatever we like. We're bilingual, more or less, like you, and nobody's done a French song yet, so how about *'Vive la Canadienne'* which means something like 'Hurrah for the Canadian girl.' She has pretty eyes and everybody's going to dance at her wedding, and that's about all there is to it. Surely you know this one, Dafydd."

That was wicked of her. Dafydd must know lots about girls with pretty eyes, but little about weddings. People caught the joke and Janet forgot to be self-conscious. The tune was merry and easy. With Dafydd coming in on the chorus, she couldn't help sounding good enough to be encored. Then Sir Emlyn started her off on the sad, tender ballad of "Evangeline." Janet sang it well, but this was no way to end a joyous day. She turned again to Dafydd.

"Let's do *'Alouette'* and ask everybody to join in."

"Couldn't be better. I'll start off, then you come in with the necks and beaks."

So Janet explained about the lark that was to have its feathers either put on or taken off, she'd never been sure which, and away they went: first the head, then the nose, the beak, the neck, the back, the wings, the tail, and at last the feet, all tacked on one by one and repeated after the latest addition with a good, loud, drawn-out "ohhh" in between, and the fiddle jigging and everyone keeping up with it however they might, and Sir Caradoc beating the time with both hands and feet and getting up at the end to give hugs all around. And now that Wales had surrendered its heart to Canada, there was nothing to do but wish Sir Caradoc Happy Birthday yet once more, and go get another cup of tea.

Chapter 12

"It's high time we put Dorothy to bed," said Madoc.

"It's also high time I got out of this dress," said Janet. "If we're coming back for the Beltane fire, I'm coming in something warm and woolly."

"Well, I'm not coming at all," said Lady Rhys. "I've had quite enough excitement for one day, and more than enough food. I'm ready to curl up with a book in front of a fire that nobody's planning to jump over. I daresay Uncle Caradoc feels the same way by now, though he's borne up marvelously. What about you, Emmy? You do want supper, don't you?"

"I do, but not another whacking great meal like the last one. There's Alice coming out with a platter of something, they must be setting up a buffet in the barn. Why don't you and I snatch a bite now while Jenny's putting Dorothy to bed, then go along and baby-tend so that she and Madoc can come back?"

"What a splendid idea. Aren't you glad we're such old fogies, Jenny?"

"Tickled to pieces. I'll see you at the house, then. Don't hurry, she's going to need a bath. Madoc, you stay here and visit if you want."

"You can't manage the pram alone on this rough ground."

Of course she could, but Mary, who'd been mercifully quiet during the concert, was now heading their way and any excuse to escape was better than none. They said good night to Gwen, who'd been coaxed into driving to Bangor for a night or two with an old school chum, exchanged pleasantries with some other people who were leaving, told a few more they'd be back in a while, and went on down to the manor.

A coddled egg would be a good supper for a tired baby, Janet decided. Betty, Alice, and Megan must all be up at the barn, so Madoc stopped in the kitchen to fix it while she took Dorothy upstairs. With her child in her arms the room felt welcoming enough, even though Danny the Boots hadn't been around to light the fire.

That was all right, Janet could scratch a match as well as the next one. By the time Madoc came up with the egg, the room was toasty and Dorothy was sitting in the big china basin getting the day's accumulations sponged off. When the grandparents arrived, she was into her sleepers, listening to her father's bedtime story about an enchanted grizzly bear while Janet changed out of her party clothes.

"Well, this is cozy." Lady Rhys took the armchair Madoc pulled up beside the fireplace for her, and propped her feet on the fender. "Go on, Madoc, what happened to the grizzly bear?"

"A princess kissed him and he turned into a frog."

"What a disgusting thing to tell a child."

"Not at all. She was a frog princess and they lived happily ever after, zapping bugs with their tongues. 'Night, Dody, don't give your grandma a hard time. My private stock of brandy's on the shelf in the wardrobe, Tad, if you feel a thirst coming on. Ready, Jenny?"

"No, but it's getting dark and who's to see? Is anything left at the buffet, Mother? I wouldn't have thought it possible, but I'm getting hungry."

"Not to worry, there's enough to feed a regiment. You're not planning to jump the fire in that lovely skirt, Janet?"

"Not with a polyester slip underneath, I'm not. Suttee isn't my idea of fun. I don't see how Mary's going to manage without setting fire to her petticoats. She appears to be wearing quite a few."

"Ah, but they'll be woolen. Wool doesn't blaze up like cotton or synthetics, you know. If she does catch a spark, the cloth will just smolder till she can beat it out. Mary's no fool; at least I've never thought so until this trip. If she doesn't watch that tongue of hers, she won't get asked back here again, that's for certain. You two missed the scene of all scenes a few minutes ago. I really thought Iseult was going to scratch Mary's eyes out."

"What about?" asked Madoc.

"Something to do with Iseult's emeralds. I'm not sure whether Mary was calling them fakes or intimating that Iseult had acquired them under unladylike circumstances, or some of each. They were both talking at once by the time we came along."

"Loudly," Sir Emlyn added.

"That, my dear, is one of your typical understatements," said his wife. "They were yowling like a pair of fishwives, though I must say the only fishwife I've ever known personally was a model of decorum. Anyway, Mary was virtually incoherent and Iseult was coming out with some fairly picturesque language until that Williams man told her to shut up. Which she did, much to my surprise. You don't suppose he means to marry her, Emmy?"

"After that exhibition, he'd be a fool if he did. But

135

one never knows. Perhaps that's just the way film folk carry on. It's Mary I'm shocked by. She was always something of a bore, but never a pest on the grand scale, till now. You know, Sillie, I shouldn't be surprised if Mary's going the way her mother did, poor soul. They had to put her in some kind of looney bin for the gently reared. I should think Bob would have taken steps, he's such a mass of pomposity. Mary must be a terrible embarrassment to him, carrying on like this."

Lady Rhys was quietly amused. "I expect Bob will be able to endure the carryings-on as long as Mary's also able to carry on with her gem-cutting. According to Tom Feste, who always knows everything, they haven't a bean except what she brings in."

"You can't go by what Tom says," Sir Emlyn objected. "You know what he's like."

"Well, perhaps, dear. Anyway, one can't see Bob dipping into his own money while he can still get his hands on Mary's."

"But all those irresponsible insinuations she's hurling about might land them in a lawsuit."

"I don't know whether you could take an insinuation into court," said Madoc.

"Oh, stop talking like a policeman," snapped his mother. "Go get your supper, wretched boy."

"I don't expect we'll stay long," said Janet.

"That's all right, Jenny, take your time. Look at that little sweetikins, nodding off already. Was she her granny's darling, then?"

Obviously they weren't needed here, and Janet did want to see the lighting of the Beltane fire. Out behind the farmhouse, the scene had changed. Most of those who'd stayed must be inside the barn, its doors were open, the glow of lantern light showed through. Out in the middle of the lawn, a few young ones were fetching sticks and laying a small fire under Huw's direction. Others were clustered around Owain's middle son, who was twanging inexpertly at a guitar and whining out some ballad in such a confusing blend of English, Spanish, and Welsh that most of his audience probably hadn't a clue as to what it was about.

Not that they cared, Janet didn't suppose. The kids appeared happy enough, after having sat patiently through the afternoon's concert, to be hearing their own kind of music, if such it could be called. Far over toward the west, another small glimmer of light was flickering. She touched her husband's arm.

"Look, Madoc, somebody must have lit the candles on the altar. Do you suppose we ought to go see?"

"Mary could be jumping over the candlestick for practice. I suppose it wouldn't hurt to have a peek. We needn't go in."

Yes, the candles were lighted and yes, Mary was there. So was Bob. What they were up to was anyone's guess, but they weren't just fooling around. Both were working hard, their doughy faces shone with sweat. They had sprigs of some leafy plant in their hands. Janet guessed it might be mistletoe, though she couldn't tell in so feeble a light. Anyway, they were weaving the sprigs in and out and betwixt and between as they pranced solemnly around the altar first clockwise, then widdershins.

This had to be some kind of mystic rite; they wouldn't be going to all that bother just for exercise. Janet began to feel ashamed; she stepped back lest they catch her spying on them. Madoc was glad enough to follow; he could feel the sweat running down his spine.

"What do you suppose it's all about?" she whispered once she and Madoc were away from the window.

He wrinkled his nose. "Some kind of purification rite,

perhaps, or else a spot of fire insurance. Let's eat."

Janet was more than ready; all the same, those she-nanigans in the chapel had left her with an eerie feeling. However, once inside the barn, it was easy enough to let herself be pleasantly distracted with Rhyses hailing them right and left, Alice pressing them to try the Welsh rarebit, and Mavis chauvinistically offering Madoc a glass of Patagonian beer.

At least half the crowd must have left; there didn't look to be more than thirty or so here now, most of these either home folk or near neighbors. Tom was with Lisa down at the end of the left-hand table, where drinks had been set out. Each had a glass, but only the man was drinking. Janet and Madoc stopped to say hello.

"Uncle Caradoc had enough, has he?" said Madoc. "I don't see him around."

"No, he was getting tired, and about time," Lisa answered. "Dafydd walked him back to the house a little while ago. Dafydd's fagged out himself, he said he was going to bed."

"He didn't specify with whom," Tom added.

Lisa was not amused. "You had to put that in, didn't you? Dafydd has every right to be tired. He was performing all afternoon while you were lolling around getting squiffed. Why don't you go and eat some ham or something to soak up the alcohol?"

"Because I am a rigid vegetarian. You will find me drinking Brut like a tutor on a toot. You will find me drinking ale like an agrarian. You will find me drinking gin—what a perfectly splendid idea." He picked up a bottle and waved it around in a manner presumably intended to beguile. "Gin for you, Jenny *mia*?"

"Nothing for me, thanks. Have you tried the rarebit, Lisa?"

Janet hoped she hadn't taken Tom up too short, but

she didn't care for being leered at by vaguely connected in-laws who'd had too much to drink. Lisa was fairly ticked-off too; she was scowling down into her glass.

"I don't know why I took this. I don't want it, but I hate to leave an unfinished drink sitting around. It looks so wasteful."

"Pour it down a crack in the floor," Madoc suggested.

"As a sacrifice to the earth spirit? Why not? Tonight's the night."

Lisa let drop the scarf she'd thrown around her shoulders and bent to pick it up. When she rose, the glass was empty. "And there we are. I thought I heard a faint hiccup from down underneath, but it may have been only a toad. Yes, Jenny, by all means let's try the rarebit. I love scooping food out of a chafing dish, it makes me feel so baronial."

She was putting up a front, turning on the chatter to hide the inward smart, Janet decided. Where the heck had "inward smart" come from? More important, what was Lisa smarting about?

Her stepbrother, most likely. Tom was prancing around in front of Iseult now; he'd switched his Flaming Youth outfit for tweed plus fours and a Norfolk jacket. The actress had changed out of her mermaid disguise into dark green wool slacks and a bulky green pullover with a wide cowl neck, not forgetting a long, heavy gold chain with chunks of emerald set into it every few links. She'd let her hair down, Janet rather hoped she was planning to jump the fire. Iseult should make quite a picture with that red-gold mane streaming out behind her.

The rarebit was lovely. Lisa chased the last bite around her plate. "I'm glad we got to this when we did; there wasn't much left. I've a notion to go back and scrape the dish."

"Go ahead," said Janet. "Lick the spoon while you're about it. I dare you."

"Don't think I shan't. I may be a glutton, but I'm not a coward."

Lisa was making good her boast when Bob and Mary marched in like a couple of drum majors who'd got strayed from the parade. Janet expected Bob to make a beeline for the by now depleted buffet. Instead he planted himself squarely in the center of the vast room, took three or four deep breaths, and roared, "The time has come!"

"God, he sounds like the crack of doom." Iseult's comment came loud and fuzzy. She'd had a couple too many herself, from the sound of her. "Time for what?"

"Time to light the fire, of course." Reuel, who'd been slumped over a glass of Mavis's beer, pushed back his chair. "I want to see this."

They were all going to see it whether they wanted to or not. Bob and Mary were harrying everybody out of the barn like collies driving a flock of sheep to pasture. Janet had the distinct impression that either of the pair might nip at her heels if she didn't move fast enough.

No matter, she was quite willing to go. The sky was all but jet black now. The stars were coming out; the moon was a thin golden sickle. Too bad Uncle Caradoc couldn't capture it and pin it up in the dining hall. Somebody back in the pack was muttering about a silly waste of time. Maybe so, but this particular silliness had been going on since long before the Cistercians were here, long before the Rhyses were here, perhaps even before the Druids. Who could tell? Janet felt the excitement mounting, she gripped Madoc's arm and squeezed.

"Have you ever jumped the fire, Madoc?"

"Oh yes, when I was a kid. It was just something one did. Getting the urge, love?"

"Not till I see how big the fire is. I suppose it would be something to tell the folks back home. They'd think I was either lying or crazy, I expect. Who goes first, or doesn't it matter?"

"I don't remember any special protocol, we just lined up and took our turns as they came. One waits for the fire to die down, of course, unless one's a champion high-jumper. Dafydd pole-vaulted over the fire once, I remember, but he made a rather spectacularly ungraceful landing. He'd forgotten about some bramble bushes on the other side."

"Dafydd's always had a tendency to leap before he looks."

That was Lisa, sounding more acerbic than Janet would have thought the observation called for, but Lisa knew Dafydd better than she did. "I hadn't quite realized it," she said, "but you and he must have more or less grown up together, didn't you? Have you always lived where you are now?"

"Pretty much," Lisa replied, "when I wasn't off at school, except for a short while after I got married. Dafydd used to come and stay with Sir Caradoc quite often during the holidays when we were kids. He and Tom would go off and not take me with them, they made me furious. Oops, brace yourselves. Here comes another speech."

Bob tried, but he didn't get far. He'd made the mistake of standing with his back to the piled-up sticks; he'd barely got his mouth open when one of the youths who'd been lurking in the background sneaked up behind him and lit the fire. Janet had got a glimpse of the culprit's face when the sticks flared up; she was pretty sure it was Dai, and who better?

Actually this hadn't been the smartest thing to do, Bob had been pretty close to the fire. His own leap, once

141

he'd felt a spark hit the back of his neck, was impressive enough to draw a round of applause that did not assuage his wounded dignity.

The bonfire was not a big one, Huw had seen to that. The dry sticks burned down quickly; then the long-legged youngsters came hurtling over, yelling and laughing. Maybe this pell-mell dash was not according to Bob's notion of the Beltane ritual, but Janet had the feeling that she was seeing the ceremony as it had been back at the beginning of time: a raucous, half-savage celebration of youth and agility and the power of life and light. The jumpers would have been half-naked and half-wild, all of them young because hardly anyone lived long then, wearing only short tunics and no shoes. Now it was jeans and expensive sneakers, but the wildness was still there. Tib and Dai, pretty Annie and her burly brothers, their Patagonian cousins, all the brave lads and bonny lasses, they were like colts let out to pasture. Why couldn't the grown-ups leave them alone to celebrate their own rite of spring?

No, the grown-ups must have their share. Iseult was up there now, having cannily waited till the fire burned low enough not to singe her emeralds. She must have studied ballet at some time in her theatrical career; she hitched up her slacks and sailed over the coals lightly as a firebird, her flame-colored hair and her golden chain flinging out around her. The boys were applauding, susceptible as very young males always are to the charms of an older woman, especially when that woman happens to be an actress with lots of glamour and lots of emeralds.

Now Alice, stalwart and matter-of-fact in her dark dress and brightly woven shawl, walked up to the fire and hopped over neat as a pin without so much as agitating her perm, and Betty after her amid loud rejoicing, and Lisa with the cowl of her jersey pulled up over her nose so that she wouldn't sneeze from the smoke. Then Madoc swung Janet up in his arms so her polyester slip wouldn't catch fire, and leaped high and handsome, and landed safely, moreover; and jumped back again and kissed his wife quite shamelessly in front of the lot of them.

And on they came and over they went, but still Mary hadn't leaped. Janet could make out her tall steeple hat back there in the dark. It looked as if some people were urging her on—there was a little bustle around her— but Mary was taking her time, waiting her moment. The fire needed more wood now and got some, maybe a little more than it ought to have had because the young chaps were flaunting their muscles in front of Iseult. No matter, the blaze would soon settle down. At the moment, it was casting a flickering brightness over the entire scene. Janet could pick out everyone in the little crowd of watchers; she was surprised to spy Dafydd standing apart from the rest. She thought he looked rather strange, but then so did everybody else in this eerie play of glare and shadow.

But now the flames were dying back, and here came Mary on the dead run, high hat and all. And now she leaped, straight through the middle of the fire. And now—great God! A violent *poof*, like a giant's sneeze. A huge ball of searing, blazing light. An acrid smell, a great puff of whitish smoke rising high toward the sickle moon. And Mary, what was left of her, sprawled face-down across the Beltane fire.

Chapter 13

Nobody screamed. That was the oddest part, nobody screamed. Janet wished somebody would, the sound might help to unfreeze her legs. She couldn't herself, her heart must be blocking her windpipe. She felt as if it would be impossible to move. Not that she had to. Madoc was moving, he and his Uncle Huw and Huw's son, Owain, shouting at the rest to keep back, lifting Mary off the coals, laying her out on the ground away from the smoke, raising her head, laying it back.

Now Huw was running toward the farmhouse. To telephone a doctor? No, not the doctor, not from the way Madoc had put Mary's head down. It would be the police Uncle Huw would have to call. Janet knew why. So must everyone else, with the smell of gunpowder hanging so heavy in the air.

Now there was screaming. That was Bob. Owain was trying to shut him up, but he kept on and on, shrieking out the one word over and over. "Sorcery! Sorcery! Sorcery!"

Huw was back, carrying a sheet or a tablecloth or something to cover Mary with, thank God. Trust Huw Rhys to observe the amenities. He was glaring at the fire as though it were his personal enemy, but he couldn't stamp it out because they needed the light.

Now a man was coming forward. Janet recognized him as the local doctor. He'd sung a funny song this afternoon, or maybe he'd just sung a song funnily; anyway, people had laughed. They were making way for him, released from their shocked silence by the magic of his little black bag. Huw was hailing him with a relief you could almost reach out and touch.

The doctor was pushing up Bob's sleeve, baring the fat arm, swabbing the flabby, pallid flesh with something out of a bottle. Alcohol, Janet assumed. Now Owain was holding the arm, and the doctor was filling a hypodermic syringe out of a tiny vial. Now both Owain and Huw were trying to hold Bob steady while the doctor stuck him in the arm.

At last Bob was stopping that horrible screaming. Owain and Huw had him propped up between them, walking him back to the farmhouse. Dai was behind them, trying to help and being shooed away. The doctor was bending over Mary, raising the sheet, shaking his head, covering her up again. Now Dai was at the doctor's elbow, pestering. Madoc at least was willing to talk to Dai, he got the boy's attention, started asking questions. Janet had known he couldn't resist getting in a spot of police work. Dai was shaking his head, waving his hands, beginning to fall apart. The doctor was pointing over at the farmhouse, telling him to go in and keep an eye on Bob, or take an aspirin and go to bed, or just get out from underfoot. More likely to phone for an ambulance. They couldn't leave Mary's ghastly remains just lying there.

Where would they take her? There'd have to be an autopsy, even though the cause of death was only too hideously obvious.

Having grown up in hunting country, Janet knew a little about gunpowder. Mary must have had a pocketful, to cause a reaction like that. Gunpowder wasn't hard to get hold of, back home you could buy it by the pound at any sporting-goods shop. It came in different grains: coarse, medium, and fine. Sam Neddick back home had an old muzzle-loader he fired off every year on the Queen's birthday, and on various other occasions when the mood seized him. He'd ram coarse-grained gunpowder down the barrel, then put a pinch of a specially fine-ground powder in the priming pan to set off the discharge, since it was only the finest grain that could burn fast enough on its own to create the necessary explosion and detonate the rest. Coarser powder, if ignited directly, would simply fizz and burn itself out.

Sam had explained to Janet once how careful a person had to be not to get the different grinds mixed up. If he were to make a mistake and ram a whole load of fine-ground powder down the barrel, it would cause a big enough explosion to blow up the musket. And himself with it, like as not. Could Mary not have realized what a dangerous substance she was monkeying with? Had somebody else been better informed than she?

The remains of Mary's clothing would have to be examined as well as the remains of Mary herself, of course; that was a job for a forensic specialist. Since her costume had mostly been made of wool, there might, with luck, be enough left of the garments to show where the powder had been stashed. Mary would have had to be pretty crazy to carry gunpowder on her knowingly when she performed her allegedly famous leap; but who was to say she wasn't? She'd bragged about her expertise as a gemologist; she'd been absurdly self-congratulatory over her prowess as a fire-leaper. Mightn't she have felt cocky enough to think she could jump safely over, then perhaps flick the packet of gun-powder behind her just as she landed to create a spec-tacular effect, little realizing what kind of effect she'd be likeliest to create?

Her timing would have had to be on the button, assuming she'd been deft enough to pull it off; any sort of gunpowder would have flared up the instant it hit the fire. Gem-cutters must surely have to possess great skill with their hands, but that wasn't to say they had to be fast. Dai had been Mary's apprentice; maybe he'd have some information about where the gunpowder had come from. Probably Madoc had already asked him. Madoc wouldn't be handling the case, of course; but he'd go on bird-dogging from sheer instinct until whoever was in charge locally showed up.

Somebody did show up. One constable on a bike. Typical British understatement. Well, how many cops did you need to start an investigation? How many did you want charging around, disturbing the peace of an influential old gentleman like Sir Caradoc Rhys on his ninetieth birthday?

Thank God Uncle Caradoc had gone to bed before the Beltane fire was lighted. When you came to the end of a perfect day, you didn't need one hideous memory to spoil it. What would the verdict be: accident, suicide, murder, or sorcery?

Uncle Huw was the local magistrate. Would he have to preside at the inquest? No, more likely it would be the county coroner. Madoc would know. Janet wished she could go over and talk to him, but she knew enough not to. She might better occupy herself going back to the main house and breaking the news to his parents before they got a garbled account from somebody else.

No, she mustn't leave. She was a witness, and po-tentially a more reliable one than some of the others present, since she hadn't had anything stronger than tea to drink. Besides, Madoc might need her here at the scene, if only for a look or a nod. This must be even worse for him than it was for her. After all, Mary was family, he'd known her more or less all his life. Oh, why did this awful thing have to happen tonight?

And when else could it have happened? How many Beltane fires would Mary have had the chance to jump in the course of a year?

The constable had his notebook and pencil out, Huw was putting more wood on the fire so that he could see to take notes. The blaze was making people uneasy, making them want to get away, and who could blame them? Huw was answering the constable's questions now. Janet worked her way around to where she could catch Madoc's eye, and he came over to her.

"All right, Jenny love?"

"Bearing up. How about you?"

"Hanging in. Want to talk to the constable?"

"Yes, I don't mind. What's his name?"

"Rhys the Police, what else? He read a poem this afternoon—you slept through it. Cyril's a nice fellow, we used to play football together. Did you get a good view of what happened?"

"Too good." Janet had to swallow hard before she could speak again. "I don't have to look at her, do I?"

"God, no." He stood with his arm around her till Huw had got done talking, then spoke up. "Cyril, would you like to talk to my wife? Jenny, you remember Constable Rhys, he was at the party this afternoon. We're forty-third cousins, I think."

Janet and the constable expressed their mutual pleasure at meeting again so soon and their regret at the reason for their unanticipated reunion. Then she, being Janet, got straight to the point.

"I suppose the first thing is to find out where Mary got hold of fine-grain gunpowder. Have you asked Uncle Huw?"

"Fine-grain gunpowder, Mrs. Madoc?"

"Oh yes, it must have been, to have acted the way it did. Didn't Madoc tell you? There was this great, loud poof, then a ball of flame like a bomb going off. Not that I've ever seen a bomb explode, but that's what it made me think of."

"Could this explosion not have been caused by petrol or some other volatile substance?"

"No, I'd have smelled petrol. What I did smell was gunpowder, strong as anything. I was downwind of it, so I got a good whiff. It lingered in the air for a bit afterward, other people must have smelled it too. And there was that big puff of white smoke, the way gunpowder burns. Remember, Madoc?"

"Yes, love. I remember. How do you know so much about gunpowder?"

"Sam Neddick, mostly. Sam's my brother's hired man back in New Brunswick, Constable. He hunts a lot."

In and out of season, but one needn't go into particulars. "I shouldn't be surprised if Mary'd had a pretty good load of it in her skirt pocket or someplace like that right next to her body, to have been burned so—" Janet swallowed again. "She might even have had some sprinkled on her clothes, or inside that steeple hat she was wearing. Your forensic lab can do powder tests on the clothes, can't they?"

"That will be for the chief constable to be deciding," Rhys the Police replied somewhat stuffily. "But why would the lady have done such a mad thing?"

"Why, Jenny?" said Madoc.

"Madoc, you know the way Mary'd been carrying on ever since we got here. I'd say she might have done just

149

about anything to get people's attention. Night before last, Constable, she was bragging all through dinner about what grand leaps she'd made over other Beltane fires and what a show she was going to put on this time around."

Madoc gave her a squeeze to help steady her voice, and she went on. "Mary claimed that the right way is to jump back and forth through the flames three times in a row. I'm wondering, and mind you this is nothing but speculation, whether Mary might have meant to put on some special effects after she'd got the range, as you might say. She could have brought the gunpowder along with her, not realizing what a terrible risk she was taking. Ordinary coarse-grained gunpowder doesn't ignite all that easily, you know; she may simply not have realized she'd got hold of the wrong kind."

"That is a possibility to be sure, Mrs. Madoc. Assuming your idea is right, would there have been anybody she might have let in on what she was planning, do you think? Somebody feckless enough not to stop her?"

Somebody disgusted enough not to stop her would be a more likely way of putting it, Janet thought. Mary must have worked her way on to plenty of hate lists with her antics today alone. Janet hedged.

"I suppose it's possible Mary said something to her brother. I don't know whether Madoc told you, but she and Bob were conducting some kind of mystic rite in the chapel before he came out to light the bonfire. At least we assumed that must be what they were doing—they'd lit candles and were prancing around the altar waving branches. We watched them for a minute or so through the window."

"A mystic rite?" The set of Constable Rhys's mustache showed what he thought of mystic rites. "And where is Mr. Bob Rhys now?"

150

"In bed, I expect. The doctor had to give him a shot to quiet him down, and Madoc's cousin Owain helped him into the farmhouse. He'd gone straight into orbit when—well, you could hardly blame him, considering. He kept yelling 'Sorcery! Sorcery!' They couldn't get him to stop."

"Mystic rites and sorcery? That is bad, Mrs. Madoc, very bad. He will not have been putting you on, you will not think?"

"He sounded pretty convincing to me. I got the impression Bob thought somebody had ill-wished their charm and caused it to backfire. Which sounds crazy, but he and Mary both seemed to be fairly well hipped on that stuff. I probably shouldn't even be saying this; I only met them two days ago. You'd do better to talk to their nephew, Dai. I gather they've more or less raised him from a kid and he's been working as Mary's apprentice. For that matter, I expect practically anybody here could give you more reliable information than I."

"I would not be too sure about that, Mrs. Madoc, but I shall have to question them all."

The constable sounded fairly dismal about the prospect, Janet could understand why. "Then I expect you'll want to get everybody into the barn. There's light enough to see by, and you could do your notes sitting down at the table. I don't know if the tea urn's still hot, but we could make you some fresh easily enough."

"Tea is always helpful."

To Rhys the Police as well as the next one, like as not. Half-incinerated corpses didn't sit comfortably on anybody's stomach. The constable blew a rousing blast on his whistle to collect everybody's attention and addressed the gathering in stentorian tone.

"It will be necessary for me to be taking statements from everybody, so nobody must go away without first having been questioned. You will all please go into the big barn now and sit down. I will ask Mr. Huw Rhys to go and put in a call for Mr. Davies the chief constable, and I will ask Detective Inspector Madoc Rhys to help with the questions if he will be so good, and that way we can get through this painful business without taking all night. Mrs. Madoc has offered fresh tea," he added on a hopeful note.

"Then it is me you will have to be excusing long enough to bring out the hot water," Alice called out. "And the cakes."

That struck a chord. People were looking a shade less pinched as they straggled in and took chairs around the long board that had been so festive earlier on. The lanterns were still burning, possibly as a deterrent to certain types of reveling among the young fry.

Their gentle light was a welcome change from the darkness outside that was still being interrupted by an occasional spurt of flame from what was left of the fatal bonfire. The supper mess had been cleared away, but an array of clean cups and saucers still stood beside the tea urn. Constable Rhys decided it would be quite in order for both Iowerth and Betty to assist Mrs. Madoc in her errand of mercy. As things turned out, all Janet did was fetch the refilled cream jug and some writing materials for Madoc, but her good offices were given full honor by one and all.

Madoc started working one side of the table, Constable Rhys the other. By the time the police ambulance arrived from wherever it had had to be summoned from, with the chief constable tagging along behind in a snappy red Jaguar, they'd pretty well finished their interrogations and each had two cups of tea in the bargain. Madoc had passed up the cakes, but Rhys the Police had shown his gratitude for the women's kind endeavors by eating a whole plateful all by himself.

"And there is no way, Doctor, of questioning Mr. Robert Rhys until he wakes up of his own accord?" The chief constable was a shortish, sixtyish man in country tweeds who somewhat resembled the late Earl Lloyd George of Dwyfor except that he seemed inordinately shy of women and had shown palpable uneasiness on being introduced to Mrs. Madoc.

"I don't think it would be much good trying to rouse him now, Mr. Davies." The doctor had stayed on with the rest lest anyone should turn faint or, more probably, fall victim to a surfeit of cakes and tea. "He'll be in reasonable shape by morning."

"Then we shall just have to wait." Mr. Davies didn't look too upset about the prospect. "Now, Mrs. Madoc Rhys, you say you believe the victim may herself have put gunpowder in her pockets?"

"I didn't say I believed it, I only suggested it as a possibility."

He quailed and turned to the nervously hovering Dai as a less daunting prospect.

"And you, Dai Rhys, you were Miss Mary Rhys's nephew and also her apprentice."

"It was her idea. The apprenticeship, I mean. I didn't want to be."

"Oh, you didn't want to be? May I ask why not?"

"Because I—I just didn't."

"Was it perhaps that you did not get on well with your aunt, who, with her brother, had taken you in as an orphan and given you food and shelter and education and set you on the path to a respectable career as a gem-cutter?"

"They didn't! I mean, they did, but it wasn't as if I'd

been Oliver Twist or somebody. My father left—" It apparently dawned on Dai that he was not making the best possible showing in front of the chief constable, he proceeded to make a bad matter worse. "I know what they did for me. I just got sick and tired of hearing about it all the time."

"So you stuffed your aunt's pockets with gunpowder?"

"Me? Where would I get gunpowder?"

"A very good question, Mr. Dai Rhys. Can somebody here give us an answer? Mr. Huw, would there be gunpowder on this estate?"

"Only in a few shotgun cartridges. None loose, not in my house and not, to the best of my knowledge, in my father's."

"You would submit to a search of your house and barns?"

"If you deem it necessary, Mr. Davies. I can't speak for my father. I only hope you won't go waking him up tonight, because he is an old man who has had a strenuous day."

"But suppose we were to search only the bedroom that Miss Mary Rhys was occupying, in the hope that we may ascertain without further ado whether she brought gunpowder with her when she came?"

"I should say that would be a sensible thing to do," Huw replied with some relief. "I understand the advisability of the room's being searched before somebody gets in there and starts mucking about, and I have no objection, provided you don't disturb my father."

"Which room was Mary sleeping in?" Owain asked.

It was Lady Rhys who replied. "The one next to my husband's and mine. We're at the opposite end of the manor from Uncle Caradoc, so there shouldn't be much risk of your waking him unless you go shouting and thumping about. I should suggest you take my son Madoc with you instead of Cyril, Mr. Davies. His tread is far the more catlike of the two. And perhaps my daughter-in-law also, if she doesn't mind, so that Mary's ghost will not be embarrassed by seeing a strange man rummaging among her undergarments unchaperoned. I expect she's hanging about up there by now, itching for a chance to haunt somebody. Poor thing, one does hope Mary gets more fun out of the body than she ever did in it."

The chief constable obviously had not bargained for Lady Rhys. He had to blink and hem a few times before he could manage a reply.

"Thank you for your suggestion, Lady Rhys. I should welcome the assistance of Detective Inspector Madoc Rhys, and also that of his lady wife, should she care to accompany us in our search. Constable Cyril Rhys, you will please remain here and complete the taking of statements."

"Yes, sir."

Rhys the Police stood up and saluted smartly, though not without casting a regretful glance at his depleted plate and empty cup. As the search squad left the barn, they met Alice hurrying back in with fresh supplies.

"The investigation is proceeding with decorum and dispatch," Madoc muttered in Janet's ear.

"Of course," she murmured back. "I expect your mother's right about Mary's ghost. Come on then, it's not polite to keep a specter waiting."

Chapter 14

"**S**o you did find the gunpowder?"

Sir Emlyn's beautiful white hair was in disarray, he must have been taking a nap on the red-room bed before they woke him by barging in with the dreadful news. Madoc nodded.

"What was left of it. Jenny found it, actually, a cardboard box that could have held a pound or more, with only a spoonful or so left in the bottom. The box had simply been tossed into the fireplace, which could have been rather exciting for whoever happened to light the next fire."

"Exactly the feckless sort of thing Mary would do. Not to speak ill of the dead, but you know as well as I what a featherhead she was." Lady Rhys started gathering up her needlepoint materials. She was embroidering a pillow with a unicorn on it for her granddaughter's room, judging that by the time she finished, Dorothy would be out of bunnies and kitties and into her unicorn stage. "I must say I'm extremely relieved to have the matter settled so quickly, Madoc. Now you won't have to go around detecting things and upsetting people. The Condryckes' friends are still snubbing us, you know, over that time in New Brunswick."

"Yes, Mother. Did Dorothy wake up?"

"Just once. She wasn't wet and she didn't seem hungry, she just wanted her old granny to cuddle her a bit. So I did, and she dropped off again, the lamb. I do so wish Dafydd were as commonsensical as you, Madoc, about settling down and raising a family. Can't you quietly take him aside and have a nice, brotherly chat?"

"No, Mother. Would you care to join me in a nightcap? We've that duty-free brandy, if Tad hasn't drunk it all up."

"A fine way to talk about your own father in front of the baby. Just a spot, then. Poor old Mary, I cannot get over her having done such a gruesome thing. She must have been batty as a—a what, Emmy?"

"A bat, perhaps? Thank you, Madoc. Cheers. Mary may not have been one's favorite relative, but one wouldn't have wished such a death on one's worst enemy. I do hope she hadn't time to suffer."

"I don't see how she could have," Janet reassured her father-in-law. "Mary was certainly dead by the time Madoc got to her, and that was in virtually no time at all. The shock alone would have killed her, I should think. It was quite something when that powder went off. I hope we get to see the lab report."

Lady Rhys raised her eyebrows. "I suppose, being married to a policeman, these things rub off. It's so good of you to take an interest in Madoc's work, Jenny," she added out of politeness.

"Jenny's a natural-born detective," Madoc protested. "She was chasing down a murder before I ever met her. Remember that jar of string beans, love?"

"How could I forget? Those beans got me a husband, didn't they? Have you had any company this evening, Mother?"

"Just Uncle Caradoc."

"How was he feeling?"

"Weary but happy. He said Dafydd had walked him back to the door, but was going on to Lisa's. They neither of them had any desire to stay for the bonfire, which was a great blessing. Of course Dafydd's never cared for bonfires, not since that time in Winnipeg when he was a little boy and that awful child who lived next door— what was their name, Emmy? The ones who kept the pack of bloodhounds that used to bay at the moon."

"I can't remember. They didn't stay long, thank goodness."

"Anyway, they were burning rubbish or something and that ghastly boy got hold of some shotgun shells the father had left lying around, which just shows you the sort of people they were. You surely remember that much, Emmy? Dafydd just missed being killed. He had buckshot in his leg, his hair was all singed in front, and his left eyebrow was burned right off. We were afraid he'd be scarred for life, but mercifully he healed without a trace. Outwardly, at any rate. Well, darlings, I expect you want to get to bed. We'll see you at breakfast. Night-night."

Madoc had his shirt unbuttoned before his parents were fairly out the door. Janet couldn't settle. She fiddled with her earrings, brushed her hair for no good reason, wandered around picking things up and putting them down. Madoc, sitting on the edge of the bed taking off his shoes and socks, watched her till he couldn't stand it any longer.

"All right, love, what's eating you?"

She put down the nightgown she'd been turning inside out, though she had no idea why, and came to sit beside him. "For one thing, I can't help thinking what a cinch it would have been for anybody at all to sneak upstairs and toss that box into Mary's fireplace. The help were out at the party along with the rest of us, the house was wide open, and had been all day long. Mary herself never changed out of that rig she came down to breakfast in, I doubt whether she ever went back to her room. She must have stayed right on the job the whole time, judging from the show she put on and the number of backs she managed to put up. So that means she'd been carrying that gunpowder around all day long, or else—"

"I know, Jenny. I've been thinking about it too. Anything else?"

"Madoc, Dafydd did go back to the bonfire. I saw him out there, right after the explosion."

"And so?"

"And so nothing, I don't suppose. He probably just didn't care for sitting over there at Lisa's by himself after all, and decided he might as well come back to the party. Only he didn't stay. I noticed he wasn't around when Constable Rhys called us into the barn. Not that that means anything either. Maybe seeing Mary get blown up gave him an attack of the old horrors, and he was afraid of disgracing himself in front of the company. You certainly couldn't blame him for that, could you?"

"No, Jenny. Whom was Dafydd with when you saw him?"

"Nobody, he was off by himself. You know how people were bunched up on one side or the other of the fire. Dafydd was about halfway between. I only happened to notice him because the fire flared up when Uncle Huw put more wood on. I was more or less opposite him, on the side where you were. I was trying to sidle up and catch your eye."

"Why, love?"

"Because. Oh, you know why. Give me a kiss and tell me I'm being stupid."

"Since you insist. I don't know what more we can

do tonight, we'll just have to wait and see whether Bob makes any sense in the morning. Who gets to change Dorothy this time?"

"She's not wet. She'll wait till we're nicely asleep, I expect."

"Rotten kid. Come on, love, I could use a spot of wifely consolation. Assuming you're in the mood."

"Coax me."

So the long birthday ended pleasantly after all. Morning was harder, somebody had to tell Uncle Caradoc. Huw would have been the obvious person. However, he'd made no objection when Sir Emlyn offered to do it, since he and Elen were already stuck with Bob, not to mention the tidying up.

A person could not have lived as long as Sir Caradoc Rhys without having become fairly well inured to tragedy along the way. He was distressed, of course, but not enough to be put off his bacon and eggs and sausage. His main concern was for Dai, because the young took things so much harder. When Danny the Boots came in with a scuttleful of coal for Betty's stove, the old master sent him upstairs to see how the nephew was doing.

"He is curled up like a dormouse," was Danny's report. "Dai Rhys will be sleeping the day away, I am thinking."

"That is a good thing. Let him sleep until we need him. Do you go now and tell my son Huw that I wish Bob Rhys to be sent here as soon as he is awake. They have enough to do up at the farm, and it will be better that any questions to Bob come from me. Madoc, you will perhaps wish to be present when I talk to him."

"Certainly, Uncle Caradoc. You'll want Constable Rhys too, I expect. Cyril's an able chap, he was at the barn last night taking statements. I don't know whether

Tad mentioned that. The chief constable also came by."

"Cyril read well yesterday. His poem was one of the worthier efforts, did you not think? We will indeed have Cyril Rhys, I would not wish to slight a kinsman. There is no reason to trouble Mr. Davies again."

Madoc should have known. Some years back, hot words had been exchanged between Sir Caradoc and the chief constable in a matter of sheep. Sir Caradoc was not a vengeful man, but neither was he a forgetful one. That Davies had invaded his premises without his leave was an affront; whoever had let the man come should have known better. He went on eating his eggs and sausages in awful silence until Dorothy, who had inherited her grandmother's gift for smoothing over awkward moments, offered him a bit of her toast. Things went merrily enough after that, until Owain delivered Bob.

It was as well they'd pretty much finished breakfast; the bereft brother was a sight to kill anybody's appetite. Nobody had thought to take Bob a change of clothes, perhaps he hadn't even been undressed last night. He was still wearing his John Dee getup, and a fine mess it was. His beard was every which way, his gray hair lay in greasy strings across his scalp, his features seemed to have melted and run together.

This was the way a witch's waxen malkin would look after it had been set by the fire to toast, Janet thought. She'd seen Bob coming by the window, a shapeless mass of black bundled into a wheelbarrow that Owain was trundling, with Huw walking beside. The father and son between them had got him into the kitchen, dumped him into a chair, and been out the door even before Betty could offer them a cup of tea. They must be thoroughly fed up, and no wonder.

Anyway, Betty was quite ready to take over. "It is

plenty of sugar you will be wanting this morning, Mr. Bob. Is it myself who will be putting it into the cup for you?"

Bob must be in even worse shape than Janet had thought, he wasn't even talking. He did finally manage about half a nod, but by then Betty had the sugar all scooped and stirred.

"There you are, then. Do you be drinking while it is still hot, it will be putting heart into you."

It was going to take more than oversweetened tea to stiffen this one's backbone. Either Bob was still dopey from the doctor's knockout drops, or else he was working up to a full-scale depression. Having a fit of the guilties, perhaps, over the hocus-pocus in the chapel. Maybe the gunpowder had even been Bob's own idea—not that he'd have wanted to murder Mary if she was the family breadwinner, but because he'd been too cocksure of his own omniscience to realize how dangerous it was.

Well, no point in speculating now, Janet decided, Dorothy was getting reckless with her porridge. "Come on, baby," she coaxed. "Into the mouth, not on the floor."

Betty put a plate of assorted comestibles in front of Bob; he stared at it blankly, then turned his head away like a sick animal. Lady Rhys had appeared by now, she picked up the teacup and held it to Bob's flaccid lips. He managed a swallow or two, then shook his head. It was a painful thing to watch. Lady Rhys set the cup down.

"All right then, if you won't, you won't. Would you like to go up to your room?"

He didn't respond.

"Perhaps we'd better get the doctor back here," said Janet.

"Try a spot of brandy," Madoc suggested.

The brandy worked, but not the way they'd hoped. Once he'd gulped it down, Bob laid his head on the table and bawled. Dorothy, either frightened or sympathetic, started crying too.

"I'd better take her outside," said Janet. "She doesn't usually do this."

"Neither does he, I don't suppose," said Lady Rhys. "Let me take her, Jenny, you haven't finished your tea. Bob, do you want to go outside with me and the baby?"

"Wha—ah, tea. I will drink my tea."

He was dabbing at his wet, blubbered face with his napkin, making a pitiful attempt at pretending to be back in control of himself. The tea Betty had poured for him earlier was still standing there beside the untouched plateful, stone-cold by now. She sloshed it into the sink and poured him a fresh cup, hot from the pot she'd kept sitting on the back of the stove. This time Bob drank avidly, but he still had no stomach for food.

That was all right, at least he was back among the living, more or less. The rest of them went on with their breakfasts, making careful chat about nothing in particular, skirting any allusion to the events of the previous day. It was a relief to them all when Sir Caradoc pushed back his chair.

"I am going to work on my accounts. Madoc, when Cyril comes, will you bring him into the office? Bob, would you like to come with me?"

It wasn't really a question, Bob was rational enough to sense that. He heaved himself away from the table and shuffled after Sir Caradoc into the small room where the old man did most of his paper work and much of his napping.

Bob's lack of appetite had put Janet off hers. She finished her tea and refused more toast. "Now what, Madoc? Do I make myself scarce or hover in the background?"

"Hover, I think, if you can bear it. What are you and Mother doing this morning, Tad?"

"I don't know," Sir Emlyn replied. "Sillie hasn't made up my mind yet. That was a nasty piece of business just now. I wonder if Bob is going a little daffy like his sister. Actually what I would like is to spend some time with Owain. We haven't had much chance to chat since he and Mavis got back. You don't need me here, do you?"

"No, go ahead. Jenny and I will probably straggle along in a while. I'd better go bring in the kid so you and Mother can get along."

"Not on your life, my boy. We'll take Dorothy with us in the pram."

"Not with porridge all over her face," Janet objected.

"Oh, Sillie can sponge her off. Anyway, what's a little porridge? Ah, I see that the strong arm of the law is about to be amongst us."

Rhys the Police was indeed heaving into view, the badge on his bicycle agleam in the morning sun and all his buttons atwinkle. Today was going to be hot and fine like yesterday, Janet thought. Too nice to be shut inside, poking questions at a slobbering bowl of jelly who might at any moment slip round the bend.

No, nothing that dire was going to happen today, not with Uncle Caradoc running the show. They might as well go ahead and get it over with.

Chapter 15

"According to information received by Chief Constable Davies and conveyed to me this morning via the telephone, he being engaged for a game of golf with three other gentlemen whose names he did not tell me, the sad demise of Miss Mary Rhys was occasioned by her having had gunpowder of the most volatile kind in the pockets of her skirt and sprinkled here and there about her person, as has been determined by a laboratory analysis of the clothing Miss Mary Rhys was wearing. Said gunpowder became ignited upon contact with the bonfire whilst Miss Mary Rhys was in the act of leaping, and burned so fiercely that severance of the mortal coil was instantly effected."

Before Constable Rhys had got down to business, the usual courtesies had been exchanged. Bob had got through his part listlessly, now he was bold upright, quivering with outrage.

"Gunpowder? That is ridiculous! That is impossible!"

"With all respect, Mr. Robert Rhys, I must tell you that, in the fireplace of the very bedroom which Miss Mary Rhys had been occupying here in the house of Sir Caradoc, was found discarded a green cardboard box containing approximately one half-teaspoon of fine-grained gunpowder."

"You are prevaricating to me! Mary could not have had gunpowder. She told me nothing about gunpowder."

"It was then Miss Mary Rhys who was always telling you everything, is it?"

Bob hesitated. "Perhaps not everything. No, not always everything. It is not everything I should have wanted to hear."

"Then the circumstance of Miss Mary Rhys's not having told you anything about gunpowder, look you, is in truth no guarantee that she was not in fact having gunpowder in her possession, Mr. Bob Rhys?"

"I cannot gainsay you. Nonetheless, I maintain that gunpowder is not a thing Mary would have had. Unless," Bob appended with a glint of craftiness in his small black eyes, "she would have had it without telling me. Mary has become subtle of late."

"Subtle, you say? Can you explain in what way Miss Mary Rhys was having become subtle?"

"She has teased me with inscrutabilities. She has hinted."

"Of what manner of thing was Miss Mary Rhys having been hinting?"

"That I cannot tell you. There were knowing looks and enigmatic nods. It was an atmosphere of 'I could an if I would.' As though, in short, she had a tale she could unfold, but she was not unfolding it. This is a game Mary has played before, to get my attention fixed upon herself when my thoughts would fain have rested upon higher matters. Often have I found it necessary to direct my sister's wayward mind into more uplifting channels."

"Was that what you were doing with Mary in the

chapel before you went to light the fire?" Madoc interjected gently.

Bob was rather pleased than offended. "You saw us then?"

"My wife and I. We'd noticed the candlelight shining out through the windows."

"Yes, the candles were necessary. Why did you not come and join with us?"

"We wouldn't have known what to do."

"I would have instructed you what to do."

"But we might not have followed your instructions. What if the ceremony was not done properly?"

"It was done properly."

"Then why were you screaming about sorcery after Mary was killed in the fire?"

"I was not screaming about sorcery. This is police-brutality tactics. You are trying to intimidate me."

Madoc did not press the issue. It was quite likely that Bob had no recollection of the way he'd carried on last night. If he did remember, one could hardly blame him for pretending he didn't.

Sir Caradoc had been listening quietly; now he decided it was time for him to speak. "Bob, would it not have been courteous of you to ask my permission, or at least to inform me of your intention, to conduct a ceremony in the chapel?"

"But it was for your protection, Sir Caradoc."

"And what made you think I needed protection?"

The butchered ram, perhaps? The one thing Sir Caradoc wasn't supposed to know about? Madoc felt a stab of apprehension, but Bob came up with a more esoteric reason.

"The golden sickle, surely. Had you been aware of what dark forces you were stirring up, Sir Caradoc, you would not have dared to touch that sickle without having first performed the proper rites. Look you what has happened to the monks who wrested from the Druids their magical tools. Gone, all gone, and the bats nesting in their once-proud chapel."

"We do not know for how many centuries the sickle may have lain hidden inside the monastery walls before the monks were driven out, Bob. Nor do I think I can fairly claim responsibility for the bats in the chapel. However, I thank you for your kind intention. I can only hope that Mary did not become sufficiently carried away as to convince herself that self-immolation would be a useful adjunct to your rite. You must understand, Bob, how essential it is that we find out why Mary had gunpowder on her person when she performed her leap."

"Yes, yes! If her death should be proved to have been caused by suicidal impulses, then it will be resulting that those rapacious fiends at the insurance company will not pay what is owed to me. Mary would not have spited me this way, she knew too well what I would—" He stopped short.

Janet hoped she wasn't going to vomit. Even gentle Sir Caradoc was having a struggle not to show the disgust he must be feeling. Madoc, on the other hand, appeared merely interested.

"But you're not going to starve to death in any case, are you, Bob? Surely a provident fellow like you will have something put by. My mother says you had an income from your parents' legacy, but lived mostly on Mary's earnings. That was from gem-cutting, right?"

"From the gem-cutting and from the annuity. And that is another tragedy!" Bob's voice rose again. "The annuity will stop now, just when it was about to get bigger!"

"What annuity was this, Mr. Bob Rhys?" demanded

the constable. "Why was it going to be getting bigger, and why will it now be stopping?"

"I do not know why the annuity would have got bigger. Mary said only that it would. She was smug and self-satisfied, she was bragging. The annuity will stop because it was for her and for her only."

"You mean she bought it herself, out of her earnings?" said Madoc. "My father seems to be under the impression that she used to turn all her earnings over to you."

"Those moneys that came from the business, yes. It was our father's business and we inherited jointly. Therefore I was entitled to my share."

"Even though your sister did all the work?"

"Ah, but I bore the responsibility. The female brain has not the power to deal with matters of finance. Mary understood that she was not to be trusted with money because she was a female and therefore stupid. I made the reason plain to her."

"But in fact Mary was your sole source of income, outside of whatever interest you've been earning on the money your parents left you. How much is this insurance you hope to collect?"

"One hundred thousand pounds. I would not have you suppose I held my dear sister's life cheap."

"Nothing could be farther from my mind," Madoc assured him. "And you insured your own life for a similar amount?"

"I insured my life for nothing at all. Where would have been the profit in that?"

"It never occured to you that, since Mary'd been supporting you all these years, she might deserve to have some provision made for her old age should you predecease her?"

"But she would have had the annuity," Bob argued.

"The annuity she's supposed to have bought from the earnings you took away from her? How did she manage that? And why did she say the annuity was going to get bigger?"

"I told you I do not know why. And I did not say Mary bought it, Madoc Rhys. She claimed only that it came through Arthur."

"You mean Lisa's husband Arthur? The gem dealer?"

"Oh yes, Arthur was doing business with us for many years, and his father with our father before us."

"So this was another insurance deal pertaining to the business, was that it?"

"No, that was not it," Bob sputtered. "If the annuity had been related to the business, I would have had a legal claim to half. As it was, I had to take only what Mary chose to give. It was a great humiliation."

"So what it boils down to"—Madoc was still trying to be patient—"is that Arthur simply bought your sister an annuity out of the goodness of his heart?"

"Mary did not say that Arthur bought the annuity, she said only that it came through him. I have already told you this."

"And when did she start receiving it?"

"Soon after Arthur died, of course."

"Then it was a legacy? She inherited through his will?"

"Mary did not inherit through his will. There was nothing in the will about Mary Rhys. Arthur's estate was all for Lisa and the daughter, barring some small bequests to servants and five thousand pounds to Arthur's own sister. Naturally I went to Somerset House and saw for myself. I am not a fool, Madoc Rhys."

"You are obviously an expert at handling your own

affairs, Bob. But if Arthur didn't buy the annuity, how could it have come through him?"

"That is what Mary would not tell me. Once she got her hands on money, I could not control her. She grew bold and insolent in her manner. She angered me so that I would sometimes wish the annuity had never been. Arthur must have done this in some devious and underhanded way to spite me; he knew Mary would become froward and disrespectful. He never liked me."

"But he must have been fond of Mary," Janet put in.

"No such fondness was ever apparent in his behavior toward her. There would be words, often there would be words. Arthur would accuse Mary of taking too much for the cutting, of not following his instructions, of sometimes even exchanging good stones of his for flawed stones from other dealers and getting paid extra by his competitors for having worked the deception on him. Mary thought Arthur was disloyally taking his best stones to other cutters in order to cheat us out of the profits, notwithstanding the agreement that had existed since the time of our fathers and grandfathers even. She was irate about this, she said she was going to spy on him and catch him in the act."

"And did she?" asked Sir Caradoc.

"I think not, though I could not be sure. In those days, she would often be required to travel abroad, to Amsterdam and other places. I would not be going with her, you see, because that would have meant paying two fares and I do not like to stay in pensions or cheap hotels or to travel tourist class, which is no class at all. To have pleased myself would have been to give Mary expensive ideas. I would therefore make the reservations in advance and send her alone. Unfortunately

I had to allow her certain sums for pocket money. Although I demanded always a strict accounting, Mary could have lied to me about how she spent the money. She could even have cashed in a ticket and gone somewhere else. Women are never to be trusted, but what else could I do?"

"So Mary was still doing a fair amount of traveling when Arthur died?"

"A fair amount, yes. In fact she was abroad at the time of his death, though fortunately elsewhere."

"Where?"

"Ostend, I believe. I cannot say for sure."

"Couldn't you tell from her passport?"

"After Arthur was killed, Mary Rhys burned her passport and vowed she would travel abroad no more because foreign lands were too dangerous. And she did not."

"That's right," said Janet. "She mentioned night before last that the world came to her."

"That was what Mary liked to believe. Unfortunately not enough of the world has been coming of late. Had it not been for the annuity, I might have had to dip into my reserves. There have been worries, I can tell you, my life has not been easy. And now I am beset with further troubles. The only balm in my Gilead is that I have made Dai a bonded apprentice. He will have to carry on in Mary's stead. It is regrettable that he has not Mary's gift nor Mary's reputation; he will have to make up for his lack by greater industry. I shall have my work cut out, keeping him ever busy."

"But what if Dai doesn't want to be kept ever busy?"

Bob had clearly talked himself out of his depression; now he favored Janet with a calm and complacent stare. "Dai Rhys will do as I tell him. And now, Sir Caradoc, it will be best that you send for Dai Rhys at once. He must begin packing for himself and for Mary, and also for myself since I am prostrate with grief, as you plainly see. We will require a modest repast and then the car at half-past two to carry us to the station. I shall want a little extra time to deal with the stationmaster about the return half of Mary's ticket. I have dire forebodings that it may not be easy to obtain the reimbursement due to me."

"And I have dire forebodings that you and Dai will not be allowed to leave," the old man replied. "Is this not so, Constable Rhys? Will Bob and Dai not have to remain here until after the inquest?"

"That is my personal belief, Sir Caradoc, sir. It will be for Chief Constable Davies to be deciding. I am to be reporting to him this afternoon about what we have been able to learn from Mr. Bob Rhys. If we have in fact learned anything other than that Miss Mary Rhys's death may result in a diminution of Mr. Rhys's income," Rhys the Police added with a certain amount of grim satisfaction for which Janet certainly didn't blame him.

"But I am promised this evening to address the Friends of the Lesser Demons, which is a very important society, look you," wailed Bob. "And what about the return tickets? They are for the special rate, they will be forfeit if we do not leave today."

Sir Caradoc was having some trouble keeping the lid on. "You and Dai are guests in my home, Bob. When it becomes possible for you to leave, I will make sure you both get home without further strain on Mary's insurance. Now you must go up to your room and rest your troubled spirits. I will have food sent up to you; you need not come down again until we have heard from Chief Constable Davies what he wants done with you."

That's telling him, Janet thought. Disgusting old toad.

Even the toad looked taken aback, but only for a moment. "Wait, I am cogitating. I am examining the evidence, I am making deductions. You have thoroughly searched the room Mary was occupying?"

"We have," said Madoc. "Constable Rhys, my wife, and myself, with Sir Caradoc's permission."

"And you found only the box that had contained the gunpowder? There was no other thing that caught your interest?"

"Such as what, Bob?"

"Such as a suicide note, that is what. You would have noticed a suicide note, surely."

"Oh yes, we'd have noticed. There wasn't any note. There was no written matter of any kind, only a book that Mary had been reading."

Madoc did not speak ill of the dead's choice of reading matter. Bob was triumphant.

"Then, Madoc ap Emlyn, there was no suicide. You have known Mary. Do you believe it would have been possible for her to have killed herself wantonly and wickedly without making a great hurrah about it? She would have papered the room with notes! She would have written in giant letters all across the walls and ceiling. She would have flung herself into the fire with a dirge upon her lips and a wild and dreadful shriek, and flaming torches in both hands. And she would have composed herself a funeral elegy, moreover, that she would have expected me to read at the obsequies. And she would have left instructions for a funeral that would have put an Egyptian pharaoh's to shame, and she would have sent out invitations in advance to everybody she ever heard of. Is this not true, what I have said?"

"You do have a point, Bob," Madoc conceded. "So your argument is that Mary didn't commit suicide because she left no writing on the ceiling."

"Or elsewhere. I am saying that, yes. And I am right, you know I am right. And it must go on the police record that I am right, Cyril Rhys. You must make the insurance company understand that there is to be no nonsense about suicide and therefore no delay in their paying me my one hundred thousand pounds."

"It is not for me to be telling them," the constable objected. "It will be for you to be putting your argument to the coroner at the inquest, and for the jury then to believe you or not, as the case may be. They will wonder, I have to tell you. They will be asking themselves, if Miss Mary Rhys was not intending to commit suicide, why was she jumping into that bonfire all covered with gunpowder?"

"Oh, that is simple. Huw Rhys is to blame for that. Huw is against the building of the Beltane fires, look you. He thinks they are a pagan custom and therefore to be abandoned, which is very foolish of him and also dangerous because the old gods will turn against him and then where will he be? He would not even help me assemble the nine men to collect the nine different woods. He said there was already wood enough to build a small fire, and a small fire was all there was going to be because he does not hold with my nonsense. And this to me, who am renowned among the Friends of the Lesser Demons and other learned groups for my knowledge of the Beltane fires and have written papers, mind you. And also on other subjects which I will not mention because I am thinking profoundly on the subject of my sister and the gunpowder. Do you understand me, Constable Cyril Rhys?"

"No, I do not understand you, Mr. Bob Rhys, and you need not keep telling me who I am. What has Mr. Huw Rhys's opposition to a big bonfire to do with what happened to Miss Mary Rhys?"

"It is because Huw would permit only a small fire that my sister meant to make it bigger, do you see? She had lamented earlier to me that leaping a small fire would not give her scope to display her consummate skill and make her the cynosure of all eyes. Furthermore, if the blaze was not of impressive proportions, it would not be noticed by mystical beings whose names I must not repeat aloud in this unhallowed place. Mary at least had some understanding of occult matters, thanks to my inspired tutelage. Being a woman and therefore foolish, however, she was wont to put her own interpretations on them. Ergo. Ergo, I say."

"Yes, Bob, you've said it quite nicely," said Madoc. "So what was Mary's interpretation, then? That she should blow herself up to placate those mystical beings?"

"No, no, not at all. It would only have been to make the fire burn brighter that she carried the gunpowder. She would have believed she could accomplish this without scathe to herself. Mary thought, you see, that she had gained mastery over fire."

"Good Lord, did she really? Because you'd encouraged her to think so?"

"Not I. You cannot accuse me of such a silliness. I did not support my sister's belief in her mastery over fire; I would never have given her that satisfaction. It was all in her own head. Mary brought destruction upon herself, yes, but she did so only because of her false belief that she was an adept like me. This was death by misadventure, plain and simple. And let her demise be a lesson to all who dabble in magic without knowing what they do."

Bob stood up, having neatly talked himself out of any reason to feel shocked or depressed over his sister's terrible end. "So all I need to do is explain to the coroner that this unfortunate incident was all due to Huw Rhys's intransigence and my sister's mistaken trust in powers she did not have. He will then instruct the insurance company that I am to be paid forthwith and that will be the end of this sorry matter. Now I will telephone the Friends of the Lesser Demons at your expense, Sir Caradoc, to explain why I cannot come to talk to them tonight. And then I will betake myself upstairs to study my grimoire for information on how to lay Mary's ghost so that she will not go lurking about these ancestral halls and scaring the daylights out of people. I know what is due to my gracious kinsman, Sir Caradoc, and thus I will repay your hospitality."

A cool nod was the most his gracious kinsman could manage.

"Come along then, Bob," said Madoc, "I'll go up with you and wake up Dai. You'll want to question him next, won't you, Cyril?"

What Madoc himself wanted was to ask the one question he hadn't wanted to pose in front of Uncle Caradoc. He followed Bob into the fat man's by now stuffy and disordered bedroom and shut the door after them. "Now then, Bob, what can you tell me about the killing of a ram in the chapel night before last?"

Bob gaped at him, eyes abulge and jowls awobble. "A ram? Is it a sacrifice you are meaning?"

"Please answer my question."

"How can I answer? In what way was this killing performed?"

"The head was cut off and set up on the altar. The body was left on the floor."

"And the blood? Was the blood drained into a sacrificial basin?"

"No, it was all over the floor."

"And the carcass not heaved up on the altar, even? It sounds to me like a shabby and ill-managed affair. Was the head at least crowned with a garland?"

"No, it was crowned with Padarn's old cap, and his pipe was stuck in the mouth."

"Then it is ignoramuses who have done this outrageous bumble, and they have achieved nothing by it. Why was I not sent for to consult? It is an affront, I tell you. What would the Friends of the Lesser Demons say? I will not tolerate so rude a slight, I will shake the dust of this house from my feet and I will never darken its door again. And you may tell that to Sir Caradoc Rhys for me!"

Well, here was an ill wind that had finally blown some good. None the wiser but somewhat cheered, Madoc went to wake up the nephew.

Chapter 16

Well, *you sure look like the morning after the night before.*

Janet didn't say so out loud; Dai Rhys was an abject enough specimen without having to be reminded. He'd put on some clothes; yesterday's shirt and jeans picked up off the bedroom floor after they'd spent the night as a bed for Betty's cat, from the look of them. Madoc hadn't allowed him time to shave, though; Janet found his intermittent sprouts of whisker oddly moving. The poor kid couldn't even grow a convincing crop of stubble. How old was Dai anyway? She went and got him a cup of tea.

When she came back with a tray, Janet got the impression that she hadn't missed much. Dai appeared to be answering Constable Cyril's questions mainly by blank stares and pitiful moans. She set a full cup and a plate of cakes on a taboret close to his hand, and pulled up a chair next to him.

"For Pete's sake, Constable, let up on the boy till he's got a little something inside him. Here, Dai, drink your tea while it's hot. I expect you must feel pretty awful, like the rest of us. Would you believe your Uncle Bob was actually knocked speechless for once in his life?"

That got to him. Dai even managed a snort of what might have passed for laughter, rather unfortunately because he'd been in the act of sipping his tea. At least she'd loosened him up enough to quit acting like a zombie.

"Where's Uncle Bob now?" he asked once he'd got his tea under control.

"Upstairs studying how to lay your aunt's ghost. Here, have one of Betty's cakes. Does he honestly believe that stuff, Dai, or is he just gassing?"

"Oh, he believes it. He's balmy enough to believe anything. So's Aunt Mary. I mean—is she?"

"Oh, she's dead all right. Don't you remember, Dai? You were there when it happened."

He dived into his cup. "It's just that I was having these dreams," he muttered when he'd got his whistle wetted enough to talk. "Things got mixed up. I don't think I'm really awake yet. Is there more tea?"

"Of course." Janet gave him a refill from the pot on the tray. "Madoc, what about you?"

The question was rhetorical, even Cyril the Police was all teaed out. Anyway, the boy's eyes were almost open by now, and there was a hint of color showing among the ineffectual tufts of whisker. Madoc gave Janet a nod of thanks and got down to business.

"The thing of it is, Dai, we've discovered that your aunt had her pockets stuffed with gunpowder when she jumped into the fire."

"Gunpowder? How could she? Where did she get it?"

"We were hoping you might be able to tell us that, since your uncle couldn't. Or wouldn't. He just sat there all puffed up and gulping air like a bullfrog. You don't suppose he's trying to keep something from us?"

"He's bloody-minded enough to keep anything from anybody. Crazy old bahstid." Dai cast a furtive glance at Sir Caradoc and muttered, "Sorry. I don't know."

"Your uncle doesn't hunt, by any chance?"

"Him? All he does is talk and eat."

"I get the impression that you haven't had much use for either your aunt or your uncle."

Dai's answer was a sneer. He picked up a cake from Janet's tray and snapped at it like a ravening coyote.

"Why are you still with them, then?" Madoc persisted. "You're old enough to be out on your own, aren't you? What are you, twenty or so?"

"Almost. I have to stay, they're my guardians till I'm twenty-one. If I leave before then, I'll never get my inheritance."

"Who says you won't?"

"Uncle Bob. He says it's in my father's will." Dai finished his cake and reached for another. He was warmed up now. "My father was a geologist for an oil company in Iraq, I think it was. He died out there when I was a kid. My mother took off with some bloke when I was still very small, and my father got custody of me. He couldn't take me to Iraq with him, so he parked me with Aunt Mary. I expect Uncle Bob made Father write in his will that they were to get paid for taking care of me."

Madoc was interested. "Have you ever seen your father's will?"

"How could I? Uncle Bob keeps it at the bank."

"Then it is Bob and Mary Rhys who had taken care of you practically all your life?" Constable Cyril interjected.

"Well, they had a nanny for me, then I went to school. Only as a day boy. I'd rather have been a boarder but they wouldn't let me. I wanted to go off to college, too, but they said there wasn't enough money so I'd have to be apprenticed to Aunt Mary. I'm to serve seven years without pay, then I get taken into the firm. Only how can I, now that she's dead? Can Uncle Bob attach my inheritance for breach of contract?"

"What contract was this, Dai?" asked Madoc.

"The one they made me sign when I was apprenticed."

"But how could they do that if you're still underage?"

"I don't know. Uncle Bob said they could."

"Couldn't you have asked the lawyer?"

"There wasn't one. Uncle Bob took care of it all."

"It sounds to me as if somebody ought to take care of Uncle Bob," Janet was too incensed not to get in her two cents' worth. "What do you think, Uncle Caradoc?"

"I think we must investigate this matter on Dai's behalf," the old man replied quietly. "It is a pity you did not come to me sooner, Dai."

"I wouldn't have known what to say," the young fellow mumbled. "They kept telling me they were acting in my best interest, because there wasn't enough money in the trust fund."

"We shall see. Now we must deal with the problem of why your aunt Mary died in so unlikely a fashion. We are relying on you to help us. Madoc, do you have further questions for Dai?"

"Oh yes. What you must realize, Dai, is that you're the only one who may be able to give us any real help. So far, your uncle's testimony hasn't amounted to much. He complains that his sister never confided in him, but we're wondering whether that may have been because he never gave her much chance to talk. Did she talk to you when you were alone together in the workshop?"

Dai's shudder would have been answer enough. "God, yes! Yammer, yammer, yammer, that's all I heard the whole day long. She never shut up till dinnertime, and then Uncle Bob would take over. You're not going to make me go back with him, are you?"

"I have no authority to make you do anything, Dai. Anyway, I doubt whether Constable Rhys will allow any of us to go anywhere until we find out the real story of how your aunt died. You have no idea whatsoever where that gunpowder might have come from? Take your time, think it over. Do you want another cake?"

Dai wanted another cake. He was beginning to look almost hopeful. "Unless Uncle Bob got some to use for one of his spells. He was trying to raise a demon once. He'd taken off all his clothes and painted his—um—anyway, he'd drawn a circle with a pentagram inside it and a lot of mystic symbols done in colored chalks on the floor of his bedroom, and he was hopping around inside it making odd noises. And he was burning something in a brazier."

"Are you sure it was gunpowder?" Madoc interjected. "Was it burning very fast and hot? Did it smell like firecrackers going off?"

"Well, no, not exactly. It seemed to be just smoldering and giving off a lot of smoke, and the smell was more like dead leaves or something. Anyway, it was rather ghastly. But he might have had some gunpowder mixed in." Dai was clearly itching to pin something on his uncle. "I wasn't close enough to see."

"You weren't taking part in the rite?"

"Not likely! I was peeking through the keyhole, if you really want to know. I was only about ten at the time, I wanted to see the demon."

"And did you?"

"No, the thing was a complete bust. I heard Aunt Mary coming and had to slope off in a hurry."

"But that was ten years ago. You can't say whether your uncle has gone in for any demon-raising lately?"

"I haven't bothered to snoop. Uncle Bob's spells never work out. And Uncle Bob in the buff is no great treat, you know."

"I don't know"—Madoc was trying not to smile—"and I sincerely hope I never find out. The one thing he did tell us was that your aunt has been making extra money of late years, not through the gem-cutting business but from some kind of annuity. Did she tell you anything about the annuity?"

"Not really."

"What's that supposed to mean? More keyholes?"

Dai shrugged. Madoc persevered.

"Your uncle told us that your aunt used to hint around about the great lot of money she was getting, but wouldn't give him any concrete information about where it was coming from. Was that what she did with you?"

"She never said anything to me directly. I'd hear her dropping cryptic remarks to Uncle Bob now and then. He'd be livid because she wouldn't tell and begin shouting at her. When she talked to me, it was mostly about what a great gem-cutter she was and how I'd never be as good as she; which I don't suppose I ever will because I never wanted to be one in the first place. But she'd talk to herself a lot while she was working, and I couldn't help catching bits of what she was muttering even though I didn't particularly want to. And she'd talk to people on the telephone sometimes."

"What people were these?" Madoc asked him. "Friends of hers?"

"I shouldn't think so. I don't believe Aunt Mary had any friends. She did get business calls, of course, but these calls were different. I could always tell—she'd put on a smarmy voice, as if she was pretending to be somebody else. Whoever it was never called her, she'd always put through the calls herself."

"With you right there to hear?"

"Oh, she'd have forgotten I was around. She'd do that, you know, simply forget I was there. I always had the feeling she thought of me as some kind of puppet that she could stick on the shelf when she didn't want me for anything, and I wouldn't be able to move until she came back to pull my strings."

"That must have been very hard on you."

"No, actually those were the easy times. Being ignored was better than being picked at like a hen with a worm. Me being the worm, needless to say. I don't have to tell you, you saw her going at me yesterday, right in front of Annie and everybody. God, I wanted to die!"

"You were not wanting Miss Mary Rhys to be dropping down dead in your place?" That was Constable Rhys, back on the job.

"No, I've never ill-wished either of them. I'm too inadequate for that, I suppose." Dai scowled down at his dirty tennis shoes. "If I were to kill anyone, it would be myself. I've thought of it sometimes."

"At least you had sense enough not to try," said Madoc. "Since you've brought up the subject yourself, Dai, would you mind telling us what your aunt was laying into you about yesterday at the party?"

Dai's chin went down into his shirtfront. "It was about something I hadn't done," he mumbled.

"When were you supposed to have done this thing?"

"Then. While everyone else was at the party."

"Mind telling us what it was?"

"She'd told me to get out the golden sickles and make tracings of them."

"Get them out?" exclaimed Sir Caradoc. "How could you?"

"Easily enough, she'd given me her key to the grille. See, here it is."

Dai fished a shiny bit of metal from his pocket and handed it over. The old man stared, not believing what he saw. "But this is impossible!"

"Oh no," said Dai, "it was quite simple. Remember the last time we visited? You had the crosier out to polish and she went through her routine with the loupe. You'd laid the key on the table, as you always do, and Aunt Mary just casually reached over and took an impression of the wards with a little lump of wax she had in her hand. I don't expect anybody else noticed—people never did notice Aunt Mary unless she was making a pest of herself."

"But why would she have abused my hospitality in so mean a way?"

"Because she wanted to steal the emerald."

"The emerald? Dai, you are not making sense. If it was the emerald she wanted, why did she ask you to trace the sickles?"

"By then, she'd already got the emerald."

"Boy, you must stop telling me such stories. After I had come from my wonderful birthday party, the last thing I did before going to bed was to visit the dining hall, as I often do. The little light that illumines the grille was shining, my eyesight is perhaps not what it used to be, but it is good enough. I could see clearly the great green stone in the crosier. I thought how beautiful it looked with the freshly polished silver gleaming around it, and I vowed to myself that for whatever time I had left, I would keep the crosier brightly shined for my own selfish pleasure and to the glory of God, as the old monks must have done. I may have waxed fanciful, but I believe I was still in full possession of my wits."

"Sir, I'm not saying you didn't see a green stone; it simply wasn't the emerald. Aunt Mary must have taken the real stone the night we came. That had to be why she was so insistent about making me look through her bloody loupe, blethering on about what I was supposed to be seeing, making you all believe the stone was what it should have been. She thought I'd be too dense to catch on. She'd no opinion of me at all, you know, she was always calling me an idiot and saying I'd never learn. I'll admit I'm no great expert, but I've learned enough to tell a genuine emerald from a lump of melted glass."

"Great God in heaven! Madoc, is this possible, what Dai is saying?"

"I'm afraid it's more than possible, Uncle Caradoc. I assume she wanted the tracings so that she could fake up substitute sickles too, and pull another swap the next time she came. Right, Dai?"

"Oh yes, no question. The thing of it is, I've always wanted to be a goldsmith instead of a lapidary. I've a feeling for gold; it's something I was born with, I think, like perfect pitch or being double-jointed. I understand it, I know how to handle it."

"You're sure of that?"

"Certain sure. Every chance I get, I sneak over to the goldsmith's shop next door to ours. Armand—that's the chap who owns it—has been teaching me on the sly when Aunt Mary would go off to see clients or whatever. I haven't wanted it that way, but she and Uncle Bob would have stopped me if they'd known. Anyway, I've done a fair amount of whining about wanting to change, so finally Aunt Mary said all right, she'd give me a test.

If I could make her accurate copies of your golden sickles, I could go and apprentice myself to Armand instead of her, so long as I didn't tell Uncle Bob."

"When was this, Dai?"

"Just this past week, the day before we came. I said it was an unfair test because I'd never find the perfect shade of that old red gold. Then she said I wasn't to use real gold, but just copper with gold leaf over it, which is bonkers, but she wouldn't listen. That's what she was at me about yesterday. She wanted me down at the manor, climbing the wall to get at your sickles."

"I assume climbing the wall is a figure of speech," said Madoc. "How would she herself have got at the emerald? Did she tell you?"

"She'd got hold of a collapsible aluminum ladder somewhere, she claimed it was the sort Raffles the Gentleman Cracksman used to use. Some chap she met abroad, I suppose—I don't know if she got it off him or what. It's not really a ladder, just an expandable tube with handholds that flip out and hooks at the top to catch on with."

"But how could a frail, elderly woman be climbing an expandable tube?" demanded Constable Cyril.

Dai snorted. "She wasn't that old, and she certainly wasn't frail. Aunt Mary could climb like a monkey. She'd go upstairs on the outside, swinging from the banisters with her legs dangling out in space. I used to wish she'd lose her grip and break her bloody neck, but she never did. She'd got the ladder hidden under some shrubbery, she was afraid to leave it in her room because Uncle Bob was always snooping. I can show you where, if somebody hasn't walked off with it."

For once, Sir Caradoc was looking all his ninety years. "I cannot believe this. My own kinswoman stealing from me. Mary a criminal, climbing like a monkey.

And jumping through the balefire with gunpowder in her pockets. That is not the act of a sane person. She must have been wandering in her wits."

"We're not at all sure Mary knew the gunpowder was there," said Madoc. "Dai, have you any thoughts about that?"

The ex-apprentice shrugged. "Unless it was something to do with those weird telephone calls she'd been putting through."

Here it came; Madoc could feel the prickling up his spine. "Dai, can you remember any of the things you heard your aunt say during those calls?"

"It was more the way she'd say them. Like the way she'd been paying Aunt Iseult those little backhanded compliments on her emeralds to let people know they're not really all that marvelous. Anybody who's not a fool ought to realize they couldn't be, or Aunt Iseult wouldn't dare wear them as casually as she does. That doesn't mean anything. Lots of film stars have replicas made of their real jewels so they don't have to worry if the stuff gets stolen."

Madoc wasn't interested in Iseult's jewelry. "About the calls, Dai, can't you remember anything at all about what Mary said? Were these different people she talked to, do you think, or was it usually the same one?"

Dai had to think a minute. "I'd say it was the same one. Mostly, anyway."

"And was this person a man or a woman?"

"I've no idea. She did mention a man's name every so often, but I don't think it was the name of the person she was talking to. It was more as if it was somebody they both knew. Arthur, that was it. Arthur."

"Arthur? Would that have been Lisa's husband? The chap who died abroad and nobody wants to talk about? Uncle Caradoc, do you know what happened to him?"

"Oh yes, Madoc, I know. Arthur Ellis was found beaten over the head and strangled in an alley in Marseilles. He had been robbed of his money and presumably of gems. The reason people do not want to talk about it is that the place where his body turned up was one in which Arthur would, quite literally, not have wanted to be found dead."

"Oh." Dai was staring at the old man, his face flushed beet red. "Then I think I know what the calls were about. I think Aunt Mary was blackmailing somebody."

Chapter 17

"**B**lackmail is a terrible thing to be accusing your own aunt of doing, Dai Rhys."

Constable Cyril was not at all happy with this added complication. Why should he be? A woman who'd been blown up by gunpowder in the midst of an ancient fertility rite was no sort of corpse for a village constable to be stuck with. Making her out a crook might explain why she died, but it still didn't prove who'd stuck the gunpowder in her pocket.

Janet could see it coming. That petty satrap of a chief constable wasn't about to call in Scotland Yard. Why should he go flinging the county's money about on a pack of Londoners when here was a perfectly good Canadian whom he could stick with doing the job for nothing? Nor would Davies strain himself to help Madoc and Cyril, because they were Sir Caradoc Rhys's kinfolk and he didn't like Sir Caradoc. Mary's death would remain a family affair unless the Rhyses absolutely forced Davies to take official action, which they wouldn't because they didn't like him any better than he liked them.

But it was just plain stupid to believe a half-cracked woman who'd been systematically milked of her earnings all her working life by that leech of a brother, and had finally got the upper hand of him by milking some other victim in turn, would have turned around and committed suicide in a fit of remorse for her ill-doing. Mary had been riding high yesterday, cocksure of her ability to control a situation whose potential dangers she was too egocentric to recognize. According to her repellent sibling, she'd preened herself on having mystic powers that he was either sane enough or mean enough to realize she couldn't have possessed; power of some kind was clearly what she'd wanted more than anything else. And no wonder, after having been browbeaten all her life by that awful brother. Janet could believe Dai's blackmail story, she sensed that Madoc did too. Uncle Caradoc naturally didn't like having to think of his dead kinswoman as a crook; but after Dai's revelations about his life with Bob and Mary, a person might as well believe anything.

Dai was sticking to his guns. "I'm sorry, Sir Caradoc. I don't want to be stirring up more trouble for the family, but if Aunt Mary wasn't blackmailing somebody, then where was she getting all that money?"

"You're quite sure she was in fact getting the money?" Madoc asked gently.

"Oh yes, I know she was." Dai flushed again. "I happened to see her bankbooks one day last week. She'd left her handbag on the workbench while she went out to the back to do something, and I—I suppose it wasn't the sort of thing good lads do, but there it was, and I thought I might as well have a look. She'd been so strange, you know; I was sure she must be up to something. Anyway, the books showed over a hundred thousand pounds on deposit, and she'd just that morning put in another five hundred."

Sir Caradoc grasped at the only straw he could think

of. "But could this money not have come from her gem-cutting?"

"No, sir, not possibly. Uncle Bob has all the payments sent directly to him. He handles the bookkeeping and banking, and pays the bills. Aunt Mary didn't get to touch a penny except when she went abroad. He never wanted her to have any, he said she'd only spend it. She had to have some cash when she went on business trips, but he'd make her keep count of what she spent so he could take it off the taxes. He wouldn't even let Aunt Mary buy so much as a pair of slippers by herself; he'd go with her to the shop and raise a stink if she didn't like what he picked out. At least he used to, till she started getting that annuity."

Now that he'd got used to being the center of attention, Dai was becoming quite the raconteur. "I've thought right along there must be something awfully fishy about that. Why would anybody in his right mind want to play Father Christmas to a nasty old witch like her?"

"It was shortly after Mr. Arthur Ellis died that the checks began coming, right?" said Madoc. "You'd have been how old then? About eleven?"

"Yes, that's right. I hardly knew Mr. Arthur. He never came to the house, only to the shop, and I wasn't there much then, except on weekends to sweep out and tidy around. Aunt Mary and Uncle Bob talked about him a lot, though—they made him sound like Count Dracula. After he died, they really ripped him to pieces. They claimed he'd been killed in a—a place where there are girls who—"

Dai glanced at Sir Caradoc and left off trying to think of a euphemism. "Uncle Bob was livid, not because somebody murdered Mr. Arthur, but because the gossip about how he died might reflect badly on the business. Aunt Mary didn't say much at the time. She'd just sit there with a revolting smirk on her face, as if she knew something he didn't and wasn't going to tell."

"What did your uncle say to that?"

"I don't think he ever noticed, till the checks began coming and she told him about her so-called annuity. Then he went straight through the roof. He kept yelling, 'Where are you getting that money?,' and she'd just say 'Through Arthur.' So he charged off to that place where you look up people's wills and came back and called her a liar because Mr. Arthur hadn't left her a penny. I thought he was going to strike Aunt Mary that time, but she wasn't a bit frightened. She just smiled the way she'd do when she was telling me how stupid I was, and told him that if he ever expected to get anything out of her again, he'd better shut up and quit his bullying. She told him flat out, 'I've got the upper hand now, brother dear. If you don't like it, I'll just nip off by myself where you can't find me, and you may sit here alone and starve to death.' "

"Do you think she really meant it?" said Janet.

"Oh yes." Dai was grinning now. "After that, every time Uncle Bob tried to bring up the subject, Aunt Mary would simply pretend she didn't hear. One morning at breakfast, she got him so furious that he threatened to put a curse on her."

"That is terrible!" cried Constable Cyril. "To lay a curse is the height of impiety."

"Oh, Aunt Mary didn't bat an eyelid. She just gave him another of those forbearing smiles and said, 'But, brother dear, you've taught me how to turn a curse back on the curser, don't you remember? You have always been so ready to instruct your dim little sister, and I have always been so dutiful a pupil. Do go ahead with your curse. I'm itching to practice my lesson.' Uncle Bob was in such a rage he couldn't even talk. He sat there all swelled up and purple in the face, gobbling like a turkey. That was the only meal in their house I've ever enjoyed."

Madoc's lips twitched, partly in sympathy, partly in amusement. "Getting back to the emerald, Dai, what do you suppose your aunt might have done with it? It wasn't found last night when her room was searched."

"She wouldn't have put it there, she'd know Uncle Bob would come snooping. Why not in her handbag? That's where she kept the bankbooks."

"That's a thought, certainly. But it didn't turn up in the bonfire ashes, I sifted them myself. Jenny, do you recall whether Mary had a handbag with her yesterday?"

"Yes, she did, a soft black leather pouch that she'd strung on her belt like an old-fashioned reticule. But I'm quite sure she wasn't wearing it when she and Bob were doing their dance in the chapel. Because there were coins inside, I suppose, and metal on the belt buckle. That was one of Bob's taboos, remember? He may have made her take it off. And I don't recall her having put it back on when she leaped the fire."

"Aunt Mary wouldn't just have left it lying around, though," Dai insisted. "She'd have hidden it away where Uncle Bob wouldn't find it."

"Or anybody else, if that great chunk of emerald was inside," Madoc agreed. "Right, then, we'd better organize a hunt. Cyril, that's a job for you. And a nasty one, I'm afraid, Mary was all over the lot yesterday. She could have stuffed it down a rabbit hole or high up in the chapel, there's no telling. Dai, you'd better go with him and find that ladder of hers, you may want it to climb on. Just don't break your neck. You might recruit some of Owain's lot to help, else you'll never get through."

"Will we also be asking the grown-ups to join in the searching?" asked Cyril.

"Not yet, I need to talk to them. Particularly Uncle Huw. He'd better know what's going on."

There was also the open question of the ram. Huw wouldn't be able to keep the lid on much longer, not if Scotland Yard had to become involved, and what would be the point? That crude slaughter seemed a paltry affair now, in view of the greater horror. Unless it had, as Madoc suspected, been the first act of some quasi-operatic tragedy, and Mary's bizarre death perhaps only the second.

This was no time to sit spinning fantasies. He stood up. "We'll have to search this house more thoroughly too, Uncle Caradoc."

Sir Caradoc gathered his bones together and rose also. "Whatever may be necessary must be done. What happened last night has made it impossible for us to be nice about observing the usual courtesies. Come, Madoc, you and I will go together to the farmhouse. Dai lad, you have had nothing to eat but a few cakes. You must stop in the kitchen before you go hunting and ask Betty for some proper food to sustain you. Cyril Rhys, we are grateful for your concern and your diligence on behalf of this grievously troubled family."

The constable stood smartly to attention. "Sir Caradoc, sir, it is an honor and a privilege to be serving you. Mr. Dai Rhys and I shall be procuring from Betty some bread and cheese to be eating whilst we search, and we shall be going directly to the chapel lest some unauthorized busybody will have been finding Miss Mary Rhys's handbag before we are getting there."

It needed only a flourish of bugles. Helmet straight,

buttons all ashine, the doughty Cyril marched firmly kitchenward. The weedy Dai followed a respectful pace or two behind, as purposefully as he could manage in his scruffy jeans and wilted shirt. Sir Caradoc and Madoc went off together. Left alone, Janet decided she'd better find out what the grandparents had done with her child.

Dai and the constable were already shutting the door behind them, each carrying a great wedge of bread and cheese. Iseult was sitting alone at the long table. The older woman, and Iseult was certainly that, had a cup of tea in front of her but wasn't doing much about it. Catching sight of Janet, she shrugged and tried to work up a smile.

"No room service at this hotel. Don't look at me, I haven't put my face on yet."

Iseult hadn't put on much of anything else, if it came to that, just a slinky green wrapper over a nightgown that seemed to be, what Janet could see of it, hardly more than a figment of the imagination. It stood to reason she'd be wearing green satin mules with marabou trimming. Janet peeked under the table on the flimsy pretext of looking for Bartholomew, and she was. The shape those leg veins were in, the silly woman ought to have had on flat heels and support stockings.

This must be why Iseult was so partial to floor-length skirts and floppy-legged pants. Forty if she was a day, and maybe a few years more. Janet began to feel sympathy; at least the old trouper was putting up a good battle, even though she looked right now as though she knew she'd already lost the war.

Betty, true to form, was waving the teapot and suggesting a little something to stay Mrs. Madoc's stomach until lunchtime. Janet shrugged.

"Why not? I'll sit here if it's all right with you, Iseult.

What's happened to Dorothy? Do you know, Betty?"

"Ach, the little love will be up at the farm with Lady Rhys and Sir Emlyn. It was Tib's pram they were pushing her in, with her sitting up in her pretty bonnet like a daisy in the sun, God bless her. Is it a new-laid egg I could be poaching for you to eat, Mrs. Madoc?"

"Thanks, but one breakfast a morning's about all I can manage. I might just cut myself a sliver of your wonderful bread, though. Go ahead with whatever you're doing, Betty, I'm not that helpless. What's on your agenda for today, Iseult?"

"Good question. Things don't seem to be exactly bright and peppy around here this morning, do they? I suppose one could hardly expect fun and games after last night's horror show. I was rather hoping I might persuade Tom and Dafydd to drive me somewhere away from the smell of toasted Rhys. Have you seen them around?"

"No, nor Reuel either." It occurred to Janet that she hadn't reminded Madoc of that remark Mary had made about the scriptwriter's having profited from her program on gem-cutting. Had Mary simply been angling for more attention, or had the remark carried a double meaning? No matter. Madoc would have remembered; he always did. "Is he still asleep?" she added in all innocence.

Iseult took umbrage. "I wouldn't know, contrary to what everybody's no doubt been assuming. Reuel came with me for two reasons: one, that I needed a lift and he has a car; two, that he's supposed to be gathering local color with which to write me a script, and it had jolly well be a better one than last time, or I shall be in the market for a new writer. I'll have a slice of that bread if I may, since you seem to know how to cut it and I don't. What do you do besides mothering, Jenny?"

Janet didn't suppose Iseult actually gave a hoot, but a civil question deserved a civil answer. "I housewife. Shop, cook, bake, sew, paint furniture, hang wallpaper, chase down the odd antique. You know."

"No, I don't, thank God. Is that all?"

"Oh no, we do a lot of entertaining, what with family and neighbors and unexpected company Madoc's always dragging home at odd hours. Fredericton's a university city as well as our provincial capitol, so there's always something to go to: concerts, art shows, plays, and whatnot. On weekends we often drive over to my brother's farm, sometimes we fly to Toronto or wherever one of Madoc's family happens to be performing. This is our second trip to Wales since we've been married, I expect we'll come again before too long. This must sound awfully dull to a famous film star."

"Huh." Iseult slapped butter on her bread with a to-hell-with-the-calories air. "Do you know what film stars spend most of our time doing? We sit. That's how glamorous filmmaking is, and don't let anyone tell you otherwise. One sits until one's bloody ass of a director makes up his mind what he wants one to do next, which may take days. Then one sits some more while the camera crew try to get the right angle and the electricians fiddle around with the lights. Then one gets up and goes through some stupid piece of business and speaks one's silly lines. Then one does the same thing over again, and again, and again till one's ready to scream; all because some idiotic bit player doesn't know how to get through a door without falling over his feet. At last everything goes like a bomb, and that's when the props girl happens to notice that somebody's pushed a flowerpot two inches out of line, so it's all to be gone through yet again. And there's dull little housewife you, giving parties and buying antiques and flying around to concerts. Do you have servants?"

"Not to say servants. We have a woman who comes in to clean two or three times a week and helps out if we're having a formal dinner or something, which we don't very often. And a man who cuts the grass in the summer and shovels us out in the winter, and a neighbor who waters the plants and feeds the cat and takes in the mail while we're away. We haven't found a baby-sitter yet because we've either stayed home ourselves or taken Dorothy with us; but I expect we'll be coming to that sooner or later. What about you, Iseult? Where do you live?"

"In London, like everyone else. In a rather pleasant flat, with a daily to clean and plenty of restaurants nearby. One doesn't go in for cozy home cooking, I'm afraid."

One might look a few shades less godawful without one's makeup if one did try to get some honest plain grub under one's belt now and then. Janet didn't suppose Iseult wanted to be told so, nor did she want to break up this tête-à-tête just yet. She wasn't a gushy person, but this was a case where a spot of gush might be in order.

"Eating out all the time, I suppose you always have people rushing up to your table begging for autographs. That must be a thrill."

Iseult shrugged. "It's a nuisance, actually. They want to stand and chat, and one's food gets cold. Fortunately the celebrity game is played much less seriously over here than in America. One doesn't think of oneself as a star, you know; one's simply an actress. One wouldn't turn down a good supporting role merely because one's accustomed to playing leads. That's why one's always in work, both here and abroad."

"Do you mean in other European countries, like France and Italy?"

"Oh yes. And Spain, Morocco—one manages to get around a fair amount. One even squeezes in a bit of fun here and there."

"I should hope so. What's your favorite city?"

"Rome, I suppose. The Italians are always so appreciative. Paris can be amusing, and Cannes. I do like Cannes."

"That's down near Marseilles, isn't it? I read somewhere that if you were to sit at an outdoor café on the Cannebière long enough, you'd see everybody you've ever known walk by. Have you ever tried?"

Iseult lifted one finger, signaling for Janet to hold on till she'd taken a sip of her tea; it must be stone-cold by now.

"Oddly enough, Marseilles is one place I've never been. Now I must dash upstairs and pull myself together. You'll be around, I suppose?"

"As far as I know. What I'm planning to do right now is track down my child. If I see Dafydd or Tom, I'll tell them you'll be down and not to go off without you."

"Lovely. Pip-pip."

So they really did say "Pip-pip." Or was that just a line from one of Rcuel's scripts? Janet carried the empty cups over to the sink and left them for someone else to wash. It went against the grain, but she knew Betty'd have a conniption if Mrs. Madoc were caught rinsing them out herself. She was halfway to the farmhouse when she heard hooves clattering on the path behind her. She moved out of the way, but the rider pulled up beside her.

"Aunt Jenny?"

Janet wasn't anybody's aunt over here that she knew of, but it was polite of Lisa's daughter to grant her the title. "Hello, Tib. What's doing?"

"Mother sent me to tell you she's found a leek pie that didn't get cut, and would you and Uncle Madoc come to luncheon? Please say yes, I'm afraid Mother's about to pull in her neck. She's dreadfully shaken up about Miss Mary. Not that she liked her much because how could one? But it was a shock, you know, and Mother doesn't handle shocks very well. On account of Daddy, I expect. It's not something we talk about, you understand, but there it is. Anyway, do please say you will. And may I get to hold Dorothy?"

"Thank you, Tib, I'd love to come." Here at least was a way she might be helpful. "I can't answer for Madoc; he's busy with Uncle Caradoc. As for Dorothy, it's a question of whether I can pry her away from her grandparents. What time would your mother want us?"

"Whenever you'd like to come. One thing about Mother, she's flexible."

"Then would you tell her please that I'll be along in a little while, with or without Madoc and Dorothy, as the case may be? I'm afraid that's the best I can do right now."

"Oh, that's fine. Mother won't care so much about Uncle Madoc, she gets a bit sick of men when Uncle Tom's around. But she thinks you're lovely."

Tib wheeled her pretty mare and trotted off. Janet stood looking after her for a few seconds, then went on up to the farm. Her parents-in-law were exactly where she'd expected they'd be; sitting at the kitchen table with Elen and Mavis, drinking tea and hashing over the party, trying to avoid mentioning what had happened at the end. Dorothy was on the floor, having a serious conversation with a handsome ginger cat. Fortunately she was encountering no dearth of feline companionship in Wales so far.

Elen's hand automatically went out to the teapot. "There you are, Jenny. We were just talking about you. Sit down, I'll pour you a cup."

"No, really, Aunt Elen. I've just had a second breakfast with Iseult and Lisa wants me over there for luncheon. She's found a stray leek pie that needs to be eaten up and Tib wants a turn at holding Dorothy."

"Well, she can't have her." Sir Emlyn was growing positively belligerent over his grandchild. "Dorothy's planning to take a nap with her grandmother and me, if this Mad Hatter's tea party ever finishes. What's Madoc up to?"

"Trying to get a line on what really happened last night before the chief constable starts poking his nose in and upsetting Uncle Caradoc. Bob's in a swivet because he's been told he must stick around for the inquest, which means he won't get to speechify for the Friends of the Lesser Demons and will lose the advantage of his cheap-rate ticket. Not to be running down my husband's relatives, but I do think that man's the absolute outside limit."

"As do we all, my dear," Lady Rhys assured her. "If only Bob couldn't sing! One can't thoroughly despise even an adequate basso, can one?"

"I'd be willing to give it a try if I had to be around that tub of lard for long," said Mavis. "He and that sister of his did a right job on young Dai, didn't they? What are they saying down at the manor, Jenny?"

"Not a great deal at the moment," Janet evaded. "Madoc and Uncle Caradoc are with Uncle Huw, wherever that may be. The constable and Dai are organizing a posse to hunt for Mary's handbag. I expect they've roped in your lot by now. Iseult came down to the kitchen for a cup of tea, then went back up to put on her face in case Tom and Dafydd want to take her someplace."

"Where, for instance?" Mavis seemed to welcome a change of subject, as who could blame her?

"I don't think she cares. We did talk a bit, mostly about ourselves. Iseult was curious as to why I haven't died of boredom over in the colonies, and naturally I wanted to hear about her life as a movie actress. She told me she'd been in films all over Europe and northern Africa. I asked whether she'd ever been to Marseilles because I've been hearing oddments about Lisa's husband that nobody seems to know the whole story of; but she said no, she hadn't."

"But she has," said Lady Rhys. "Don't you remember, Emmy? We were headed for Monaco and Dafydd was on his way from Melbourne to Munich, I think it was. We'd agreed to meet in Marseilles for dinner and a quick visit. It was a wretched night, absolutely teeming. Dafydd had a flight out at some ridiculous hour and we were concerned about the weather, so after dinner we'd stuffed him into what must have been the only available taxi in Marseilles and sent him along to the airport. Then we'd gone back into the restaurant and dawdled over our coffee, hoping the storm would let up."

"Not that it much mattered," Sir Emlyn replied. "We'd nothing else to do and were feeling a trifle bereft. At least I was."

"Yes, darling, so was I. Anyway, it kept on raining. Finally we decided we might as well go on outside and try our luck. We were queued up under the awning with a few other hopefuls when this ravishing redhead came tripping along in the highest of heels and the shortest of skirts, with her head up inside one of those transparent plastic bubble umbrellas. It had a green band around it, naturally, Iseult always wears green. She was so heavily made up that the man behind us made a disgusting remark. That was when I realized the woman was Iseult."

"One realized, of course, that she'd just come from a performance and hadn't taken time to scrape off the greasepaint," Sir Emlyn put in gently.

"Of course, dear, though one also realized it wasn't the most professional thing for an actress to have done. Anyway, one didn't quite like to rush screaming after her in the rain; and just then a couple of taxis came along, so that was the end of it. But I've always remembered the incident because it was that same night Arthur Ellis got murdered, right there in Marseilles, not far from where we'd dined. Actually we didn't find out about Arthur till we got back to Wales, but wasn't that a weird coincidence, Jenny? No wonder Iseult prefers not to remember Marseilles. She'd rather had her eye on Arthur at one time. I believe; she was quite put out when he married Lisa. Well, Emmy, shall we walk Jenny back as far as the manor?"

Chapter 18

The conference with Huw Rhys couldn't have taken long. Madoc and Sir Caradoc were coming down the hill, very slowly. The old man was leaning heavily on the cane he often carried but seldom made much use of. Sir Emlyn and Lady Rhys fell back to walk with him, keeping the baby with them, Madoc came on ahead to meet Janet.

"Anything happening, love?"

"Lisa's invited us to lunch, but I said you were probably going to be busy. Is that right?"

"Yes, you go along without me." He'd save the story of the ram for when they had time to talk, if ever. "I need to search the house, and I'd like to dust that green box you found in Mary's fireplace for fingerprints. I'm guessing it will be bare as a baby's bum and turn out never to have held more than that one pinch of gunpowder."

"Then what was the point of putting it there?"

"Good question. The house was wide open all day yesterday, there were scads of people around, and you say Mary never went back to her room. Anybody or his uncle could have planted the box."

"Anybody who knew which room was Mary's, and

knew she was going to get blown up," Janet qualified. "You don't think she'd have been subtle enough to rig up a fairly obvious fake and put it there herself, just to cause trouble?"

"Don't ask me, love. With Mary's penchant for insulting people to their faces, I should think she'd have been more apt to plant the box on whomever she wanted most to spite."

"Namely her brother, I should think. Maybe she did, and he found it and put back in her room. More likely that box was Bob's idea of insuring the right verdict. He's the one who has most reason to want her death declared misadventure due to excess goofiness. Madoc, I can't swallow that argument of his about wanting to keep her alive on account of the annuity. According to Dai, Mary had a pretty hefty chunk in her savings account already, and you can darned well believe that if Dai managed to snoop into her handbag, so did Bob. He had nothing but Mary's word to go on that she'd be getting any more money from her mysterious benefactor, if there was one. In the meantime, she was acting more and more independent; she'd given him good reason to be afraid she might take off with her nice big nest egg and leave him to pay his own way for a change. As it stands now, he'll inherit as next of kin, won't he?"

"Assuming we don't get him for doing her. A murderer can't profit from his crime, of course. Or unless Mary made a will leaving her money to somebody else. I must say, I find hard to imagine Bob would let her though, after the way he handled her life insurance. What he did was common practice as far as it went; though of course he should have insured himself too. It would also have been customary for Bob and Mary, as partners, to have made wills leaving their shares of the business to each other."

"And it would have been Bob's practice to make sure Mary left him not only her share of the business but also everything else she owned," Janet agreed. "Gosh, I hope there's something in that handbag besides the emerald and the bankbooks; something you can pin him with."

"So do I, love, but it may not be that easy. There's still Dai's story about Mary's blackmailing somebody in connection with the alleged mugging murder of Arthur Ellis. That could explain where her money came from, but I can't see her working such a scam on her own brother. Can you?"

"No, but I can confuse the issue a little more. Did you know Iseult was in Marseilles the night Arthur Ellis was killed?"

"Good Lord, Jenny! How did you find out?"

"Your parents saw her. They'd made an overnight stop so they could meet Dafydd for dinner."

This was nothing remarkable; Dafydd, Gwen, and their parents were always snatching quick family visits in odd places. Nevertheless, Madoc was jarred. "Was Dafydd with them when they met her?"

"No, he'd gone off to the airport, he had a late flight to catch. It was raining buckets and they'd nothing else to do, so they'd dawdled on at the restaurant. They'd finally gone out looking for a cab when Iseult walked by. She was got up like a streetwalker and somebody near them made a rude remark, so they didn't go after her. You know your mother. They assumed she must have been performing somewhere and hadn't bothered to take off her makeup, which of course may have been true; but still—Madoc, you're not worried about Dafydd? You don't honestly think he'd—"

"How do I know what to think? Sorry, love, I didn't mean to snap at you. Is that all?"

"No. Iseult told me this morning that she'd never

been to Marseilles in her life. I mentioned it just now at Aunt Elen's, that's how the story came out. On top of that, your mother claims Iseult had had her eye on Arthur Ellis and was ticked-off when he married Lisa."

"Well, well. Thanks, Jenny."

"Don't mention it. If Dafydd's still at Lisa's, shall I chase him over here to lure Iseult off so that you can search her room? I expect she's still up there putting on her eyelashes, she's hoping Tom and Dafydd will take her someplace."

"Where?"

"She didn't specify. She may just be having the creeps about Mary, as who isn't."

"Why can't the boyfriend take her?"

"She claims he isn't."

"A likely story. All right, love, you nip along and enjoy your luncheon. I gather Dorothy's not invited?"

"Tib asked me specifically to bring her, but your father wouldn't let me. We'll be lucky if we get to take her home."

"Maybe we'd better have a few more, so Dorothy won't get worn out from a surfeit of relatives. Give Lisa my apologies and don't trip over a sheep on the way."

Madoc went into the house. Janet didn't feel guilty about not staying to help with the search; he'd have Alice and Danny the Boots and his mother, like as not, once she'd got Dorothy and Sir Emlyn settled. They all knew the manor far better than Janet did. She kept on through the gate and down the narrow road. She did meet several sheep, but they were amiably disposed, merely glancing up at her as she skirted around them, then getting back down to their grass-cropping.

Today's weather wasn't quite so perfect as yesterday's, but it was near enough as made no matter. She enjoyed her walk and was as charmed by the inside of

Lisa's house as she'd been two days ago by the outside. It was, as she'd rather thought it might be, about half-way between Anne Hathaway's cottage and Toad Hall: a fascinating jumble of family heirlooms, faded chintzes, Persian carpets, Oriental porcelains, oddments and whatnots from all over the globe, not to mention an extensive collection of tortoises in wood, clay, painted tin, brass, pottery, bone china, painted rocks, stuck-together shells, stuffed patchwork, and just about anything else except boiled macaroni.

"People keep sending them to me," Lisa half apologized, "and Arthur was always fetching home souvenirs from places he went. One doesn't like just to stuff them away."

"Of course not," said Janet. "Why should you? They're wonderful."

This could be the opening she'd hoped for. A cabinet-size photograph in a silver frame was sitting on top of a gilded grand piano with Watteauesque scenes painted around the sides that took up half the back parlor, if that was what they called it in Wales. Janet went over for a closer look, the photo showed a rather distinguished-appearing man between forty and fifty, she judged, beginning to gray at the temples. "Is this Arthur?"

"Yes," Lisa replied. "One doesn't want to stuff him away, either."

"I should hope not. Do you miss him terribly?"

"Not terribly, no. It's been eight years now, and Arthur was always away so much. But then he'd come back, you know; one does miss the coming back. We'd meet him at the station with the pony cart, Tib and I. We'd have brought hot tea or cold lemonade, depending on the weather, for him to drink on the way home. And cakes, of course. And we'd have a special meal waiting, and he'd have silly presents for Tib and nice ones for me. It was always Christmas when Arthur came home."

Lisa shrugged, a resigned little twitch of her shoulders. "Now it's just Tib and me and the tortoises."

"But your brother comes quite often, doesn't he?" Janet herself wouldn't have found Tom Feste any great consolation.

Apparently Lisa didn't, either. She answered rather sharply. "Tom's only my stepbrother. It was a second marriage for both Mother and his father, and we two came with the package. We got on well enough, mainly because Tom was usually away at school and I spent so much time here with my grandparents. I've always thought of this as my real home, I never wanted to be anywhere else. Anyway, yes, Tom does come fairly often; but one never knows when or if until the last minute. Dafydd at least phones in advance. Not that Dafydd stays here except when there's an overflow at Uncle Caradoc's, like now; but he's always sweet about taking Tib and me out for meals and things. Furthermore, he pays. You don't want to hear all this."

"Yes I do. Where are Tom and Dafydd now?"

"Tom's gone off to Billy the Grease. That ridiculous car of his is always needing something done to it, mainly because he's such a terrible driver. And it gulps up petrol faster than he gobbles money. Which reminds me, I must call Billy. Excuse me one second."

A fancy French telephone, all polished brass and mother-of-pearl, was standing among a group of tortoises, Lisa picked up the handset. Janet politely went over to look at a different group of tortoises, but she needn't have bothered. Lisa's call did in fact only take a second.

"Billy, when Tom asks for the usual, tell him no. That's right, no. Thanks, Billy. Never mind. Let him walk." She replaced the handset gently but firmly and returned to her guest.

"Sorry, Jenny. Dafydd's out singing to the tortoises."

"Singing to the tortoises?"

"Vocalizing. Doing his exercises. He has to, or his tonsils grow purple fuzz on them. You know, scales and trills and shrieks and whoofles. One can get rather tired of listening after a while, but the tortoises don't seem to mind. Dafydd says they're the perfect audience; they don't fidget, whisper, cough, or rattle their programs. He'll be in soon, leek pie's his favorite."

Janet was surprised. "Is it really? I'd have expected something more exotic. Beef Wellington at the very least."

"Heavens, no, Dafydd's as simple as they come. It's just that he keeps thinking he has to live up to his reputation. Come out to the kitchen, it's much nicer than the dining room on a day like this. You don't mind kitchens, do you?"

"Not a bit. My family's old farmhouse back in Pitcherville doesn't even have a dining room, and I can't say anybody's ever felt the lack of one. The only reason Madoc and I use ours in Fredericton is that our kitchen's rather poky. We're planning to remodel it if we can ever make up our minds what we want. Oh, Lisa, this is perfect."

It was. The low-ceilinged room with its dark slate floor could have been gloomy, but Lisa had distempered the walls in yellow and hung a Wordsworthian crowd of daffodil-patterned curtains at the many-paned bow window that looked out over the garden. Within the bow sat an oval table so right for the spot that it could have grown there. To have covered its lovingly polished top would have been a sin that Lisa had known better than to commit; marvelous old white-and-green Chelseaware dishes were set on mats just big enough to keep them from marring the wood.

Five place settings, Janet noticed; Lisa must be expecting Tom as well as Tib and Dafydd back to eat with them. Too bad, she'd hoped for something closer to a tête-à-tête. Sternly reminding herself that she hadn't been invited here to snoop, she sat down on one of the curve-backed wooden chairs that hadn't been made to go with the table but naturally did, and accepted a minuscule glass of sherry with a slight qualm.

"Thank you, Lisa, though I'm not sure I ought to have any. I'm still nursing Dorothy, when my in-laws give me the chance."

"That's barely a smidgen, it can't hurt. Arthur bought me these absurd midgets when I was carrying Tib, so that I could make believe drink with the rest and not feel conspicuous. But you may have something else if you'd rather. I can't think what, offhand. I've got to gather my wits about me and go shopping this afternoon—we're down to the nubbins."

"This will do fine. These really are doll-size, aren't they? Pretty, though. If they weren't such good quality, you might use them for hummingbird feeders."

The lead-crystal goblet, shaped like a miniature lily, was astonishingly thick for its size. Lisa was right, it couldn't hold more than a teaspoonful or so. Janet sipped a drop at a time, thinking what a considerate husband Arthur must have been. She was about to say so when Dafydd came in from the garden.

Dafydd had his charm turned off. His hair was mussed, there were lines in his face Janet couldn't recall having noticed before. A middle-aged man and a tired one, wearing the same sort of baggy slacks and pullover that Madoc might put on to slouch around the farm with Bert and Sam Neddick. She said "Hello, Dafydd." He said "Hi, Jenny," and turned to Lisa.

"Did you speak to Billy?"

"Yes, I did."

"Good. Shall I do the salad?"

"It's done. Mix the dressing if you like. Have you seen Tib?"

"She'll be in. She was just getting Mollie unsaddled."

"We'll give her a few minutes, then. Sherry?"

"Sit still, I'll get it."

It was all so commonplace, so like the trivia Janet would exchange with Madoc, or Bert with Annabelle. Dafydd was puttering with oil and vinegar, knowing where the spoons were kept, dabbing a bit of his mixture on a leaf of lettuce for Lisa to taste, watching her nibble and nod with the sort of expression on his face that outsiders should never be allowed to see. Janet felt a stab of acute embarrassment. Good Lord, she thought, so this is what's ailing him. He's in love with her.

Chapter 19

Well, here was a pretty mess. How the heck was the hare supposed to live happily ever after with the tortoise? Dafydd would keep on rocketing around from hither to yon and back again, with Lisa wanting only to dig in her heels here and stay put. Did Arthur Ellis's widow even know what was happening? More to the point, did she want to know?

Tib came in about then, to Janet's relief, smelling like a horse but clean enough as to hands and face; she must have washed under the stable pump. Lisa got the leek pie out of the warming oven, Tib cut the loaf, Dafydd set the salad where everybody could get at it. This was the way things happened back at the farm, or at Janet's own table when she wasn't having to put on the dog for some big bug from Ottawa. Too bad Madoc and Dorothy couldn't be here; this was the coziest meal she'd sat down to so far in Wales. Not that she hadn't enjoyed the others, but it was pleasant to be with a few instead of a multitude for a change.

Dafydd cut and served the leek pie with careful impartiality. Its undercrust had got a trifle soggy by now, as undercrusts will. Lisa apologized, but Janet said the pie tasted fine anyway and anybody who objected to soggy undercrust didn't have to eat it; so everybody did and liked it fine. Dafydd and Tib both had seconds, leaving none for Tom assuming he showed up.

"Let him stop at the pub and spend his own money for a change," Dafydd said callously, scooping out the last of the salad and putting it on Lisa's plate. "Want to go out somewhere again tonight, just us? And Madoc and Jenny, if they'd like to come? You can park the kid with Mother, can't you, Jenny?"

"It would be fun, Dafydd, but I don't know. They've had her all day, and there's no telling when Madoc will be free. That idiot of a chief constable isn't lifting a finger. Constable Cyril seems to be a good man and nobody's fool, but I don't suppose he's ever had to cope with anything worse than dogs killing sheep, which of course is bad enough. Let's talk about something else for a change. How did you get started on tortoises, Lisa? And when are you going to show me some of your books? I've never seen one."

"Show her *Tessie Goes to the Opera*," Dafydd coaxed. "No, Lisa; sit still, I'll get it.

"I was technical editor on that one," he explained when he came back with the book; he made sure Janet noticed the dedication. *To Dafydd, with thanks.* Very nice.

The drawings were adorable. Tessie the Tortoise made a smashing Brunhilde, though Janet herself inclined more toward *Wild-West Tessie*, in which the hardshelled heroine became a deputy sheriff and rounded up a bloodthirsty gang of corn-rustling weasels on her trusty tricycle. They'd finished their strawberries and cream and were sitting around the table, drinking their tea and thinking up insane new adventures for Tessie and her klutzy boyfriend, when Tom burst in, footsore and furious.

"Lisa! What the hell's got into you, telling Billy not to work on my car?"

Lisa had no doubt expected the onslaught; she was perfectly calm. "I didn't tell Billy not to work on your car. I merely told him not to charge the work to me."

"Why not, for God's sake? He always has before."

"I'm all too well aware of that, Tom. And you've always told me you'd settle with me later."

"And I always have, haven't I?"

"No, Tom, you have not. Never. Not once. No more than you've ever paid back one penny of all the hundreds and hundreds of pounds you've been wheedling out of me on one pretext or another since Arthur died. I've let you get away with far too much because I hate it when you go into one of your tantrums, as you well know. But what I hate worse is pouring good money into leaky barrels, and that's what you are, Tom. You think you can throw it away on any bit of nonsense that takes your fancy, and little stepsister will be fool enough to give you some more; but I'm finished, Tom. You've tried me once too often. Feel free to make a scene if you like, it won't bother me a bit. Jenny, you won't mind if Tom has a tantrum, will you?"

"Not at all. Canadians tend to be on the reserved side, generally speaking, so I don't get to hear much really inspired cussing and yelling. This is going to be a real treat."

Janet touched her napkin to her lips, laid it decorously beside her plate, and sat up straight with her hands folded in her lap, like a good little girl at a Sunday School concert. "Go ahead, Tom. Let 'er rip."

"Let what rip?" The voice, and the body that followed it, were Iseult's. "May I join the party? I've been wondering where everyone had got to."

"Sit down, Iseult," said Dafydd. "You're interrupting Tom's tantrum."

"Oh, is he having one? What's it about this time?"

"He's upset about his car," Lisa told her somewhat curtly. "There's nothing left to eat but bread and butter. Would you like a cup of tea?"

"Never mind the refreshments, let's get on with the show. What's wrong with the Daimler, Tom?"

"You wouldn't be interested," he snarled.

"Nonsense, I'm passionately interested. I was hoping to cadge a ride."

"Sorry to disappoint you, then. It's down at Billy the Grease with its brakes hanging loose."

"Oh, bother! Can't Billy tighten them?"

"That was the objective one had in mind. Unfortunately my helpful stepsister has put him off doing the work."

"But it's your car. How could she?"

"Quite simply," snapped Lisa, "by telling Billy I'm not going to pay the bill. If Tom wants his precious car fixed, he'll have to bite the bullet and spend his own money for a change. Go ahead, Tom. Let 'er rip."

"Lisa, don't be such a beast. Quit baiting the poor fellow." Iseult wasn't about to give up her outing that easily. "We could pass round the hat, I suppose. On the other hand, you're not going anywhere, are you? You never do. You might be kind enough to lend us your car."

"She's not going to lend anything," said Dafydd. "Drop it, Iseult."

"Well, get you! When did you begin singing Parsifal, Dafydd? One's always thought Don Giovanni was more your thing."

"Very funny, Iseult. In point of fact, Don Giovanni's

not a tenor role. Reports of my alleged gallantries have been grossly overstated. Moreover, I'm fully aware which two of my so-called friends have generated most of the overstating. Don't you two think your little joke is wearing a trifle thin?"

"No, indeed, we don't think so at all. Do we, Tom?"

"Far from it." Tom was grinning now like the wolf in Grandma's bed. "We've barely scratched the surface. Let's talk to Reuel, Iseult; we might get him to write a nice, steamy *roman à clef* with a handsome Welsh opera star for its key figure. He can have a little list, like the Don." Tom began to sing, wretchedly off-key, with operatic flourishes. " *'In Italia seicento e quaranta, in Alemagna duecento e trent'una, Cento in Francia, in Turchia novant'una, Ma, in Ispagna son già mille e tre!'* And that doesn't count the—"

"Oh, stop it!" cried Lisa. "Go take a walk or something, I don't want to see you around here. And you needn't come back to supper, because there's not going to be any."

"Yes, stepsister dear. I shall expect to find my jammies and teddy bear out on the front steps when I return. Or shall I take them with me now?"

"That would be nice."

Janet would have been all for getting rid of Tom too, but she thought she'd better intervene. "Just don't leave the village, Tom."

Naturally Tom put the wrong twist on her words. "Jenny darling, can't you bear to part with me? I didn't know you cared."

"I don't, but the chief constable does, or darned well ought to. The cause of Mary's death hasn't yet been established. Until it is, we're all having to be detained as possible suspects."

"My God! Jenny, you're not serious?"

"I don't tell bad jokes about murder, Tom. If you don't believe me, ask Madoc."

Oh good Lord, what had she done? Lisa's face was white as chalk. Dafydd snatched her close to him, he was glaring at Janet as if he'd like to commit murder himself.

"Damn you, Jenny! Can't you shut up? Lisa, Lisa darling, it's all right. She didn't mean—"

To sink through the floor would hardly be practical. What could Janet do but apologize? "Lisa, I'm sorry. I should have known better."

"It's all right, Jenny." Lisa was pressing herself against Dafydd's chest, wedging her head under his chin, grasping his wrists, making sure he wouldn't let go of her. "You weren't here when Arthur was killed, you can't know what it was like. The worst of it was we never found out who did it. The French police are still convinced I hired an assassin. Jenny, we've got to find out this time, no matter what happens. Get Madoc. I have to make him understand. Now, Jenny. Please!"

"Of course, Lisa. I'll be back as soon as I find him."

Janet walked fast. It would have been quicker to telephone the manor, but she needed a chance to talk with him before he had to face his brother. What in God's name was she to say?

What could she say? Tell the truth and shame the devil, what else was there? She wouldn't have to mention what conclusions a person might draw. Madoc would be a jump ahead of her, he was too much a professional to shut his ears to what he'd rather not hear.

He must have spied her through one of the bedroom windows, he was swarming down the ivy. She stopped halfway up the drive and waited for him.

"Jenny, what's up? I thought you were lunching at Lisa's."

"She sent me to get you and I think you'd better come. Madoc, we have to talk."

"If you say so, love. What about?"

She swallowed. "It's about Dafydd. Remember I told you he'd been in Marseilles on the night Arthur Ellis was murdered?

"Yes, and so what? Arthur was robbed, as I understand it. Jenny, you don't think Dafydd would kill somebody just to get his hands on a few bits of colored stone?"

How can you tell what he wouldn't do? Janet thought. You've said yourself you don't even know him. All she could say was, "It wouldn't have been about colored stones."

"What, then?"

"Lisa. He's in love with her."

Madoc actually laughed. "My brother? With Lisa? Little brown Lisa with her head tucked underneath her shell? Jenny, are you serious?"

"I'm not one to tell sick jokes, Madoc, you ought to know that. It sticks out a mile, and it's not something that's happened all of a sudden. He was showing me one of her Tessie books, that he'd helped her write. It was dedicated to him, and copyrighted nine years ago. I know because I looked."

"That doesn't necessarily mean—but then why hasn't he—oh hell!"

"My feelings exactly. I grant you it doesn't sound very plausible, considering Dafydd's reputation, but don't you think it might explain why he's been acting so strangely ever since we got here? Either he's eaten up with remorse over having murdered her husband and hasn't been able to bring himself to cash in on his perfidy, which would be a fine operatic reason why he hasn't popped the question, or—" Janet shrugged. "Or else he fell in love with her by accident and can't bear the thought of settling down into a faithful husband instead of a round-the-world Romeo. That's the best I can do, Madoc. Take your pick or think up a better one."

"The second, for choice. But it needn't be Dafydd, Jenny. We do know from what Dai told us that Mary's death may well have something to do with what happened to Lisa's husband. How did this get started anyway?"

"She had a fight with Tom. Evidently he's been hitting her up for money ever since Arthur died, and never paying it back. This morning he'd taken his car to Billy's garage—I suppose you know where that is."

"Just beyond the village. What's the matter with it? It seemed to be running fine the other day."

"Don't ask me. Anyway, when I got there, Lisa was on the phone telling Billy not to let Tom charge the work to her account, as he'd always been in the habit of doing. A while later, Tom came storming into the house, mad as a wet hornet. He started to bully her and she told him where to get off—Dafydd had given her a pep talk about standing up for her rights. So they all three got into a hair-tangle, and Tom decided to pack up and leave. I thought I'd better tell him he couldn't go far because we're all caught up in a murder investigation, and Lisa flipped. That's when she begged me to get you over there."

"Do you think Lisa knows what Mary'd been up to?"

"The blackmailing? She didn't say so, but she did say there'd been bad blood between Mary and Arthur for years. She may think there's a connection between the two murders, or it may simply be that she can't bear the thought of another one going unsolved after all she's gone through since the first one. Whatever it is, she's horribly upset and I do wish you'd come with me right this second."

"Of course, love. Hop aboard."

Janet had been too agitated to notice the bicycle Cyril Rhys had left standing at the foot of the drive, no doubt to save himself the labor of pedaling up. Madoc hoisted her up on the seat, swung his leg over the crossbar, and started to pedal for all he was worth.

This wasn't the pleasantest ride Janet had ever experienced; she clutched desperately at Madoc's belt, struggling to keep her behind on the saddle and her feet out of the spokes. She was no end relieved to find herself still in one piece when Madoc pulled up at Lisa's side door. Tib ran to meet them, with a tortoise in each hand.

"Aunt Jenny, I'm so glad you've come back! Mother's dreadfully upset. I thought I'd better take Tessie and Jonathan in to cheer her up."

"What happened to the others?"

"Iseult and Uncle Tom have gone off to the pub. Uncle Dafydd's with Mother. He just keeps hugging her and patting her back and saying it's all right, when anyone with half an eye can see it's not. Men are so helpless, don't you think, Aunt Jenny? Oh, Uncle Madoc, I'm sorry. That wasn't awfully tactful of me was it? Now that you're here, shall I take the tortoises back to the garden?"

"I think we can manage without them," Madoc assured her. "And would you mind doing me a very big favor? You see, I've borrowed the constable's bike, and I'm afraid I didn't stop to ask his permission. Could you possibly sneak it back to Uncle Caradoc's and park it down by the gate before he finds out it's gone and comes to pinch me?"

Tib grinned. "You're making me an accessory after the fact, you know."

"If I get you in trouble, I'll bail you out. Scout's honor. Oh, and you might find my parents and tell them where we've gone. Tell them I said you could hold Dorothy."

"Good show!"

She ran back down the garden path, waving goodbye with Tessie or Jonathan, as the case might have been. Madoc said, "Nice kid," and held the door for Janet.

Lisa was sitting in one of the yellow-painted chairs. Dafydd had pulled another chair close to hers, he was holding a tot glass to her lips.

"Come on, love, take a sip. That's my girl, now another."

Lisa obeyed, then turned her head away. "Ugh! Hateful stuff. No more, please, Dafydd, I'd be sick. You finish it for me. Jenny, is there any tea left in the pot?"

Trust a man not to think of the obvious. Janet lifted the lid. Down to the tea leaves, but the kettle was simmering on the Aga. She did what she could.

"There you are, Lisa, a bit weak but better than nothing. I'm putting in extra sugar, you need it. Dafydd, you'd better steady the cup for her."

Might as well give him a legitimate excuse to keep his arm around her, poor devil. Janet felt sick herself. God alone knew what Madoc must be feeling. His own brother, what a mess!

At least a little color was creeping into Lisa's face. "I'm sorry to be such a nuisance, you people must think I've gone batty. I'd thought I was over that ghastly time about Arthur, but—" She'd begun to shake again. "Oh God, is it never going to be over?"

Chapter 20

Janet grabbed for the teacup. Lisa's face was wholly buried in Dafydd's pullover, she was sobbing without any attempt at restraint. Dafydd had both arms tight around her, rocking her back and forth like a father with a colicky child. It was agony to watch, Janet turned her head away. Madoc was the only one of the four who stayed calm.

"Lisa, you sent Janet for me because you wanted to tell me something. What is it you want to say?"

"For God's sake, Madoc!" Dafydd was furious, mainly at his own helplessness, as was only natural. "Let her alone, can't you?"

"No, Dafydd." Lisa was making a truly heroic effort to pull herself together, struggling loose enough from Dafydd's grasp to grope a yellow napkin off the so prettily laid table, mopping at her wet, swollen face. "We have to tell him. We can't go on the way we've been, just never—I can't stand it! Madoc, why was Mary killed last night?"

"I don't yet know, Lisa. I think it's very doubtful that she committed suicide. If you're asking whether her death might have had something to do with your husband's, it's quite possible the answer may turn out to be yes. Dafydd, you and I need to talk, we may as well get on with it. Could we go somewhere by ourselves?"

"No!" Lisa took a firmer grip on the much-tried pullover. "Whatever it is, I have to know. More likely than not, I already do know. Go ahead, Dafydd, tell him."

"Yes, Lisa."

Dafydd was looking at Madoc as though he'd never really seen him before. This was no younger brother. This was a man used to authority, somebody in charge, somebody competent, God willing, to do what must be done. "What do you want of me, Madoc?"

"First, I need to know whether you've paid any blackmail during the past eight years."

"What? My God, that's one I didn't expect. No, of course I haven't. I've never in my life paid one pennyworth of blackmail to anybody, for any reason. Nor have I ever been approached to do so. Does that answer your question?"

"Yes, Dafydd, quite satisfactorily. Thank you."

"But why did you ask?" Lisa demanded. "Had it something to do with Arthur?"

"There's reason to believe it has a great deal to do with Arthur. According to information received a short while ago"—since he'd been shoved into performing as a policeman, Madoc decided he might as well talk like one—"about six months after Arthur Ellis was found dead, Mary Rhys began receiving substantial sums of money on a fairly regular basis, which she gave her brother to understand were some sort of annuity. Were you aware of that, Lisa?"

"No, not at all. But the money can't have come from Arthur. It certainly wasn't in his will, he'd left everything to Tib and me. You're not trying to say he'd established some kind of trust fund for Mary before he died? Why should he have done that? It's not as though she'd have been in dire poverty if he weren't around to give her work. Her father had left her and Bob amply provided for, she had other clients, and goodness knows she charged enough. Arthur used to be livid over the bills she sent. Bob sent, I should say."

Lisa was talking too fast, working herself up again, but Madoc didn't try to soothe her down. "He kept on using her services, though."

"Only because of the old family tie, and the promise he'd made to his own father. Arthur didn't even like Mary, he practically foamed at the mouth every time he had to meet with her. I know, Madoc, you're thinking he might have had something going behind my back, but Arthur had no talent for subterfuge. His mind simply didn't work that way. He was totally honest and totally decent. He didn't drink to excess, he didn't gamble. He didn't chase after other women. It was so unspeakably wrong, the way he died! He'd have loathed being found stretched out behind a—ugh! When I think of those ghastly French *flics*, insinuating that he'd been—"

"Steady, Lisa." Dafydd was minding this even worse than she. "Madoc, do you have to go on at her like this?"

"No, Dafydd, it's back to you. I understand you'd had dinner with the parents in Marseilles that same night Arthur was killed. Is that correct?"

"It is. How the hell did you know?"

"Mother happened to mention it to Jenny, and she told me. You were all in transit, she said, so it wasn't exactly a spur-of-the moment thing, was it?"

"Lord, no! We'd had to arrange it months in advance, one always does. Normally I shouldn't have been routed through Marseilles, this required some unusual ticketing. The chap in charge of bookings was quite shirty about it, as I recall."

"Did you know Arthur Ellis was also going to be in Marseilles that night?"

"How could he?" Lisa broke in. "Arthur's plans were always flexible, they had to be. He might fly to Paris, and phone me the next night from Rome or Amsterdam. Anyway, he and Dafydd weren't—they didn't know each other all that well."

"Thank you, Lisa." Dafydd's face had become a handsome chiseled mask, his beautiful voice totally unmodulated. "To answer your question, Madoc, I did not know Arthur was in Marseilles, and shouldn't have tried to meet him if I had. My sole object was to see the parents, since I hadn't had the chance for quite some time and shouldn't have again for another three months or so. I'd been singing at Melbourne and had to be in Munich for rehearsals the following day. The weather was foul, my plane was late landing, I had the hell of a time getting a cab. I got to their hotel just as Mother was about to call the morgue, we had a drink and chatted a bit, then went to dinner at some new restaurant somebody'd told them about. I forget the name. Mother might know, if it matters. I then went on to Munich by train, got to my hotel late the following afternoon, and phoned Gwen at her flat in London."

"You couldn't be a bit more precise as to the time?"

"Oh, probably half-past five or thereabouts. You might check it out with the Schwanallee Hotel. They may still have their records from eight years ago. Germans are so methodical, you know."

"All right, Dafydd. What did you call Gwen about?"

"Well, naturally I wanted to tell her about meeting the parents. We always try to keep in touch as best we can, you know that. I assumed she'd be playing that night, which she was, as it happened, and I wanted to catch her before she left the flat. She was still there, rather

228

upset. She'd learned that same afternoon about Arthur's being found dead in Marseilles and wondered if I knew any of the details. I didn't, of course."

"She didn't know what he'd died from?"

"No, I believe we decided it must have been a heart attack. He was getting toward that age, you see, and on the chunky side. It was rather a hurried conversation, I was supposed to be meeting with the Munich people and she had to get dressed. I asked about flowers and things and she said never mind. She'd called Uncle Huw to make sure it was in fact the right Arthur and asked him to order flowers from the family. She'd sent Lisa a telegram and would go to the funeral if she could get time off. I told her where to reach the parents, sent Lisa a cablegram of my own, and dashed off to my meeting, for which I was by then shockingly late, to the unconcealed annoyance of my hosts."

Madoc wasn't through yet. "You say you went to Munich by train. Mother seems to have had the impression you were going to fly."

"I'd had every intention of flying. My bags were checked straight through, and I'd gone from the restaurant directly to the airport. As I mentioned earlier, however, it was an utterly filthy night. After I'd hung around awhile, it became clear that nothing was going out. I waited a little longer hoping matters would improve, but they didn't; so I more or less swam to the railroad station and caught the midnight train to Geneva by the skin of my teeth. I shared a compartment with a carpet salesman from Namur who regaled me into the small hours with what I gathered were funny stories in either Flemish or Walloon, neither of which I either speak or understand. From Geneva, I caught the nine o'clock to Munich and arrived there at four fifty-eight pip emma, *um punkt*. I dimly recall the carpet salesman's having given me a card, but I'm afraid I didn't keep it. Sorry, Madoc."

Janet supposed she oughtn't to blame Dafydd for being resentful, though he couldn't possibly suppose Madoc was doing this for fun. A person had to admire him for the dogged way he was sticking to the job.

"So you talked with Gwen, and that was the last you heard about Arthur Ellis?"

"*Au contraire, mon vieux.* I had rehearsals the following day, rather taxing ones that I wasn't really up for, all things considered. When I got back to the hotel, looking forward to an early dinner and a badly needed night's sleep, I was greeted by a chap from the Sûreté named Javert, of all things. He was interested to learn why I'd shown the execrable taste to assassinate in so unrefined a manner the husband of my *bonne amie.*"

"Good Lord! Whatever got him on to that?"

"After a good deal of shouting back and forth, I gathered that he was acting on information received. Some anonymous benefactor had rung the station and given the *flics* an earful about Lisa and me being lovers."

Madoc gritted his teeth. "Was there any truth in the allegation?"

"You do have a rotten job, don't you? Yes, but not enough. Lisa and I—" Dafydd shook his head. "We'd been kids together, she and I and Tom. And occasionally Iseult, during school holidays. Having Iseult around was no great treat, she was older and something of a pain. I suppose I'm a cad for saying so, but there it was. Anyway, it was always clear to me that one day Lisa and I would marry. Unfortunately I messed up."

There was just so much a brother could ask. Madoc waited. At last Dafydd went on in that dead-and-alive monotone. "As you know, I had the dubious good fortune to become an overnight success at too early an age." A momentary flicker of amusement broke the rigidity. "I wasn't quite twenty-one. I'd begun doing shepherd boys and voices off, serving my apprenticeship, getting the feel of the stage. This time, I was one of Sarastro's priests in *The Magic Flute*, and just for the experience, they'd given me Tamino to understudy. Around noontime of the final performance, the lead tenor ordered kippers for breakfast and got a fishbone stuck in his throat. It wasn't so bad, I had time enough to get the costume altered, find a pair of tights that fit me, and alert the family. Even you showed up, Madoc. You probably don't remember."

"Yes, I do. You galloped on yelling that a serpent was after you, then three old ladies in nightgowns came along and killed it."

"You would remember that part. I suppose you were disgusted at my being such a coward."

"No, I assumed that was what you were getting paid for. I did think those baby-blue tights were a bit much."

"So did I, if you want to know, but I was prepared to make sacrifices. What I hadn't counted on was the celebrity thing: the interviews, the parties, too much attention from the wrong people. I"—Dafydd shrugged—"rather lost sight of my priorities. And Lisa took umbrage."

"Why shouldn't I have?" Lisa was in command of herself by now, just barely. "My father was a celebrity of sorts too, Jenny. He wrote those full-blooded novels, you know what I mean, and was always chasing after some new inspiration. Usually a pretty young female one, judging from the fights he and my mother used to have. They split up when I was eight. He went off to America, and that's the last I ever saw of him. Mother married again in a year or so, a City man. I hated London and wasn't too fond of my stepfather, so I stayed here with my grandparents as much as I could. It's not that I didn't care for Dafydd, I always had. But people gossiped, and Tom was always sending me clippings out of the nastier papers. I didn't want the sort of mess my mother'd got into. I wanted someone who'd stay put."

"So you married a chap who was at home about five days a month." And Dafydd was still bitter about it.

"But it wasn't the same," Lisa protested, as Janet suspected she'd done before. "Arthur was older and steadier, and not the sort one would have had to live up to. What sort of wife would I be for a celebrity?"

"That's a hell of a thing to say! You're a celebrity yourself, for God's sake, or could be if you weren't always hiding under your shell. What about those film people who've been hounding you to let them do a cartoon series about Tessie?"

"Yes, and having her run over weasels with army tanks and blow them up with exploding meat pies. You know why I fell apart at Uncle Caradoc's, Dafydd? That beastly Reuel was giving me this jolly scenario about Tessie murdering a whole gang of armadillos in various gruesome ways. I will not have my tortoise turned into a monster! It's bad enough being thought one myself."

"Darling, dearest angel fathead, I've told you over and over again, it's not you. I'm the villain in this production."

"And I'm the witch who's supposedly put you up to killing her husband. Dafydd, we've been through this again and again. It's not just you Javert's out to get, it's both of us."

"Javert?" said Madoc. "You mean the Sûreté's still on your trail?"

"Oh yes," Dafydd replied wearily. "He pops up every so often, twirling his big mustache and wondering when I'm going to crack. His great ambition is to send me to the guillotine. Offing an opera singer for a *crime passionel* would be his passport to fame, fortune, and promotion, one gathers."

"He comes after me now and then too," said Lisa. "Trying to get me to admit that Arthur was cruel or unfaithful or impotent, even that Tib is Dafydd's child. You can't imagine what that beast has put us through, just because some vicious, spiteful, lying—"

Dafydd covered her writhing hands with his own. "So far, Madoc, Javert's accomplished one thing. He's made it impossible for Lisa and me ever to have any sort of life together."

His lips twisted, not into a smile. "Sounds silly coming from me, don't you think? Early on, I'd thought all those pretty women were just a perk of the position. When Lisa married Arthur, I realized how abysmally wrong I'd been, but it was too late. I was stuck playing the Duke of Mantua, I decided there was nothing left but to relax and enjoy it. After all, it's an old operatic tradition: Caruso, Scotti, all that. And one does get damnably lonesome sometimes. But it palls. God, how it palls! And I still have to keep going through the motions on account of some perverted practical joker and a French *flic* who wants his name in the papers. If I quit playing the field, Javert will have an excuse to start spouting off that it's because of Lisa, and she'll be put through the mill again. God, I'm so sick of acting the role of a buck rabbit! Madoc, is there nothing we can do?"

"Well," said Janet, "I suppose we could boil up another kettle."

They needed the laugh, any excuse would have done. "Why not?" said Lisa. "We can have some of Dafydd's ginger biscuits for dessert, he always brings me a packet."

Lisa wasn't yet ready to separate herself from Dafydd. She was combing his hair with her fingers, fussing with the crumpled shirt collar that showed above the neck of his pullover. "Can you remember where you put them, Enrico?"

"You're funny, aren't you." Sharing the load must have done him some good; this time the smile, though not wide, was genuine. "Of course I can. You know I've a memory like an elephant."

He probably did, Janet thought, he'd need one to retain every word and note in his large repertoire. There'd also be the stage business: when to come on, when to go off, when to stand or sit or charge around being heroic or cowardly as the case might be. Not to mention keeping track of what city he was in at any given moment, where he must go next, and when, and how, and with whom. Poor Dafydd! She'd been rotten to misjudge him so totally.

Assuming that tale about the relentless Javert was not another grand-opera libretto. Please, God, Janet prayed, let it be the truth, and let Mary Rhys's ghastly death be linked with that of Arthur Ellis, and let the guilty be found and this eight-year nightmare brought to an end.

At least one step had been taken. Thank heaven Lisa'd had that fight with her stepbrother, and that Tom and Iseult had gone off to the pub. Dafydd would never have opened up in front of them. Now if they'd only stay where they were!

Lisa had washed her face at the sink and scrubbed it dry on a yellow-checkered tea towel; now she was putting biscuits on a plate, calmly and deliberately. "Just as well Tib isn't here, these would be gone in a minute. I wonder where she got to?"

"I sent her up to the farm on an errand for me,"

Madoc explained. "She's likely joined the hunt, which reminds me that I'd better find out whether they've had any luck. May I use your phone, Lisa?"

"Of course. Go straight on through to the front, it's on a little stand next to the fern. I keep meaning to have another put in the kitchen, but I never do. What are they hunting for, Jenny?"

"Mary's handbag. She had it hanging at her waist all day yesterday, as you may remember, but she took it off later and nobody knows where it's got to."

"Does it matter?"

"It could. Her nephew claims that she'd stolen the big emerald out of Uncle Caradoc's crosier and left a lump of green glass in its place. Dai says Mary kept valuables in her handbag because her brother was in the habit of searching her room, which I must say I wouldn't put past him. So Madoc has Constable Cyril and Owain's lot out combing the grounds."

"That's better than having them huddled in corners whispering about Mary's getting blown to bits, I suppose." Lisa sighed. "It's so hard to know if one's doing the right thing."

"I'm sure you are," said Janet. "Tib strikes me as a pretty sane youngster. I wonder how Madoc's making out in there."

Chapter 21

"Not too badly," Madoc told them a few minutes later. "They've found Mary's collapsible ladder and her belt. At least Mavis claims it's the belt Mary had on yesterday, and she's probably right. She says Uncle Huw's mobilized the lot of them, including the sheepdogs. He's taken charge of the hunt and they're all going at it like beagles, so I've sent Cyril on a different errand. That girl Patricia, Dafydd, can you tell me any more about her?"

"Not really. Let's see, I'd come the day before you, rather late. Lisa and Tib picked me up at the train, we had dinner at the pub and spent a jolly evening chopping leeks."

"Liar," said Lisa fondly. "You conked out in front of the telly five minutes after we'd got home. We practically had to carry you upstairs. Tom blew in the next day just as I was dishing up a very late luncheon—his sense of timing is infallible when it comes to free food. Patricia was with him, I don't think he ever mentioned her last name. They'd stopped at the manor and he'd shown her around the grounds, but they hadn't gone in to see Uncle Caradoc. I made a rather pointed remark about not having an extra bed unless Tom cared to sleep up next to the cistern, which I knew he wouldn't, but he said it didn't matter. Patricia wouldn't be staying, she'd just come to see the sheep. I could believe it, she didn't talk about anything else all through the meal."

"Nor did she let anybody else get a word in," said Dafydd. "If she made one sensible remark, I didn't hear it. Then Mother phoned down from the manor to remind me about picking you up, which I was only too glad to do. I'm meant to borrow Lisa's car, but Tom said why didn't I take the Daimler instead. It's not often he makes a spontaneous gesture of generosity, so I snapped him up on it. Then Patricia suggested we all go and give you a great big welcome, all banging on kettles and cheering our heads off."

"And scaring Dorothy into fits?" Janet was not amused.

"The thought did cross my mind," said Dafydd. "Anyway, Tom wanted a nap and Lisa said she'd things to do and no kettles to spare, so I wound up stuck with Patricia. She babbled freely all the way to the station, but didn't actually say much. I gathered the vague impression that she's an actress of sorts, but that may have been because Tom's women generally are. This isn't helping, I don't suppose."

"Not much. What happened after you'd dropped us off?"

"Which was rude of me, but I couldn't see turning that talking machine loose on the family. You know what it's like to be trapped with someone who has nothing to say and insists on saying it anyway. I could see you all being painfully polite, dying to get down to the family gossip while some total stranger burbled on and on about nothing at all. My thought was to take Patricia back and dump her on Tom, but she wasn't having any. She insisted on stopping at the pub to play darts. That wasn't so bad, in fact she was surprisingly good. Better than I, to be brutally frank— she took fifty pence off me. So I paid up and bought her one for the road and said I expected she'd want to be off to wherever she was going. She said Swansea, I said the train service was excellent, and drove her to the station."

"Did you go in with her?" Madoc asked him.

"I did not. Why should I?"

"To carry her bags and buy her ticket?"

"She had no bags, just a carryall thing which she managed quite capably by herself. And I'd already bought her two pints of bitter and a sausage roll, mainly in the vain hope of stopping her mouth for a while. I'd have been willing to open the car door for her, but she bounced out before I could get to it. So I tooted a mildly enthusiastic farewell and came on home."

"The Daimler was running all right, was it?"

"Like a breeze. I can't think why Tom had to take it to Billy. He's an abominable driver, of course. Oh, God! Here they come back, and that ass Williams with them. Got any boiling oil handy, Lisa?"

"Don't kill them yet," said Madoc. "We have to talk."

It was too late anyway, they were in the kitchen, all three fairly well sauced. Iseult gave Williams a roguish shove forward.

"Look what we found. Can we keep him?"

"So long as you don't expect me to feed him," Lisa told her. "There's tea and precious little else. Sit down, Madoc wants to talk to you."

"Oh goody! We're going to be grilled by a real, live Mountie."

"No we're not," said Tom. "You're only the law in Canada, right, Madoc?"

"Wrong, Tom. I've been given temporary constabulary status by the local magistrate."

"Who happens to be your uncle."

"Exactly. And who's given me sufficient authority to run you in on suspicion if you don't cooperate."

"Suspicion of what, for God's sake?"

"Murdering Mary Rhys by putting gunpowder in her pockets before she leaped the balefire."

"What? That's crazy!"

"Oh yes, but it's what happened. We've had a report from the county coroner."

"But why?" demanded Iseult. "I grant you Mary was a bore and a nuisance, but that frowsy little mouse? Why should anybody have wanted to kill her?"

Madoc glanced at Janet and shrugged. He saw no sense in holding back, not with half the family already in the picture. They might as well have it straight from him instead of garbled via the grapevine.

"What it seems to boil down to is that Mary knew how and why Arthur Ellis was murdered in Marseilles eight years ago and was systematically blackmailing the person who killed him. We're working on the hypothesis that the killer got tired of paying."

"Bloody hell! Who'd have thought the old trout had it in her?"

Tom's voice held more than a hint of admiration, Janet thought. She wasn't surprised.

"I'm amazed you didn't think of that yourself, Tom," drawled Iseult.

"Oh, I did. My problem was that I didn't know whom to put the bite on. Sorry, Lisa, I'm being despicable again. But who could have imagined it? Mary was always such a soggy doormat for that disgusting brother of hers. 'Yes, brother dear. Whatever you say, brother dear. Hit me again, brother dear.' Ugh! I can see Bob as a blackmailer far more easily than I can Mary. Are you sure she wasn't just fronting for him, Madoc? He could be laying it on her to shield himself, couldn't he?"

"Evidence of the blackmailing didn't come from Bob, Tom. He maintains he knew nothing of what his sister was up to."

"And you believe him?"

"I'm willing to entertain the possibility, because he's so bloody-minded about money. I don't think Bob would have cared a pennyworth how Mary got it, what infuriated him was that she wouldn't give him the handling of it. Bob had always kept total control of the family cash, despite the fact that Mary was the sole breadwinner. According to Dai, he wouldn't even let her buy a pair of slippers unless he went along and picked them out. Since she started getting this mysterious independent income, she'd become increasingly inclined to flout his authority, to the point where she was threatening to clear out and leave him to live on what he'd already grabbed."

"Which would have made excellent sense," said Iseult. "But if Mary didn't start getting paid off until after Arthur was offed, and Bob wouldn't give her a bean to travel with, she could hardly have been at the scene of the crime, could she? So then how did she know whom to blackmail?"

"That's a good question, to which Bob has provided a plausible answer. As a gem-cutter, Mary actually does seem to have had a certain reputation. She was asked occasionally to take on special assignments in other countries, and she was on the Continent at the time. Bob thinks she was supposed to be in Ostend; but he suspects that she might have lied to him, cashed in the ticket he'd bought her, and gone to Marseilles instead. He can't say for sure because, after Arthur died, Mary burned her passport and vowed never to travel again."

"A likely story! You're not intimating that she and Arthur were have an *affaire*? That greasy-faced frump?"

"No, Iseult, nothing like that. According to Bob, Mary suspected Arthur was cheating her out of some of her fees by holding back his best stones and getting somebody else to cut them. Could that have been possible, Lisa?"

"Yes, but it wouldn't have been cheating. Arthur and Mary weren't in any legal partnership, you know; it was just that their fathers had had a long-standing gentlemen's agreement about the buying and cutting. After the old men died, Arthur felt honor-bound to carry on with the arrangement even though he detested having to do business with Bob and wasn't always satisfied with Mary's work. She insisted on doing everything her own way, and sometimes hers wasn't the best way."

"Do you mean she'd spoil his stones?"

"Not spoil them, exactly; but not cut them as Arthur thought they should be done. Sometimes she'd wind up with a less impressive cut than he'd expected. That would mean a smaller profit, of course, which wouldn't go down too well. After a while, he got tired of always having to fight with her and began quietly taking his more important stones to a different cutter. There was no reason for him to lose money just to keep Mary pacified, but naturally she wouldn't have seen it that way."

"Then Bob's suspicion that Mary meant to follow Arthur in the hope of catching him cheating on her, as she saw it, might not be so far off the mark?"

"Knowing what their relationship had been ever since Arthur's father died, I'd say it was quite likely. But if Mary actually did follow Arthur to Marseilles and watched him die, why in God's name didn't she come and tell me? How could she simply"—Lisa's voice was starting to crack—"simply sit back and smirk, and trade my husband's life for a new pair of slippers?"

Chapter 22

"**O**h, come off it, Lisa!"

Now that he'd burned his bridges, Tom wasn't bothering to be civil to his stepsister. "You appear to be taking one hell of a lot for granted. Why should there have been any connection between Arthur's death and Mary's, shall we say, fund-raising activities? The French police, not to mention the French *juge d'instruction*, decided he'd simply been mugged and robbed according to time-honored local custom by some thug who either knew he'd be carrying valuable gemstones with him or else just happened into a stroke of luck. Why can't you accept their verdict, for God's sake?"

"Because it wasn't that simple."

"All right, Lisa. I grant you the whole business was a ghastly horror story, but why turn it into a long-running serial? Mary could have been lying when she told her brother the money was coming in on account of Arthur. If brother Bob had her booked for Ostend that day, I for one can't picture her slapping on a false mustache and chugging off to Marseilles after Arthur, much less her knowing which of its many bawdy houses he'd be most apt to frequent."

"Very amusing, Tom," snarled Dafydd, "but hardly enlightening."

"Then let's try a different scenario. Do you remember what Mary said night before last about gem-cutters being able to recognize individual stones? What if somebody had stolen some fairly impressive specimens, pried them out of the dowager's tiara or wherever they'd been, and sold them to Arthur, who in turn brought them to Mary to be recut?"

"So that they wouldn't be spotted as stolen goods when Arthur tried to peddle them again?" Lisa's voice was cold as death. "You're saying Arthur Ellis was a fence who worked with thieves?"

"It was only a supposition."

"Then kindly keep your suppositions to yourself."

Iseult, for some reason, elected to play peacemaker. "Oh Lisa, do quit sniping at poor Tom. I can't say I find his suggestion so awfully farfetched. Arthur needn't have known the jewels were stolen. But Mary would have stuck her clever little eyeglass into her beady little eye and seen at once that these particular stones could only have come to Arthur via some highly respected nobleman who'd have been kicked out of his clubs and warned off the cricket crease should it become generally known that he was running a sideline in upper-class thievery. Like Raffles, the Gentleman Cracksman. You'd have made a superb Raffles, Dafydd, you were always quite good at cricket, for a tenor. You didn't happen to be in Marseilles on the night, by any chance?"

"Yes, I was, and Madoc knows all about it. I had met my parents for drinks and dinner. I had to be in Munich for rehearsal the following day, so I left them about half-past nine and spent the night on the train to Munich. After I'd checked into my hotel, I telephoned Gwen in London, and that was the first I knew of Arthur's death."

"Gwen even telephoned me at the studio," Tom broke in, "which was more than anybody else bothered to do. I was out of my office at the moment, as it happened, so I didn't get to speak with her, but I remember thinking it was awfully decent of her to leave the message. Sorry, old boy, I didn't mean to interrupt."

Dafyyd's studied calm had come unstuck, he was halfway to the boil by now. "In short, Iseult, I did not murder Arthur Ellis: firstly, because he was someone I liked and respected; secondly, because I would not have wished to cause Lisa grief; thirdly, because I was not then and am not now an amateur cracksman; and fourthly, because I simply wouldn't have had the time."

Iseult still wasn't giving up. "Oh, but you would, if you'd flown to Munich instead of going by train."

"I'm well aware of that, thank you, and so is Madoc."

"How nice for both of you."

This was too much for Janet. "You were in Marseilles yourself that night, Iseult."

"I was not!"

Iseult had packed enough temperament into her scream to have kindled another Beltane fire, but she wasn't fazing Janet a whit.

"Oh yes, you were. You walked past a restaurant not far from where the body was found, about half-past ten that same night. You were wearing very high heels and a tight miniskirt, and carrying a transparent bubble umbrella with a green band around it. What made you tell such a silly lie this morning, Iseult?"

"I didn't lie to you! Why should I? Where did you get this faradiddle? From Dafydd?"

"No, I got it from Lady Rhys. After they'd put Dafydd into a taxi, she and Sir Emlyn had stayed on at the restaurant. They'd finally got ready to leave and were out under the awning trying to hail a cab for themselves when you walked by. They didn't speak to you because some man standing next to them made a rude remark. You had your face so plastered with makeup that he evidently took you for a streetwalker, and you know how Dafydd's mother feels about his father's position. I should add in fairness that they both assumed you'd been performing and hadn't taken off your stage makeup."

"How charitable of them. It's all rot, of course. Whatever that woman may have been, she certainly wasn't I. Lady Rhys had better get her lorgnette adjusted."

"My mother has excellent eyesight," said Dafydd. "She never forgets a name or a face, she never gets people mixed up, and she is not a malicious liar. Where in Marseilles were you performing that night, Iseult?"

"*Et tu, Brute?*" Iseult pushed back her chair and stood up. "If this is the liveliest entertainment you have to offer, I think I'll stroll back down to the Gas and Gaiters and seduce the village idiot. One does need to keep in practice. Coming, Tom?"

"If Madoc's quite through with his inquisition. One doesn't want to flout his authority. Not that he really has any to flout, Uncle Huw to the contrary notwithstanding. Do you, old boy? Why don't you go back to Canada and try it on the Esquimaux?"

Madoc was not at all ruffled. "I've been deputized to help Cyril Rhys because Uncle Caradoc prefers to keep the investigation in the family as far as possible. If you'd prefer to have the chief constable call in Scotland Yard, I expect that could be arranged."

"Oh, don't trouble on my account. What about it, Williams? You're not family, come join the grilling session. Cousin Madoc wants to know why you blew up Cousin Mary last night."

"Oh? Why does anybody blow up anybody? That

reminds me, Mrs. Ellis, I have a message for you. Your daughter wanted me to say that she'd got the constable's bicycle back without being pinched and she's going to stay and help hunt the handbag. Is that another old Welsh custom?"

"No, the Welsh custom is for ladies to keep a very tight grip on their handbags," said Tom. "Right, Lisa?"

"Quite right. Thank you for telling me, Mr. Williams."

"Not at all. Sorry I didn't think of it sooner. By the way, I'd planned to drive Iseult back to London today, but I'm told we aren't allowed to leave. For how long, does anyone know?"

"Until you're either blown up or carted off to the jug," Tom replied. "Which would you prefer?"

"The jug, please. At least I might be able to get some work done there. Regardless of all that about Arthur Ellis, it must have been the brother who killed her, don't you think? Motive incestuous lust, I hope. Incest's rather high on the list just now in what we scriptwriters laughingly refer to as our profession. Insanity's passé, and money's so trite. Did she have any, by the way?"

"Money, or unnatural yearnings?"

"Ridiculous question. Money, of course."

"Pots of it. Too bad you missed your chance, Reuel old chap. Where were you when the lights went out?"

"In the dark, as I so often am. Who gets the oodle: the brother, the nephew, or you?"

"I should be so lucky. Bob, of course. He has a natural affinity for money, however come by. Madoc's going to arrest him as soon as we've finished our game of cops and robbers. Aren't you, old boy? Or do you incline to the loaded pistol in the library, since it's a matter of saving the family honor?"

"Good question, I haven't quite decided. How long

have you and Iseult known each other, Mr. Williams?"

"Too long, I sometimes think. About—what, Iseult? Four years? Four and a half? Shortly after I got back from the States, anyway."

"And how long were you in the States?" Madoc's voice was still mild.

"Almost twelve years. I'd got tired of writing documentaries; that one I did with the late Miss Rhys was the first of far too many. I'd become locked into that particular slot, you see, and I wanted out. I knew any chap with a British accent would be leapt upon with cries of joy in Hollywood, not because of our skill with the language but because we add such a nice touch of class to the producers' wives' indiscretions. Anyway, I decided to try it long enough to redefine myself as a scriptwriter, so over I went. The climate was appalling but the money was good, so I stayed on, as one does, you know. Got married and all that. When the marriage broke up, I decided it was time to come home. Not very interesting, is it?"

"You did come back for visits, however, or on special assignments?"

"Lord, no. I don't make visits unless somebody pays my way, and Hollywood film moguls wouldn't dream of sending Brits to Britian. That would be far too obvious. We got shipped off to Malaysia or the Sea of Okhotsk, places like that, suffered nasty afflictions from the native foods, and came back to tacos and guacamole. I believe what really precipitated my return to the homeland was that I'd developed an overwhelming yen for a plate of bubble and squeak."

"Naturally one would. This was about five years ago, you say?"

"Yes, that's right. I sailed back on the *QE2* to give myself a few days' worth of image-polishing, and passed my fortieth birthday sicking up in the Newfoundland Basin. I'm forty-five now, God help me, so that does it, doesn't it? Anyway, I got a job at Goldilox Flix on the strength of my American accent. Iseult was there on loan from Curvaceous Cinema at the time, her script wasn't right, and I was given a go at fixing it. That worked out, so Iseult moved over to Goldilox and it got to be more or less taken for granted that I'd be doing her scripts. So back I am in another rut. At least this one's drier than the Sea of Okhotsk. Part of the time, anyway."

"And there's no dearth of bubble and squeak," Madoc replied understandingly. "Did you ever meet a gem buyer named Arthur Ellis?"

"I had a lovely time in Caracas once with a girl named Stefanya Ellis, only I'm not sure that's how she spelled it. No relation, I don't suppose?"

"Probably not. Have you ever been to Marseilles?"

"Oh yes, quite often when I was in my documentary period. I was there again just a few weeks ago, as a matter of fact, for the first time since I got back to the old sod. Had a rather touching encounter, by the way. I dropped in at a place over near the Cannebière that I'd frequented as a golden-haired stripling, and the old girl who runs it remembered me. She stood me a bottle of awful champagne and we got quite matey, reminiscing about the dear dead days of long ago. She asked what I was doing these days, and when I said writing for the flicks, she opened another bottle. Seems she'd had this gorgeous *rousse* working there for a while, who'd gone on to become a famous film star. She appeared to take this as a personal triumph, she'd even kept a scrapbook. It wasn't something she showed to everybody— one had to be discreet, after all—but with an old friend like me and one actually in the business, *eh bien, pourquoi pas?* So we had quite a cozy time looking at the

249

photos, and it didn't cost me a cent. Madame Fifine, she calls herself."

"God damn you to hell, Reuel Williams!"

It was a shriek to shatter windows. Reuel Williams gazed across the table with an air of polite dismay.

"What's the matter, Iseult? Have I said something inappropriate?"

Chapter 23

"**S**o that's why Mary Rhys was blackmailing you."

Tom made it a statement, not a question. Madoc wasn't standing for interference.

"Let me handle this, please, Tom. Mr. Williams, did Madame Fifine tell you, or were you able to determine from material in the scrapbook, exactly when this gorgeous redhead was employed in her establishment?"

"It was only for a short period, not more than a few months. I could put through a call to Madame Fifine if you think it's important."

"I didn't realize you despise me this much, Reuel." Iseult spoke not resentfully but wearily, the fight gone out of her. "Actually it was more a matter of weeks than of months. I was researching a part, trying to get the feel of—oh, hell, what's the use. I'd been let down over a job, I'd dropped what little money I had trying to win back my fare home, and it was a matter of take what you can get. In France they're more civilized about such things."

"Nobody's judging you, Iseult." Lisa sounded worn-out too. "We just want to get at the truth for once. Were you in Marseilles on the night of April twelfth eight years ago, as Lady Rhys claims you were? You might as well say. Madoc will find out anyway."

"Thanks to my pal here. I know. Yes, I was there. When Lady Rhys saw me, I was out for a stroll with one of Madame Fifine's regulars. She didn't allow anything really kinky, she was quite the gentlewoman in her way, but this chap had a relatively harmless little thing about trotting along behind a girl and pretending to pick her up. He was a bit on the prissy side, he wouldn't have dreamed of approaching anyone to whom he hadn't been formally introduced. I didn't mind, it made a change. Anyway, he trailed me back to the house and business continued brisk from then on, so you see I have an involved alibi. I didn't kill poor old Arthur because, like Dafydd, I simply wouldn't have had the time. Not that I would have anyway, he was such a pet."

"When did you find out Arthur was dead?" Madoc asked her.

"It was after daybreak, I know, because I was just getting to bed. Unaccompanied, that is to say. My room faced out on the alley. I heard a bit of commotion and looked out the window, as one naturally would. A couple of *flics* were down there, bending over a man who was lying on the ground. I could see a wallet and a few calling cards or some such scattered around him, it was fairly obvious he'd been beaten to death and robbed. Then one of the *flics* stepped aside and I got a look at the man's face. I recognized Arthur Ellis immediately and decided that this was not the place for me."

"So what did you do?"

"I knew Madame would be up and about; she never missed a trick in more senses than one; so I went and told her I'd got another job and must leave for Paris *tout de suite*. She knew I was lying, but she also knew I hadn't killed the man in the alley. Anyway, she didn't want a scandal any more than I did, so she paid me off, told me there'd always be a bed waiting should the new job not suit, and wished me bon voyage."

"That was sweet of her," said Reuel. "I'm sure you were sadly missed."

"I shall see to it that you wind up writing documentaries again," Iseult replied through clenched teeth. "Preferably in Okhotsk."

"You don't know how Arthur happened to be just there?" Madoc persisted.

"No. Arthur definitely had not been one of Madame Fifine's customers, neither she nor any of the other girls recognized him. The police assumed he'd been pushed into the alley as he walked by, or else struck down on the sidewalk and dragged in there to be searched and robbed. Madame Fifine was of the opinion that he'd been killed somewhere else and brought there by one of her competitors to make her look bad. I had to listen to a tirade before she got round to counting out my money. It was rather nerve-wracking; I did want to be off."

"Where did you go once you'd left the house?"

"I took a bus to Cannes. That was Madame's idea, actually. She thought it might look too obviously like flight if I went scuttling off too far too fast. As usual, she knew best, Cannes turned out to be the best stroke of luck I've ever had. I met a producer from Curvaceous Cinema on the beach, and my career took off."

"Along with a few other things, no doubt," drawled Reuel.

"Too bad your scripts aren't so clever as your repartee. Can't you arrest him, Madoc?"

"I may. We'll see. When did you first hear from the blackmailer?"

"Just about the time advance publicity for my first really big film began to appear. It was a note, clumsily printed in purple ink on cheap paper, all correct and according to protocol. It started with a modest request for fifty pounds, along with a threat to divulge not only my short career as a lady of the evening but also my connection with the death of Arthur Ellis if I didn't pay up. I wasn't about to risk any unfavorable publicity then, of all times, so I paid. The following month, I got a polite thank-you note and a request for another fifty pounds. And so it went. The amounts were bearable, so I kept on paying. As my career burgeoned, the price went up."

"How much was your last payment?" Madoc asked her.

"Five hundred, once a month. By that time, I was getting polite telephone calls instead of notes. It hadn't been raised for almost a year. Neither had my earnings, in case you were about to ask. Actors over here don't earn at the same scale as Americans do. Some Americans, at any rate. And much as I hate to admit it, I'm not quite the blazing star Reuel's old girlfriend apparently thinks I am. It costs a bomb to live in London and keep up appearances, Tom can bear me out on that. I was feeling the pinch, and wondering what to do if the price went up again. And to think all the time it was only that silly old Mary. Why didn't I recognize her voice on the phone? Because I'd never heard her say anything but, 'Yes, brother,' I suppose. Gah! If I'd known, I'd have killed her myself. Go ahead, Madoc, arrest me."

"Sorry, Iseult. As of now, there seems to be no provable case against you. How many of those evening strolls with your client had you taken?"

"Not many. Three or four, I suppose. I told you I hadn't been there long."

"But there would have been time enough for somebody to spot you and track you to Madame Fifine's. Somebody who was aware that you knew Arthur Ellis, for instance. You'd gone about with him at one time, didn't you?"

"Yes, but not for long. I made the mistake of bringing Arthur out here one weekend to impress him with my aristocratic relations, and he met Lisa."

"You weren't too happy about that?"

"Not thrilled to the marrow, no. What woman would be? But that was ages ago."

"People have been known to hold grudges. You continued to visit Sir Caradoc frequently?"

"Not frequently, but from time to time. A baronet in one's family is good for the image, you know."

"I suppose so, I'd never thought of it that way. During your infrequent visits, then, did you ever express yourself on the subject of Arthur Ellis?"

"I may have dropped the odd remark. If not, I'm sure somebody else did. Madoc, you're not accusing me of having killed Arthur out of spite because he'd thrown me over for a crawl of tortoises."

"No, I'm just wondering whether some bright soul might have thought your presumed disappointment over Arthur would constitute an adequate motive to set you up for a potential murder charge, in case a scapegoat should be required. Didn't that ever occur to you?"

"God, no! You don't mean Dafydd would—"

"Of course Dafydd wouldn't." Lisa was sticking her neck out now, good and proper. "Dafydd only plays grand opera, he doesn't write the silly plots. You've told a very touching story, Iseult, but I can think of a few different twists that would fit your scenario just as easily. For instance, while you were out on that little stroll, you happened to bump into Arthur. He liked to walk, you know, and he wasn't afraid of anything, not even in Marseilles. You surmised he'd be carrying gems and you saw a way to solve your financial problems in a hurry.

You managed to lose your follower briefly, which wouldn't have been hard in such awful weather as Dafydd described, and accost Arthur. He wouldn't turn his back on an old acquaintance, much less a relative of mine. You're no pigmy—you could have shoved him into that alley, bashed in his head with a cobblestone or whatever, and robbed his body; then picked up your chap again and gone back to work."

"So I could, and thanks for the compliment. For that matter, Lisa darling, it's not inconceivable that you could have flown over to Marseilles with an artistically faked-up passport and killed him yourself. Wasn't that what the French police were thinking for a while?"

"Until they found out I couldn't possibly have managed it, yes. Iseult, I'm sorry. I don't really believe you killed Arthur. Only I know it couldn't have been Dafydd, because—"

Because, that was why. This argy-bargy wasn't getting them anywhere, Janet decided. Dafydd wasn't about to see Lisa pull her neck in again. "Madoc," she said, "why haven't you told them about the emerald?"

Iseult's green eyes glittered like a wildcat's. "What emerald?"

"The big one out of the crosier. Mary stole it and put a dummy stone in its place."

"She didn't! My God, Jenny, I don't believe this. But why? She said herself the stone wouldn't be marketable even if it was cut in half a dozen pieces."

"Only because Mary would have recognized the pieces as having come from Uncle Caradoc's stone," Janet reminded her. "That wouldn't prevent Mary herself from stealing it. But if somebody else found out she had it and stole it from her they'd have to kill her before they'd dare start peddling the stone. With Mary out of the way, the risk wouldn't exist any longer. I'm sorry, Madoc, I didn't mean to butt in."

"That's not butting in, love, you've made an excellent point. Go ahead, tell them the rest."

Well, I don't know whether everybody here realizes that Dai Rhys was Mary's apprentice?"

"That skinny kid with the pimples," Iseult amplified, mainly for Tom's benefit. "Mary's nephew. He looks a bit dim to me."

"Dai's all right," Janet protested. "He's taken a lot of abuse from his aunt and uncle and I don't suppose they've ever fed him right, but he's not so dumb that he can't tell a genuine emerald from a chunk of bottle glass."

"Is that what it was?" Iseult sounded not only shocked but even somewhat frightened. "Then why didn't he say so when she was putting him through that asinine business with the loupe?"

"Because he didn't care to be made a fool of in front of Uncle Caradoc and the rest, for which you can hardly blame him. Dai was smart enough to realize Mary was using him to fortify that tall story she was handing us."

"And we fell for it."

"How could we know? As you said yourself, Iseult, the stone wasn't all that exciting to look at. I remember feeling let down when Uncle Caradoc showed it to me the first time I came. We're too used to seeing precious stones cut and polished the modern way."

"I suppose so. But then why did you have to drag in all that about blackmail?" Iseult was working herself into a fury. "It's so bloody simple. Somebody saw Mary taking the emerald out of the crosier, stole it away from her, and blew her up so that she wouldn't be able to identify the pieces after it had been cut. Or else she was acting in collusion with someone who put her up to swapping the stone for a fake, then killed her so that he wouldn't have to split the profits. Could that be what Mary was getting at yesterday, about what you'd learned from her gem-cutting film, Reuel?"

"You bitch! All I ever learned from that old hag was not to be too blasted polite to ill-favored women."

"Am I ill-favored, then?"

"You're ill-tempered, ill-informed, ill-equipped to be a decent actress, and too damned ready to ill-wish anybody who gets across you. You're the only one of this crowd who's mad enough about emeralds to kill for one."

"What do you mean, this crowd? I thought you'd never met them before?"

"Granted, I don't know. Maybe you're all in it together. Maybe the whole bloody show's a pack of thieves and murderers. By God, Iseult, that's it! Mrs. Ellis, is there something I can write on? I've got to get this down before I lose the drift. Melissa? Medora? Marbella? I always have to start with the woman's name. Merinda, that's the ticket! Malicious Merinda, vicious Merinda. Damn your soul, you harpy, you'll knock 'em dead at the box office. You'll have to dye your hair black."

"Like hell I will. Black's too aging."

"Oh, Christ! You and your bloody vanity. Face it, Iseult, that last face-lift's slipping already. You're all through playing sweet young heroines. This one's for you, pet, a role you can really get your teeth into. Or whosever teeth you're wearing nowadays. Brace yourself, Issy baby, this is going to be a biggie. Where do you hide your typewriter, Mrs. Ellis?"

Lisa cocked an eyebrow at Madoc. He nodded. "Go

ahead, Williams. Just don't let your inspiration carry you away from the village."

Iseult shrugged. "Oh well, writers are born crazy. He'd better be right this time, damn him. I look like the wrath of God in black. Where do we go from here, or don't we? Are you going off and detect some more, Madoc?"

"I don't have to go off. My mother's probably searching your room about now, she'll phone me here if she finds anything."

"What? Of all the cheek! She can't do that."

"Yes, she can, Iseult, and most capably. You know my mother. Lisa, I'm going to have to poke around a bit. Do you mind?"

"I'd be delighted. Anything to get this ghastly tangle sorted out. Is there any way I can help?"

"You can open any drawers or cupboards that need to be unlocked."

"There are none, we never lock anything. Shout if you want me."

"Actually I'd as soon you came along, to make sure I don't pinch the tortoises."

"Jolly good show!" Tom was on his feet. "Come on, Iseult. Now's our chance to watch the great sleuth sleuthing."

"May we?"

"Everybody's welcome."

Madoc was quite good-natured about it, Janet surmised that he'd rather have them under his eye than off tampering with evidence. "So long as you keep out of my way and don't touch anything. Otherwise you'd have to stay here in the kitchen. You too, Jenny love, you can be acting constable."

Reuel could be left alone safely enough. He was

pounding away nineteen to the dozen, the noise would keep Madoc informed of his whereabouts.

"We'll start in the bedrooms," said Madoc. "Standard police procedure."

It probably wasn't, Janet thought. He was just hoping he'd run across something before he wound up having to check out all those tortoises.

Either Lisa was a model housekeeper, or else she'd had someone from the village in to oblige that morning. Her own room was both charming and immaculate; Tib's was no more disastrous than might be expected of any normal teenager. Tom's had been rather perfunctorily tidied; there were a couple of dust kittens under the bed, the straw boater he'd had on at the concert was hanging by its elastic from the doorknob, and his hairy Norfolk jacket was tossed over the one straight chair. He was wearing the plus fours again today, with Argyle socks and a Fair Isle pullover, he looked like a member of the Drones Club up for the weekend and about to go off and scratch the back of the earl's prize pig.

So far, nothing of interest. Dafydd's room was next. His homey touches were on a different level: silver-backed brushes, a little leather case holding his tooled-gold cuff links and studs, a silver shoehorn on the dresser, a copy of the *Mabinogion* on the bedside table with a bookmark in it and a pair of reading glasses beside it. The wardrobe held his black frock coat and trousers, the not-too-tweedy tweed suit he'd no doubt traveled in, a pair of gray flannels, and a navy-blue blazer for taking Lisa out to dinner. There was nothing in any of the pockets.

A pair of dress pumps, a pair of town shoes, and a pair of leather traveling slippers were lined up under the garments. There was nothing stuffed into a toe. There was nothing in the dresser drawers but a genteel sufficiency of shirts, socks, and underwear, all carefully folded. Dafydd's pajamas were under the pillow, also properly folded. There was nothing else under the pillow, nothing under the mattress, nothing taped to the back of the wardrobe, nothing pinned behind the curtains.

Iseult yawned. "How boring."

"That's all?" said Tom. "Are you quite sure there isn't a hollowed-out secret compartment in the back of the clothes brush?"

He took a step toward the dresser, caught his foot in the small bedside rug, and stumbled. "Oh sorry, Lisa. Clumsy of me. Madoc will have to put it straight, I'm not allowed to touch anything."

"That's quite all right, Tom." The gibe was missed, Madoc seemed amused. Janet caught on—that short piece in the aged floorboards was easy enough for anybody who'd grown up in an old farmhouse to spot. Madoc knelt, opened the blade of his jackknife, and exposed the cache. "Is this it, Jenny?"

"Looks like it to me, a soft black leather pouch with handles. It can't have been there more than a day or so, there's not enough dust on it."

"Never mind the dust," shrilled Iseult, "what about the emerald? Oh, look! She really did. But, my God, gunpowder in her pockets. Dafydd, how could you?"

Chapter 24

Dafydd Rhys was fit to be tied and didn't care who knew it; the sheepmen must be hearing him even in the highest pastures. Tom Feste was trying to help, in his usual way.

"Of course it's a frame-up, Dafydd. We know you didn't do this. That brother of hers must have popped down here whilst the rest of us were hopping in and out of the fire. Before Mary did her smashing grand finale, that is. By the way, where were you? I don't recall having seen you amongst the merry leapers."

"I was tired," Dafydd growled, "I got there late."

"Oh really? And left early, one gathers. You weren't in the barn for the grand grilling."

"No. I was being sick in the hedgerow, since you ask. One finds one's not too stiff-upper-lipped at watching people get blown to death. After I'd given it all I had, I crawled back here and flopped into bed. I wasn't trying to dodge the questioning, I just felt too bloody awful to talk to anybody. I can't see why you're dragging Bob into this, Tom. He was at the fire when I got there—I know because I deliberately stayed as far away from him as I could. He certainly wasn't in this room when I came back. I saw nothing out of the way, and I would have, you know. I'm a neat chap, it's one of my few virtues. I'll take Jenny's word that this is in fact Mary's handbag, but I swear to God I've not the remotest idea how it got here, nor that there was a secret hiding place in the floor."

"Wait a minute, old bean, get hold of yourself. There's no sense in telling a tale you're sure to get caught out on. Of course you knew about Lisa's secret cache, we were both in and out of this room often enough as kids."

"What the hell are you getting at? We certainly were not in and out of this room. At least I never was, and you damned well ought not to have been. This used to be Lisa's bedroom, her grandmother would have raised holy hell if she'd caught one of us boys so much as walking slowly past the door. Speaking of which," he interrupted himself, "who's coming? Oh, hello, Cyril, you're just in time. You knew Lisa's grandmother as well as I did, probably better. Didn't you cut her grass or something?"

"Yes, I would often be working in her garden. That is true, Dafydd, what I heard you shouting. It is a very carrying voice you have. Mrs. Daniel was indeed a very proper lady, she would not have been countenancing any laxity in the behavior of the young whoever. She would often be lecturing us in the Sunday School, though we would not always be listening. Furthermore, Dafydd, you were seldom in this house except sometimes for tea. It was at Sir Caradoc's you would always be staying, with him being your own father's uncle and you being related to the Daniels almost hardly not at all, even."

"That's right, Lisa and I are practically strangers." Dafydd was looking a good deal less grim at the moment. "I don't think I've slept in this house more than four times, and then it's been only when there was an overflow at Uncle Caradoc's, like now. And never before in this room; it's always been a cot in the boxroom behind the cistern. You and I slept up there together once, Madoc. Remember?"

"Oh yes, very well, The cistern gurgled all night long, and you kept singing *'Bella Figlia dell' Amore'* in your sleep. At least I supposed you were singing. I couldn't recognize the tune, of course, but I managed to catch the words about the fourteenth time around. To repeat my brother's question, Tom, what are you getting at?"

Lisa took it upon herself to answer. "He's getting at Dafydd, or trying to."

"Thank you, sister dear." Tom was having a hard time not to yell. "What I'm trying to get at are the facts of the matter so that we can all quit sniping at each other and get on with the party. It's obvious enough what happened. Bob Rhys couldn't stand not getting control of the money Mary was screwing out of her blackmail victims, so he blew her up and tried to make Dafydd the villain. Can't you simply arrest Bob, Cyril, and put an end to all this tiptoeing around?"

"It will not be that simple, Tom Feste. We are still needing the final proof of perfidy. You say blackmail victims in the plural form?"

"How much perfidy do you need, for God's sake? What about the green box with the gunpowder in it that you found in Bob's wastebasket?"

"What about it, indeed? I think we will be needing to explore further ramifications of this extremely complicated affair. Do you not agree, Inspector Madoc?"

"By all means. Did you bring any ramifications with you?"

"Indeed, it was exactly as you had hypothesized and no trouble at all. I was acting upon information received from my cousin Johnny the Tickets, Sir Caradoc was lending me in his great kindness the Vauxhall for more speedy execution of your instructions, and Lady Rhys was deputizing herself to assist me, sending Sir Caradoc to help Sir Emlyn mind the baby in her stead and he acquiescing with every indication of pleasure. She has shown the ramification into Mrs. Ellis's parlor, and they are admiring the tortoises together. Will you be wanting me to escort them to this room?"

"No, we'll go down. It's already too crowded up here. We've found Mary's handbag, by the way. We'd better take it with us."

"I'll get it." Tom's hand moved fast.

Madoc's was faster. "Let it alone, Tom, this is police business. Lisa, would you happen to have a pair of tongs in the house? Not fire tongs, small ones that we could pull this out with?"

"Would sugar tongs do? Arthur and I got six pairs for wedding presents, one from each of my mother's aunts. None of the six was speaking to any of the others at the time so they couldn't compare notes beforehand. All six dropped me like a hot potato, thank goodness, once Arthur had the bad taste to get himself murdered. I'll get them."

"Just bring the strongest," said Madoc patiently.

"Why all the pother? Can't we just pull it out?" Tom made another snatch.

This time it was the constable who forestalled him. "If you are trying that one more time, Tom Feste, I will have to be pinching you for trying to tamper with the evidence. This is not fun and games we are having here. You had better come downstairs with me and quit playing the Merry Andrew."

"If Lady Rhys is here, I'd better go first," said Lisa. Dafydd was right with her, the rest close behind.

Tom Feste wanted to slide down the banister, but Cyril Rhys wasn't standing for any more nonsense. With a stern constabulary eye on him, Tom was fairly subdued, until he walked into Lisa's front parlor."

"Patricia! What the bloody hell are you doing here?"

"Oh hi, Tom. Looking at tortoises. Don't you love this pink one with the eyelashes? Hi, Dafydd. Having fun with your girlfriend?"

"Er—I thought you were going to Swansea."

"I did. Then I came back. There's the cutest pub at Llwerfylldydd, and the rooms are fab."

"You did not come back from Swansea," Cyril Rhys contradicted. "You have never been going. You were buying from my cousin John Thomas Thomas a ticket to Llwerfylldydd only. You were going directly to the Slate-Cutters' Arms, whence you departed at ten o'clock pip emma on the nose, having won four and six at darts to the chagrin of all others present. You were walking one and three-tenths of a mile precisely to Gallows Crossing, where you were picked up in a gray Daimler registered to Thomas Feste."

"Who says?"

"We are having our methods, Miss Patricia Jones of 222B Shaker Street, London. When accosted by the inn-keeper's wife who was observing you crawling in your window at twenty-eight minutes after two o'clock in a state of dishevelment, you were telling her a tale of having been watching badgers by moonlight, there being no moon to speak of, and no badgers whateffer in the vicinity."

"Well, how was I to know? There could have been badgers."

"There could have been hippogriffs also, I am not doubting. You, Miss Jones, are what is known in the cinema as a stuntwoman, your talent being to perform deeds of derring-do whilst pretending to be the actress who is afraid to do them herself. Your father is a knacker in Dwyferlli. Before you were getting taken on at the films, you were wont to assist in slaughtering old farm animals and cutting them up for cats' meat, look you. It was not for your charms, I am thinking, but for your expertise that Mr. Tom Feste was bringing you here."

Patricia shrugged. "Well, you know Tom. Anything for a laugh."

"Very funny, Pat," drawled Tom. "Now tell them the truth. She put one of her dart-playing boyfriends up to pinching my car. Slaughtering that ram was her own little joke. I had nothing to do with it."

"Really?" Lady Rhys elevated her eyebrows as high as decorum allowed. "What ram was this, Tom?"

"Why, the one that was found in the chapel the morning before—" Tom noticed the bewilderment on faces around him, and faltered. "People were talking about it. Didn't you hear?"

"Nobody was talking about it," said Madoc. "Nobody knew, except myself, Uncle Huw, and Padarn, the old chap one of you two tried to kill when he interrupted your jolly prank. Unfortunately for you, he's doing nicely."

"But he couldn't have seen," Patricia argued. "I was inside, in my birthday suit." She giggled. "Tom was outside, casting his cookies. He couldn't take it when the head came off and the blood gushed out. When the old boy ambled along, Tom whacked him with a stone before—oh gosh, Tom, I shouldn't have said that. Sorry."

"She's lying, of course." Tom was still trying. "I'm sure you'll find the chap who helped her back at the Slate-Cutters' Arms, Cyril. As to how I knew about the ram, I happened to take an early morning stroll and saw it there dead. The body was on the floor and the head was stuck up on the altar with a cap on its head and a pipe in its mouth. Patricia's notion of a jolly jape, but that didn't occur to me at the time. I naturally assumed Bob and Mary Rhys had been having a game of witches and goblins, and came away."

"What time was this, Tom?"

"I couldn't say, exactly. Half-past six, maybe."

"That does it, I'm afraid. I was there myself at quarter to five. Uncle Huw came along right after me, he'd been awakened by the crows, as I was. They were making a great racket, flying in and out, scavenging the ram. We cleaned up and got rid of the carcass, by half-past six there'd have been nothing to see. If you'd come earlier we'd have seen you."

"At half-past six, Tom was snoring like a pig," said Lisa. "And had been for some while, I was afraid he'd wake Dafydd. Half-past six isn't early in the country, Tom, I should have thought you'd know that by now."

Tom wasn't even listening any more, he was concentrating on Mary's handbag, which Madoc had placed on a small table that happened to be relatively free of tortoises. They were all gathered around it, Iseult in particular was eyeing it as a crow might eye a dead ram. "Never mind all that, Madoc," she urged. "What about the emerald?"

"Yes, let's have a look." Tom's hand snaked out; Madoc grabbed it back.

"I should think not," said Lady Rhys. "Bag-snatching on top of sheep-killing is a bit much. Don't you agree, Jenny?"

"Tom wasn't snatching the bag, Mother, he just wanted us to see him touching it. He's afraid he may have left a stray fingerprint while he was hiding it in Dafydd's room. That's Mary's bag, you see."

Tom was scared now. "She's cracked! Why shouldn't my fingerprints be on it? Mary dropped her bag yesterday and I picked it up."

"What time did you perform your act of courtesy, Tom?"

"Sometime yesterday afternoon, while Mary was flitting about making a pest of herself. I'm afraid I can't pinpoint the precise moment."

"It doesn't matter," said Janet. "Nobody would believe you anyway. Mary was wearing her handbag as part of her costume, fastened by its handles around her waist on a heavy leather belt with a good, sturdy brass buckle. She couldn't have dropped the bag without either unbuckling the belt or cutting the handles. Bob said day before yesterday that the men who were supposed to gather the wood for the Beltane fire mustn't have any metal about them. I expect he'd have made Mary take off her belt and handbag before they performed their rite in the chapel."

"How was I to know about any rite in the chapel?"

"Easily enough, I should think, if you were following Mary around. Dai says Mary used to make odd phone calls, I expect some of them were to you. You may have twigged on this weekend that she was your blackmailer and been planning how best to get rid of her. Or you hoped she'd be carrying precious stones in her bag, the way Arthur Ellis used to. Or maybe you went yourself to pinch the emerald out of the crosier and caught her beating you to it. Anyway, as you doubtless know, Madoc and I watched her and Bob for a while at the chapel. They were so taken up with what they were doing that you could have marched in there, picked up the bag, and walked out with it again, and they'd never have noticed. I don't suppose you'd have run the risk, though. Why should you? It would have been a cinch to poke a long pole in through one of those unglazed windows and hook the bag from outside."

Tom tried a supercilious smile. "It would have been even simpler for Bob to pick up the bag as they left and offer to take care of it while Mary was leaping the fire."

"According to Dai, she'd never have trusted him. Anyway, that can't be what happened. Bob went into hysterics the second that explosion went off. The doctor gave him a shot to quiet him down, and he was put to bed in the farmhouse. He was still so groggy this morning that Owain had to trundle him down to the manor in a wheelbarrow. Since then, he's been right under Uncle Caradoc's eye. Furthermore, both Lisa and Dafydd have been here all morning, so Bob would have had a fat chance of sneaking upstairs unbeknownst even if he'd been in any shape to try."

"You don't know what sort of shot the doctor gave him," Tom insisted. "Bob might have been only lightly sedated. Mightn't he have slept it off in a few hours, slipped down here and done the doings, then gone back to Huw's and taken a sleeping pill?"

"Assuming he had one to take. Bob's own luggage was at Uncle Caradoc's and I don't suppose Aunt Elen leaves things like that sitting around where her grandchildren might get at them. First, he'd have had to get out of Huw's house without waking the dogs or any of the people who are staying there. He'd have had to get past the manor, he'd have had to know about Lisa's secret hidey-hole. He'd have had to sneak into this house, find his way to the right bedroom, open the cache in the dark, and hide the bag practically under Dafydd's nose without waking him or anyone else. Has Bob visited you often, Lisa?"

"Never, that I can remember. He's no connection of

mine, you know. I don't see how Bob could possibly have known about my cache, much less got into it."

"There you are, Tom. You, on the other hand, have been coming here for a good many years. I'm sure you found out Lisa's hiding place ages ago because that's the kind of snoop you are, and you had free rein to sneak back here with Mary's handbag while Lisa, Tib, and Dafydd were all up at the fire. And furthermore, that green box with the gunpowder in it hasn't been generally mentioned. The only way you could have known about it is if you planted it yourself."

The fact that the box had turned up in Mary's room, not Bob's, was a detail Janet didn't bother to mention. Tom had probably pulled that trick during the concert, while Bob was singing his solo and Mary was listening. Bob would have spied the shiny bright green box when he went up to his room for the toe of frog and wool of bat or whatever other necromantic ingredient he'd needed for his rite in the chapel. Since his natural impulse had always been to stick his sister with the dirty work, he'd have transferred it to Mary's fireplace on general principles. Janet was almost sorry Tom hadn't got away with that one.

"So there it is, Tom. Over to you, Madoc."

"For God's sake," shrieked Iseult, "quit nattering and open that handbag!"

"Since you insist."

Using Lisa's sugar tongs, Madoc released the catch and flipped open the bag. There it was, a green chunk the size of a dropcake, wrapped in a pink tissue. He plucked it out and held it up. "Here you are, Iseult."

"Oh God! Let me hold it, just for a second. Please."

"Certainly, for as long as you like. Chuck it in the wastebin when you're through."

"What? Are you mad?"

"No, just unconvinced. Dafydd, how are you at de-bagging?"

"Splendid." Dafydd never forgot anything; he'd certainly remembered how to apply an effective armlock. He had Tom helpless and screaming; Madoc dealt deftly with the plus fours.

"Shut your eyes, Mother."

"Don't be silly, Madoc. My brothers used to hide things in their knicker knees too. Ah, I see it. May I?"

"By all means. Handle it carefully—that's the real one if I'm not mistaken. Mary must have made up an extra duplicate. Maybe her first try wasn't quite up to standard, or else she'd planned to plant it on somebody, as Tom did."

"And I was your obvious choice, wasn't I?" Dafydd gave Tom's arm a wrench that must have been excruciating. "You bloody son of a bitch, you're the one who set the Sûreté on me, aren't you? Admit it, you—"

"All right! All right! You're killing me. Jesus, Dafydd, can't you take a joke?"

Chapter 25

"So there was the story, nicely packed up in Mary's old black handbag: her bankbooks, her will, and even a pocket diary, each of them slathered with Tom's fingerprints. Quite a happy hunting ground."

Madoc had every right to be pleased. He was back in Betty's kitchen addressing a tableful of Rhyses, all of them drinking tea and slaughtering a fresh batch of Betty's Welsh cakes at record speed. Janet had managed to wrest Dorothy out of her grandparents' clutches and settled down for a hugging session, but Dorothy had elected to get down under the table and hang out with Bartholomew instead. How soon the fledglings left the nest!

"But what took you so long, Madoc?" Lady Rhys wanted to know.

"Mother, it's not that simple. Poor old Cyril had never taken in a murderer before, he wasn't even sure of the drill. We had to haul Uncle Caradoc's pal the chief constable off the fourteenth tee by brute force, and then there was the usual mess of paper work to get sorted through. At least, thank heaven, I don't have to get involved in the scut work, and neither does Cyril."

"What's that?"

"Tracking down such oddments of proof as where Tom fenced the gemstones he'd stolen off Arthur Ellis that night in Marseilles and where he'd bought the gunpowder he used to blow up Mary Rhys."

"I suppose it was understandable that he'd want to blow up Mary. But why Huw's poor old ram?"

"That seems to have been part of Tom's unnecessarily involved plot. The idea was to make us think some kind of witch cult was going on with Mary and Bob at the head of it, so that Mary's getting blown up would be seen as just another rite that went wrong.

"What trick?" asked Reuel Williams, who'd still been typing madly when Tom was carried off as a prisoner and Patricia Jones as a material witness.

"Patricia didn't say. One gathers that she has minimal interest in anything that doesn't involve an inordinate amount of physical energy and, preferably, an element of danger. Rustling and decapitating a pugnacious great animal she found rather a lark; but having to listen to Tom explain why they were doing it was not something that held her interest. So after they'd created that ghastly welter in the chapel, they bathed in the stream to wash off the gore and went for a spin in the Daimler. That's how she burned out Tom's brakes for him, demonstrating how a stunt driver goes over a precipice."

"They must have had quite a lively evening, by and large," said Janet. "Have you read Mary's diary, Madoc?"

"Enough to get the gist. It's written in Welsh, in the tiniest hand I've ever seen off the head of a pin. We had to leave it with the chief constable, he's going to get somebody to make a transcription for the inquest. It's not a day-to-day account—Mary simply recorded the high points, of which she didn't appear to have had many until she became obsessed with the notion that Arthur Ellis was cheating on her. Eventually she nerved herself up for a bold stroke. She managed by devious methods to save up a little cash, lied to Bob about her travel arrangements, and followed Arthur to Marseilles."

Madoc told the story as he'd heard it read out by Cyril Rhys, whose reputation as a poet eclipsed even his exemplary but hitherto unremarkable record as an officer of the law. Cyril's elocution had been eloquent and Mary's diary had afforded full swing for his talents. Madoc's summing-up was probably pallid by comparison, but it was riveting enough for his listeners.

Mary had traveled on the same train as Arthur; she'd trailed him to a meeting with another gem dealer, from whom he had, as might have been expected, bought a number of stones. She'd lurked in the shadows while the transaction took place. Mary hadn't been close enough to see what sorts of stones they were, but she'd surmised from the large wad of cash that changed hands—Arthur always dealt in cash—that their value must be considerable.

Arthur had then done nothing more sinister than to go into a restaurant and eat his dinner. Mary had lurked outside, wet, hungry, and frustrated; peeking in the window from time to time, watching him work his way methodically through soup, entree, and salad, with a half-bottle of wine. He'd eschewed dessert but taken coffee. Then he'd emerged, comfortably fed but not vulgarly sated, turned up the collar of his mackintosh, and braved the by now more than inclement weather. As Mary had essayed to follow him, she'd become aware that somebody else was following him too.

Here was a turn-up indeed. Quite sensibly, Mary had

decided she didn't want to be the ham in this sandwich and elected instead to follow the follower. Her danger had been great, but her reward for intrepidity (Mary's own words) had been greater. She'd actually seen the follower slip up on Arthur, throttle him from behind, and shove him into the alley. She'd heard Arthur's one brief, choking outcry, she'd seen the blow that stilled his voice forever. She'd watched with breathless absorption as the murderer ripped open Arthur's clothing and possessed himself of the little chamois bag into which Arthur had poured his so recently purchased stones.

Now how was she going to get them away? Dared she tackle a murderer? She had no weapon save perhaps a loose cobblestone. Would a cobblestone be adequate for a stunning blow, or would the villain—for this was indubitably no villainess—snatch it away and use it on her?

While she stood there dithering (Mary had of course not used the term "dithering"), the successful mugger had solved her problem for her. After having robbed Arthur's wallet of whatever money it still contained and spread the rest of its contents artistically around the now drenched and cooling body, he'd been unable to resist a glance at his booty. His cigarette lighter had flickered for one brief moment, but that was enough. Mary had seen the glint of the stones, and fine ones they were. Far more potentially valuable, however, was the glimpse she'd got of the killer's face.

It was a face she knew well, and her fortune was made. Why should a clever lady like Mary Rhys risk her life on a desperate attempt at a coup when all she had to do was go home and write a letter? And another, and another. Arthur Ellis had just assured her of a comfortable competence for as long as Tom Feste's funds held out. And everybody knew that film producers made pots and pots.

But the frosting was still to go on the cake. Mary had very sensibly hidden herself behind a wastebin, giving Tom plenty of time to leave the alley and be well on his way before she'd dare to emerge. She'd just about decided the coast was clear and that she'd go back to the train station, since her meager resources wouldn't run to a room for the night, when who should come mincing along through the downpour but—"

Madoc suddenly realized he was talking not only to the person involved but also to a number of her most respectable relatives. Lady Rhys, ever reliable in time of crisis, came to his rescue.

"Let me, Madoc. I was there, after all. It was such a surprise. There we were, Emmy and I, stuck under an awning in the pelting rain praying for a taxi, and here came Iseult with a camera crew. One couldn't even spot the photographers, they do it so simply these days. Just a couple of chaps carrying those video things perched on their shoulders, you know." Lady Rhys favored her hearers with a bland and innocent smile and went on with her tale.

"Iseult was made up as a lady of the evening. She did look smashing, I have to say. No skirt to speak of, stilt heels, fishnet tights, black lipstick. And of course that marvelous hair, with a transparent umbrella to keep it dry. Naturally we didn't speak. We knew we mustn't interrupt the shooting, and anyway our cab came along right afterward. One assumes she must have gone past the alley where Arthur was assaulted. Mary, being Mary, poor thing, naturally would have taken fantasy for reality, as was her wont, and I certainly wouldn't have put it past her to make of it what she could. Most unfortunate for Iseult, just when her career was taking such an upward turn. I'm sure we all feel for her. Go ahead, Madoc, what happened next?"

Madoc continued his excerpts from Mary's diary. A puffing elderly man had appeared, pretending (his own words) to solicit Iseult's favors; they'd gone arm-in-arm into the house that stood next to the alley. Mary had emphasized that she was not the silly innocent Bob liked to think she was; she'd been around enough foreign cities to realize what sort of house this one must be. She'd made careful note of the address and decided she'd best not hang around this wicked but potentially lucrative neighborhood any longer.

Thus it had begun and on it had gone. Ever more pleased with herself had been brilliant, gifted, increasingly wealthy Miss Mary Rhys. She'd been clever enough to realize that Bob must never be allowed to catch sight of her passport, with the French Customs stamp on it where the Belgian one should have been. Because of the uproar created by Arthur's violent death, no word of her excursion to Marseilles must ever get around to anybody. She'd handled that small difficulty by burning her passport in a fine burst of dramatics and vowing never to travel abroad again.

Mary had been clever all along the line. She'd deemed it unwise to begin her fund-raising activities too soon after Arthur's death. She'd waited to make sure Tom Feste had got back safely from Marseilles, that he was telling lies about having been in Morocco instead, and that he was still gainfully employed at the same studio. Of course he was; Tom would have been insane to quit his job now that he'd splurged on that new Daimler and moved to a more glamorous address. How then would he have been able to explain the sudden burst of affluence that must have been generated by the sale of the stolen gems?

278

Mary had taken Iseult's well-publicized new contract with Curvaceous Cinema as a signal to annex a second client. Payment had come faster and more steadily than she'd dared to hope, she hadn't even had to do much bullying. Her one big problem had been how to spend her money. Never having had any before, she'd been stumped about what to do with all this cash, other than to flaunt it at Bob.

His first reaction, as she'd expected, had been to demand the handling of his sister's new income. Mary had laughed in his face and told him nothing doing. He'd then insisted that she contribute to the household expenses; she'd taken further pleasure in reminding him that she'd been the family breadwinner all along. Nevertheless she'd coughed up, because there was less money from the gem-cutting now that she was refusing to travel, and because it was so delightful to make Bob come groveling to her for money to cover the butcher's bill.

Bob had had no idea how much Mary was accumulating. He'd have been absolutely beside himself if he did. He'd have had to know sometime; Mary had dwelt fondly and at length on whether her brother would literally burst with rage on that fateful day or settle for an apoplectic stroke. She'd prayed she'd be alive to see, but supposing she wasn't? What should be her final taunt? The obvious answer had been to draw up a will leaving him precisely one shilling, and the rest to the person whom he'd most hate to see getting it. But who?

Not the Friends of the Lesser Demons, certainly. They all thought Bob Rhys was a magus, and would have taken it for granted that Mary's big brother's good offices, or else his necromantic art, had tipped the scales in their favor. He'd then at least have got the pleasure of basking in undeserved glory, and that would never have done.

Not Sir Caradoc, he was too old and much too deserving. Not Huw nor Owain nor Sir Emlyn, far less their wives and children; they were also numbered among the worthies. Not Lisa or Tib, they'd have thought Mary had remembered them out of respect for Arthur Ellis, of which she'd felt not a jot.

Not Dai Rhys. Mary had already bestowed on Dai the inestimable benefit of her skill and knowledge; he had so far shown himself less than overwhelmed by the honor. Anyway, Dai had a fairly respectable fortune of his own, should Bob ever be persuaded, or more likely forced, into letting him have it. Not Reuel Williams, he was a cad, a rotter, and a gay deceiver; he'd led her on and let her down. She hadn't explained just how, perhaps because there hadn't been much to explain.

At last Mary had hit upon, of all people, Iseult. Iseult was as unworthy as any recipient could be, at least anybody in Mary's limited acquaintance. Mary had taken pleasure in stipulating that the money be used to buy real emeralds to replace the unconvincing imitations with which Iseult had been trying to bolster her image as a highly paid star instead of a second-rate actress in third-rate films. It would be an act of charity, Mary had written, to heap coals of fire upon that artificially enhanced head. What with her extravagant lifestyle and her contributions to Mary's secret fund, Iseult would not have been able to set much aside against the time when her face, her figure, and her popularity rating would all come tumbling down.

It was all there in Mary's will, Madoc said, duly witnessed and notarized. Which meant, Janet added privately, that Iseult was now heiress to her own money, not to mention Tom's and quite likely a fair chunk of

Lisa's, considering how Tom had been sponging off his stepsister ever since he'd murdered her husband. The lawyers ought to have a lively time with this one.

Thus the tale was told. It was Lady Rhys who came up with the *mot juste*. "Bizarre! Iseult, my dear, I hope you don't mind Mary's rude remarks. I'm sure what she really meant was that her conscience was hurting her because of the cruel trick she'd played on you."

To everyone's surprise, including her own, Iseult came around the table and kissed her ladyship with genuine affection. "Thank you, Sillie darling. I refuse to concede that Mary had a conscience, and I don't mind her bitchiness a whit, provided I get to keep the money. Not to be crude, Madoc, but how much?"

"You'll have to take that up with the Inland Revenue. According to Mary's passbooks, she'd squirreled away more than a hundred thousand."

"My God! Tom must have got skinned far worse than I, no wonder he was always dunning Lisa. And you think the will is valid?"

"Don't ask me. It looked all right. If it came to a suit between you and Bob, I should say you'd have the stronger case."

"Then let's get him down here and watch him explode!"

"Not in my kitchen!" Betty, who'd been listening spellbound, made no move to refill the teapot. "Sir Caradoc, it is no dinner I will be cooking for you tonight unless I will be having my room to prepare it in, asking your pardon, sir. Megan, you will cease gaping like a fish and be shelling out the peas. Mrs. Madoc will be wanting you to sit with Dorothy at dinnertime, I doubt not. Is it some nice bread and milk she will be having for her supper, Mrs. Madoc, or would an egg sit better on her tiny stomach?"

"She had a big luncheon of chopped chicken and vegetables at Elen's," said the doting grandma. "Perhaps a little gruel, don't you think, Jenny? With some stewed fruit perhaps? Could you manage that, Betty?"

"Is it my larder your ladyship has ever found wanting? Muesli, then, with apricot puree to strengthen her baby bones. Sir Caradoc, will I be fixing a tray for Mr. Bob Rhys, or will he be taking the five o'clock train now that we know it was not he who will have been blowing up his sister?"

Sir Caradoc, who'd said hardly a word through the long palaver, sat up straight and beamed like the setting sun. "That is an excellent question, Betty. I will go at once and tell Bob what has occurred, then Danny the Boots will drive him to the station. He can dine on the train and still be in time to address the Lesser Demons. Dai may go or stay as he pleases; we shall have to look into that matter of his father's bequest. Tell Danny to hurry, no time must be lost. I will leave it for the lawyer to tell Bob about Mary's will," the old man added as he walked swiftly from the kitchen. "If he is to burst, let it be somewhere else."

"Father is a great man," said Huw, getting up to leave.

"And Reuel is a cad and a rotter." Iseult was in high spirits now, quite understandably. "What did you do, Reuel, seduce the poor innocent maiden?"

"Not bloody likely! I was just trying to be civil, this being my first shot at a documentary script and a big step up, or so it seemed at the time. She mistook gentlemanly affability for grand passion and all hell was to pay. It's not an experience I care to recall. Do we dress?"

"Of course," said Lady Rhys in shocked surprise.

"Sorry, I just thought you might not care to celebrate, with a member of the family in the slammer on a murder rap."

Lady Rhys had spent much of her life on the North American continent; she was able to unravel Williams's verbiage and swift to correct his misapprehension. "Tom Feste is not a member of our family. His father married Lisa's mother, it was a second marriage for both of them. Lisa herself is only tenuously connected to this branch of the Rhyses. While we all love her dearly, the closeness of the relationship is due more to proximity than to consanguinity. We shall not be celebrating tonight, merely dining."

"Want to bet?" Janet murmured to Madoc.

"Dafydd and Lisa, you mean? Think it will work?"

"Oh yes. He's really a family man at heart, Madoc. You were the same, you know. And Lisa likes husbands who go away and come back again. It'll work, you wait and see."

"If you say so, love. Are you going to wear that blue dress tonight?"

"I guess likely, if it'll make you happy. Come on, Dorothy, time to get your bath. Bring her supper along when it's ready, will you, Megan?"

Going upstairs, they passed Bob on the way down, followed by Danny the Boots with two giant suitcases, one Bob's and one Mary's. He bade them an affable farewell and went off babbling gaily of Mary's great fortune that would come to him when the will was read.

"Old warthog," Janet muttered. "I hope a lesser demon gets him."

There was lots to talk about but they didn't say much. Madoc took his bath while Dorothy was having hers, then Megan came along with the muesli, and Madoc had to dress in the bathroom so he wouldn't embarrass her. Then Megan got to feed the baby as a special treat while Janet bathed; then Megan took the dish away while Janet nursed Dorothy and Madoc told them both a bedtime story; then Megan came back and Janet finished dressing, and by then it was time to go down to dinner. They were almost to the stairs when Janet grabbed Madoc's arm.

"Look," she whispered. "There it is!"

At the far end of the hall, a grayish mist was collecting. As they stood watching, it formed itself into a cowled shape. Madoc whispered, "Stay here," and charged headlong. Joke or not, Janet felt panic rising in her throat as Madoc clutched at the apparition.

His hand came away empty. He flung open the heavy draperies, pawed among the folds. He stretched on tiptoe to grope for wires or strings. Janet was with him now, they both searched along the baseboard. They found nothing whatever, but they both felt the sharp chill in the air.

"So there it is, love," said Madoc. "Just a plain old run-of-the-mill ghost."

"My, my," said Janet. "Won't that be something to tell the folks back home. Come on, darling, we mustn't keep Uncle Caradoc waiting."

CHARLOTTE MACLEOD

America's Reigning Whodunit Queen

PRESENTS

Art Detectives Max Bittersohn and Sarah Kelling

THE FAMILY VAULT   49080-3/$3.50 US/$4.50 Can

THE PALACE GUARD   59857-4/$3.99 US/$4.99 Can

THE WITHDRAWING ROOM   56473-4/$3.99 US/$4.99 Can

THE BILBAO LOOKING GLASS 67454-8/$3.50 US/$4.50 Can

THE CONVIVIAL CODFISH   69865-X/$3.50 US/$4.50 Can

THE PLAIN OLD MAN   70148-0/$3.99 US/$4.99 Can

Professor Peter Shandy

REST YOU MERRY   47530-8/$3.99 US/$4.99 Can

THE LUCK RUNS OUT   54171-8/$3.50 US/$4.50 Can

WRACK AND RUNE   61911-3/$3.99 US/$4.99 Can

SOMETHING THE CAT DRAGGED IN

          69096-9/$3.99 US/$4.99 Can

THE CURSE OF THE GIANT HOGWEED

          70051-4/$3.50 US/$4.50 Can

Short Story Collection

GRAB BAG   75099-6/$3.50 US/$4.50 Can